ate r

NEW PENGUIN SHAKESPEARE
GENERAL EDITOR: T. J. B. SPENCER
ASSOCIATE EDITOR: STANLEY WELLS

WILLIAM SHAKESPEARE

*

THE TAMING OF
THE SHREW

EDITED BY
G. R. HIBBARD

PENGUIN BOOKS

PENGUIN BOOKS

Published by the Penguin Group
Penguin Books Ltd, 80 Strand, London WC2R 0RL, England
Penguin Putnam Inc., 375 Hudson Street, New York, New York 10014, USA
Penguin Books Australia Ltd, 250 Camberwell Road, Camberwell, Victoria 3124, Australia
Penguin Books Canada Ltd, 10 Alcorn Avenue, Toronto, Ontario, Canada M4V 3B2
Penguin Books India (P) Ltd, 11 Community Centre, Panchsheel Park, New Delhi – 110 017, India
Penguin Books (NZ) Ltd, Cnr Rosedale and Airborne Roads, Albany, Auckland, New Zealand
Penguin Books (South Africa) (Pty) Ltd, 24 Sturdee Avenue, Rosebank 2196, South Africa

Penguin Books Ltd, Registered Offices: 80 Strand, London WC2R 0RL, England

www.penguin.com

This edition first published in Penguin Books 1968
Reprinted with a revised Further Reading 1995
31

This edition copyright © Penguin Books, 1968, 1995
Introduction and notes copyright © G. R. Hibbard, 1968
Further Reading copyright © Michael Taylor, 1995
All rights reserved

Printed in England by Clays Ltd, St Ives plc
Set in Monotype Ehrhardt

CONTENTS

INTRODUCTION

I

THE note that is sounded in such a line as 'The course of true love never did run smooth', that haunting lyrical expression of sentiment which is such a pronounced feature of much Shakespeare comedy, is not to be heard in *The Taming of the Shrew*. There are no songs in this play, apart from the snatches of ballads that Petruchio sings after he has arrived home with his bride; and the one moment of real tenderness in it drops like a casual parenthesis between a concession and a plea, taking the form of a simple monosyllabic jingle. It comes at the end of the first scene of Act V when, under pressure from Petruchio, Katherina at last kisses him, saying as she does so, 'Nay, I will give thee a kiss. Now pray thee, love, stay.' At this point the long struggle between them has reached its end. Katherina has finally accepted her natural role as a wife; hostility, petulance, and recalcitrance have been replaced by affection, good humour, and partnership. In the final scene, which follows immediately on this action, husband and wife face the rest of the world as allies, not enemies, working together to score a signal triumph over it. And their triumphant alliance is sealed by the longest and most eloquent speech in the entire comedy, Katherina's proclamation of the submission of wife to husband as a law of nature, something essential to the harmonious working of the universe, and therefore to be accepted gladly, not rebelled against grudgingly.

This explicit statement of the play's moral has, however, something of the set piece about it, as has Petruchio's direct address to the audience, at the end of IV.1, in which he takes them into his confidence, explains in considerable detail, and with evident gusto, the methods he intends to use in order to bring his newly married wife to her senses, and then invites anyone who knows of a better way of proceeding to speak up and tell it. Indeed, there is more of this same set excogitated quality about the other passages that linger in the mind when the play is over: Biondello's description, in III.2, of the broken-down nag, a prey to all the diseases that horse-flesh is heir to, on which Petruchio arrives in Padua for his wedding; Gremio's graphic account, in the same scene, of the wildly indecorous marriage ceremony; and Petruchio's abuse of the wretched Tailor in IV.3. All these are bravura pieces, conscious displays of the rhetorical arts of grotesque description, farcical narrative, and inventive vituperation. Language is being deliberately exploited for effect; and what, in another context, might well appear cruel, outrageous, or offensive is transformed into comic exuberance by a linguistic virtuosity that delights in the exercise of its own powers. There is, in fact, much in this play that is reminiscent of the manner of Shakespeare's younger contemporary, Thomas Nashe, whose pamphlets, such as *Pierce Penilesse his Supplication to the Devil* and *Strange News*, both published in 1592, were arousing a good deal of interest about the time when *The Taming of the Shrew* was written. Couched in a lively virile prose full of verbal extravagance and ingenious tricks of style, these works must have attracted Shakespeare's attention, and probably encouraged him to make experiments of his own in the same direction. The description of the horse looks very much like an attempt to outdo Nashe at his own game. This vigour and this assurance in the use of the rich resources of Elizabethan English are, however, confined to certain parts of the play. They appear in the Induction, where Christopher Sly's every word smacks of the Warwickshire countryside, and in the story of Petruchio and Katherina. By comparison with them most of the writing in that section of the play that deals with Bianca and her various wooers seems generally insipid, often over-ornate, and at other times flat and even clumsy, though there is one flash of truly memorable spontaneous comic utterance as Biondello tells his master Lucentio, at the end of IV.4, 'I knew a wench married in an afternoon as she went to the garden for parsley to stuff a rabbit.'

There is a good reason why the best writing in the play should be rhetorical in nature, for the main concern of *The Taming of the Shrew* is, as the title indicates, with a process – indeed, with more than one process – of conditioning. In it people are persuaded by words, and compelled by actions, all of which have been carefully planned and calculated for the purpose, to see themselves in a new light, to take on a fresh personality, and to assume a different role in life from that which they have had previously. Sly's experience in this respect anticipates and prefigures Katherina's. There is also a good reason why the writing employed in the tale of Bianca and her suitors should be comparatively tame and conventional, for here words, like actions, are not intended to create something new or reveal something latent, but to serve as a form of disguise for characters who seek to hide what they are, or to take on an identity that is not their own, in order to get what they want.

The contrast in style between the different parts of the play is, then, functional; but recognition of this fact provides little incentive for the reader who, deprived of the bustle and animation of the stage, may well find it hard to develop any very lively interest in the elaborate intrigues of Tranio, Lucentio, Gremio, and Hortensio, particularly as their names, disguises, and disguise-names make it far from easy to keep one distinct from another. He will discover much support for his dissatisfaction in the writings of those critics who have approached the play through the study rather than through the theatre, for, until fairly recently, the general reception they have given it has been either apologetic or openly hostile. Some have felt that it cannot be wholly from Shakespeare's hand, and have assigned the story of Bianca to one or another of his contemporaries; some have described it as brutal and barbarous; others have concluded that it is certainly not for all time but very definitely a thing of its own age, only intelligible in terms of attitudes to women that have long disappeared, and, even so, badly in need of special pleading. Writing in 1929, John Bailey said of it: 'It is rather strange that the play is still acted, for it is, to tell the truth, an ugly and barbarous as well as a very confused, prosaic and tedious affair' (*Shakespeare*, pp. 100–101). A year earlier Sir Arthur Quiller-Couch, in his Introduction to the New Cambridge edition of the play, had been even more outspoken. After reproaching it for being 'unforgivably coarse when it puts some of its grossest words into the mouth of Katharina', he continues:

'Let us put it that to any modern civilised man, reading . . . *The Shrew* in his library, the whole Petruchio business . . . may seem, with its noise of whip-cracking, scoldings, its throwing about of cooked food, and its general playing of "the Devil amongst the Tailors", tiresome – and to any modern woman, not an antiquary, offensive as well. It is of its nature rough, *criard* [noisy]: part of the fun of those fairs at which honest rustics won prizes by grinning through horse-collars' (pp. xv–xvi).

Yet Quiller-Couch is forced to admit, with a surprised regret that outdoes Bailey's, that 'the trouble about *The Shrew* is that, although it reads rather ill in the library, it goes very well on the stage' (p. xxv). It does indeed. More than three and a half centuries after it was written, *The Taming of the Shrew* still remains today one of the most popular of all Shakespeare's comedies in the theatre, the place for which its author intended it. Thousands of men – not to mention women who are not antiquaries – go to see it every year, not only in the English-speaking countries but also on the Continent, where it is a great favourite. Nor are the reasons for its wide international appeal far to seek. They lie in its main theme: that battle of the sexes which is as old as the Garden of Eden and as new as the latest love-affair – and in the way in which this theme is worked out. Precisely because Shakespeare's central concern in this particular play is with action, characters, and ideas, rather than with poetry and atmosphere, and because the play relies for its effect on broad and obvious contrasts between characters and attitudes instead of subtle discriminations between them, it loses much less in the process of translation than do such comedies as *A Midsummer Night's Dream*, *As You Like It*, or *Twelfth Night*. Essentially of the theatre and for the theatre, *The Taming of the Shrew* goes on living because it has, in the first place, that necessary quality of all good drama, a delight in vigorous events subjected to the discipline of a coherent, well organized, and significant plot.

2

It is no exaggeration to say that the first audience to witness a performance of the play (in 1594 or possibly two years before that – the exact dating of it is difficult and uncertain) were seeing the most elaborately and skilfully designed comedy that had yet appeared on the English stage. In what was probably his earliest piece of comic writing, *The Comedy of Errors*, Shakespeare had used two main stories, one of them, which he drew from medieval narrative, serving as a framework for the other, which he took from Latin comedy. In *The Taming of the Shrew* he employed three stories, not two, and related them to one another in a far more complex fashion. The first of them – *The Waking Man's Dream*, as it is called in one version – is at least as old as *The Arabian Nights*, where one of the stories tells how the Caliph Haroun Al Raschid has a poor man called Abu Hassan, whom he finds in a drunken stupor, carried to his palace. There Abu Hassan is dressed in fine clothes and, when he awakens, is persuaded that he is really a great man who has been suffering from temporary insanity. From whatever intermediate source Shakespeare derived this tale, he shaped it to his own purposes with consummate artistry. The beggar is transformed into Christopher Sly, a drunken tinker from the part of England that Shakespeare knew best. The concise account of his chequered career that Sly gives when he wakes up in the second scene of the Induction describes a life such as many a man born in the Cotswolds must have had, and some of the drinking cronies whom he mentions later have good Warwickshire names. Solid, earthy, and addicted to ale, Sly is a thoroughly convincing character, and he makes the perfect link between the world of the audience, to whom he would be a familiar figure, and the world of the play. Moreover, he is placed in a realistic setting. The Hostess, the hunting scene, the great house to which he is transported, with its musty rooms that need airing, and its mythological pictures or tapestries – all these carry the conviction of people and places that have been observed and absorbed by a sharp eye and a retentive memory, as for that matter does the scene in which the players arrive at the Lord's mansion.

But far more is involved than the setting of a scene and the telling of a tale. The brief yet vigorous altercation between Sly and the Hostess with which the Induction begins is a little curtain-raiser for the struggle between Petruchio and Katherina that is to follow, while the Lord's instructions to his page Bartholomew as to the behaviour he is to assume when he appears disguised as Sly's wife adumbrate the main theme of the play proper. Bartholomew is told that he must do the drunkard 'duty'

> *With soft low tongue and lowly courtesy,*
> *And say 'What is't your honour will command,*
> *Wherein your lady and your humble wife*
> *May show her duty and make known her love?'*
> Induction 1. 112–15

These lines are a succinct sketch of the ideal of wifely conduct that Katherina will ultimately acknowledge. More interesting still, there is a marked resemblance between what the Lord does to Sly and what Petruchio does to Katherina. Like Petruchio the Lord is a countryman, fond of sport, something of an actor, and much given to practical jokes. He takes Sly in an unguarded moment, and by using the varied resources that are at his disposal – his servants, his house, and so forth – succeeds in imposing a new identity on the tinker. Similarly Petruchio, through his ability to act a part, manages to alter Katherina's nature, or rather her outlook; for she and Sly have this much in common, that each of them is in some measure predisposed to take up the new role that is offered to them. It is plain from Sly's muddled attempt to impress the Hostess by saying 'Look in the Chronicles, we came in with Richard Conqueror' that he has vague delusions of grandeur and aristocratic descent which leave him open to the Lord's practices. In the same way there are evident indications early in the play proper that Katherina is not so strongly opposed to the idea of marriage as she pretends to be.

The Induction, then, lives up to its name in the sense that it does indeed lead into the play that follows. But it also has a unique interest of its own, because in no other of his plays does Shakespeare make use of this particular device. Adopted, it seems likely, from medieval narrative poetry, where it was extensively used to introduce a story in the form of a dream, the Induction was a common feature of many plays written around 1590. In most cases, however, it amounted to little more than a prologue. The two outstanding examples, prior to *The Taming of the Shrew*, of plays in which the Induction is set in a thematic relationship to the action that succeeds it are to be found in Thomas Kyd's *The Spanish Tragedy*, which was written about 1587 and is referred to on more than one occasion by Sly, and in George Peele's *The Old Wive's Tale*, which probably dates from about 1590. The echoes of *The Spanish Tragedy* placed in Sly's mouth suggest that Shakespeare had the Induction to that play in mind when writing his own, which reads like a parody of it. In Kyd's Induction the Ghost of Don Andrea relates that when he reached the underworld, after being slain in battle, Proserpine intervened with Pluto on his behalf, and obtained leave for him to return to earth. He then sits down, with the figure of Revenge by his side, to witness a bloodthirsty tragedy. Sly, on the other hand, is thrown out of the only heaven he has known hitherto, the tavern, goes to sleep on the cold ground, and awakens to find himself in a heaven on earth, where the drink is free and plentiful. There he is presented with a comedy. The Ghost of Don Andrea is passionately involved in the events that are staged for his benefit, and ultimately, after many disappointments with the way they seem to be going, expresses deep satisfaction with their outcome. Sly, in contrast, is so little taken with what is offered to him that he nods off during the first scene, and then, with a grand but despairing gesture towards aristocratic politeness, utters his damning opinion of it, ''Tis a very excellent piece of work, madam lady. Would 'twere done!'

These are his last words. The stage direction at this point shows that he remains in his place for the next scene at least, but no more is heard from him or of him. Having served his purpose as a lead-in from the reality of everyday life to the imagined world of the play, he is quietly dropped. There may, however, be more practical reasons for the suppression of his part, along with those of the other two 'Presenters'. These three roles in the Induction would require actors of ability; and only a very flourishing company could have afforded the luxury of having three of its leading performers, including a boy who could play female parts, largely immobilized on the upper stage while the main action of the play continued below. The Earl of Pembroke's Men, for whom *The Taming of the Shrew* was probably written, were in anything but a prosperous state in 1592–4; in fact, they were disintegrating. It is more than likely that Shakespeare, in characteristic fashion, has made dramatic capital out of theatrical necessity.

3

Sly's disappearance from the action is well timed, because it coincides with the moment when he might be expected to sit up, take notice, and even, perhaps, begin to make a nuisance of himself, for his final utterance immediately precedes the arrival of Petruchio and his man Grumio in

Padua, and the beginning of a tale fit for a tinker. The shrewish wife had long been established as a comic figure on the English stage when Shakespeare wrote his play, with a history going back at least as far as the miracle-plays on the subject of Noah. In poetry Chaucer had immortalized her in the formidable shape of the Wife of Bath, and numerous *fabliaux* about her were circulating during the sixteenth century. Comedy delights in the clash of theory with inescapable fact. Nowhere in life was this clash more evident than in the matter of the position of women. The official doctrine, inherited from the Middle Ages and proclaimed by the Elizabethan Church in its *Book of Homilies*, was that woman is by nature and by divine ordinance inferior to man, and that the wife is therefore subject to her husband. She owes him obedience 'in the respect of the commandment of God, as St Paul expresseth it in this form of words: *Let women be subject to their husbands, as to the Lord; for the husband is the head of the woman, as Christ is the head of the church.* Ephes. v.' This is the explicit statement on the matter that Shakespeare and his contemporaries heard when 'The Sermon of the State of Matrimony' was read in church. But life obstinately refused to be ordered by doctrine and theory. The struggle for mastery in marriage remained as a fact of existence, and also as a standing topic for writers of all kinds, some serious and some humorous, because they knew that it had a powerful appeal both for the reading public of the time and for those who frequented the theatre. Moreover, attitudes to women were gradually changing, and throughout Elizabeth's reign a long controversy was carried on between those who thought of women as the daughters of Eve, and therefore the primary cause of human troubles and miseries, and those who took a more enlightened view of them. Some of the pamphleteers involved even went so far as to write on both sides of the question in order to keep the paper battle going. An offshoot of this controversy was the large body of satirical writing, both in prose and verse, on the subject of extravagant fashions in women's dress. This is well represented in the play. Petruchio's flamboyant diatribes against Katherina's cap and gown, in IV.3, would have had a familiar ring to the ears of the original audience. They had heard the like from many a pulpit.

Before he wrote *The Taming of the Shrew*, which has the right sort of catchpenny title for a contribution to a popular debate, Shakespeare had already touched on the controversy in *The Comedy of Errors*. In II.1 of that play the two sisters, Adriana and Luciana, discuss the position of women in marriage. Adriana, who has been turned into something of a nagger by her husband's casual and unfair treatment of her, speaks up for a greater degree of equality between the sexes, while Luciana, who is unmarried, puts the more orthodox view, that men 'Are masters to their females, and their lords', in a speech which foreshadows Katherina's lengthier enunciation of the same doctrine at the end of *The Taming of the Shrew*. In *The Comedy of Errors*, however, the whole issue remains a subsidiary one and can never rise above the level of debate, because in this play of mistaken identities husband and wife hardly ever meet. In the story of Petruchio and Katherina it receives full dramatic treatment.

Whether Shakespeare adapted some existing tale to his purposes, or whether he invented the plot himself, the first thing that distinguishes his handling of the taming theme from any of its predecessors is the sophistication, the subtlety, and the ingenuity of the methods by which Petruchio achieves his end. The traditional means of subduing a shrewish woman was by the use of physical force.

In the old play *Tom Tyler and His Wife* (*c.* 1560) the domineering wife is given a thorough drubbing by her husband's friend Tom Tayler disguised as her husband. An even more cruel beating is meted out to a provocative wife by her long-suffering husband in *The Ballad of the Curst Wife Wrapt in a Morell's Skin* (*c.* 1550). Petruchio goes to work in a very different fashion. Only once does he so much as offer to use violence. This occurs during the course of his first meeting with Katherina in II.1, when she strikes him and he retorts 'I swear I'll cuff you, if you strike again.' But at this point he has momentarily been jolted out of his predetermined plan by her spirited and witty resistance. He has no further lapses of this kind, and adheres to the course he has set for himself.

His main line of attack is psychological. He perceives that Katherina, whom the men of Padua see as a devil and whom her father calls 'thou hilding of a devilish spirit', is in fact a woman of spirit who has become spoiled and bad-tempered because she has never met a man who is her equal and capable of standing up to her. He diagnoses the cause of her bad temper with immediate insight and great accuracy when, at his first meeting with her father in II.1, he says:

> *I am as peremptory as she proud-minded;*
> *And where two raging fires meet together,*
> *They do consume the thing that feeds their fury.*
> *Though little fire grows great with little wind,*
> *Yet extreme gusts will blow out fire and all.*
>
> lines 131–5

The 'little wind', that has made Katherina the firebrand that she now is, is the weak and ineffective opposition from others that her will has so far encountered. Very much the sportsman and the soldier, ever ready to take on an opponent or to lay a wager, Petruchio recognizes a kindred spirit in the spoiled girl, and welcomes the chance of meeting an antagonist who will put up a good fight. When Hortensio enters '*with his head broke*' after his ineffectual attempt to teach Katherina how to play the lute, and recounts in a piece of comic narrative what actually happened, Petruchio is filled with admiration for her vigour and cries out:

> *Now, by the world, it is a lusty wench.*
> *I love her ten times more than e'er I did.*
> *O, how I long to have some chat with her!*
>
> lines 160–62

And he means it.

Appreciating Katherina's wild, proud animal spirits, Petruchio equates her with another fierce difficult creature he is familiar with, the haggard or wild falcon. Falcons, which were much prized by the Elizabethans who used them for hunting, were tamed – and still are for that matter, as anyone who has read T. H. White's book *The Goshawk* will know – by being denied sleep. The tamer watches the bird continually until it is subdued and eventually gives way in the battle of wills that takes place between it and its would-be master, to whom, if he succeeds in his purpose, it then becomes very attached, or, as one Elizabethan writer on the subject puts it, 'very loving to the man', which is just what Petruchio wishes Katherina to be. This part of his programme – the most obvious and elementary part of it, and the one that comes closest to the traditional methods of shrew-taming – he explains to the audience at the end of IV.1 when he makes his entrance after seeing Katherina to bed. In the course of the scene he and his newly married wife have arrived at his country house, after he has hurried her away from her father's without allowing her to partake of the wedding feast. The journey has been cold, dirty, and unpleasant, and at the end of it Katherina has been packed off to bed without any supper under the pretext that the food provided is unfit to eat. Taking the spectators into his confidence, Petruchio then says:

> My falcon now is sharp and passing empty,
> And till she stoop she must not be full-gorged,
> For then she never looks upon her lure.
> Another way I have to man my haggard,
> To make her come and know her keeper's call,
> That is, to watch her, as we watch these kites
> That bate and beat and will not be obedient.
>
> lines 176–82

Two other aspects of Petruchio's plan are much subtler and, in the end, far more important. Both call for considerable acting ability from the player who takes the part. A clue to the first of them is given by the servant Peter, who observes of his master's behaviour, just before Petruchio reappears to make the speech of which part has been quoted above, 'He kills her in her own humour.' What Peter means by this is that Petruchio is deliberately outdoing his wife in his displays of perversity and bad temper. The beginnings of it are to be seen at their first meeting, where, acting in accordance with the scheme he announces immediately before Katherina appears, Petruchio takes everything that she says in the reverse sense. It goes much further in the wedding scene, III.2, where he flouts all the normal conventions, arriving late, on a horse that is a disgrace to any gentleman, dressed in clothes more suitable for a scarecrow, behaving scandalously and outrageously in church, and rushing off in the most unceremonious and impolite manner as soon as the wedding is over. When he reaches his own home, his conduct is even worse. The house is admirably run, and his servants are models of efficiency, yet he continually finds fault with everything they do, rating and beating them for actions that are his, not theirs. Tyrannical, violent, and capricious, he rejects the cap and the dress he has ordered for his wife, and abuses the Haberdasher and the Tailor without restraint or mercy.

The entire proceedings are, of course, an act. Petruchio has more than a little in common with Richard III, who is pretty much his contemporary in terms of Shakespeare's career as a playwright. Both of them adopt roles in order to achieve their ends, both take a delight in doing so, and both inform the audience by direct address what their plans and purposes are. Petruchio's aim is to make himself a kind of mirror – a mirror that exaggerates – to Katherina. His displays of temper are a caricature of hers. Absurd and unreasonable, they enlist her sympathies for those who suffer under them. When he knocks over a basin of water and then blames the servant for letting it fall, Katherina intervenes on the man's behalf, saying 'Patience, I pray you, 'twas a fault unwilling'; and when he creates an angry fuss about the meat, which, he says, is overcooked, she attempts to calm him and make him take a more reasonable attitude. She is coming to see the value of that order and decency for which she previously had no use, and also, by implication, to see herself as she is. In the same way Petruchio's apparent disrespect for all the normal conventions of social life forces her to appreciate their worth. She discovers the shame and misery of being kept waiting by her bridegroom on the morning of the wedding, the indignity of not being allowed to preside at her own wedding breakfast, the disappointment of being deprived of fashionable clothes. Just as the lack of food and sleep brings her to a recognition of the basic importance of these things which she has always taken for granted, leading her to be conciliatory and gentle to Grumio in the hope of getting something to eat, and to say, after some prompting, 'I thank you, sir' to Petruchio when he eventually provides her with it, so her enforced loss of the woman's customary rights and privileges makes her acknowledge her own femininity.

Not only does Petruchio show Katherina what she is, through his own exaggerated parody of her wild and unreasonable behaviour, but he also shows her what she might be and what he wants her to be, through the way in which he treats her and talks to her. His offensive and outrageous actions and speeches are always directed – ostensibly at least – at others, never at her. In fact, the role he adopts is that of a knight-errant coming to the aid of a damsel in distress. All that he does 'is done in reverend care of her'. The blow he deals the priest who marries them is given in defence of her modesty; when he carries her off from her father's house he is saving her from a band of thieves who would rob him of her; when he refuses to allow her to eat roast mutton it is out of consideration for her health and temper! As he says himself, when justifying his tactics, 'This is a way to kill a wife with kindness. . . .' And, while all this is going on, he also takes care to tell her the things that deep within her she really wishes to hear. Praise of her beauty flows from his lips. She is 'sweet as spring-time flowers', she looks like the goddess Diana; and in a couple of lines that give a vivid impression of how Shakespeare himself must have visualized this fierce, wayward, yet fundamentally likeable and naturally honest creature of his imagination, he tells her

> *Kate like the hazel-twig*
> *Is straight and slender, and as brown in hue*
> *As hazel-nuts and sweeter than the kernels.*
>
> II.1.247–9

Before the end of the play is reached, all that in Katherina's character which had been warped by her faulty upbringing and by the circumstances in which she found herself has become as straight as her body. And she knows how the change has been brought about, for in IV.5, the scene in which she and Petruchio on their way to Padua encounter old Vincentio, she uses her husband's methods against him. Having been forced by him to say that the sun is the moon, she is then told by him that it is the sun after all. Thereupon she retorts:

> *Then, God be blessed, it is the blessèd sun.*
> *But sun it is not, when you say it is not,*
> *And the moon changes even as your mind.*
>
> lines 18–20

She has now taken his measure, and, understanding his games, is ready to join in them, which is what she does for the rest of the play.

4

For the third element that goes to make up the elaborate plot of *The Taming of the Shrew* Shakespeare went to an entirely different source from those which he had used for the other two. In 1509 the great Italian poet Ludovico Ariosto had written a comedy called *I Suppositi*, a title that means 'The Substitutes' or 'The Impostors'. This had been translated into English by George Gascoigne, one of the pioneers of Elizabethan literature, in 1566, under the title of *Supposes*. Following Ariosto's example, Gascoigne used prose as the vehicle for his translation, and *Supposes* has the distinction of being the first prose drama in English. Moreover, Gascoigne's prose is good; varied in style, well articulated, and liberally sprinkled with quibbles, it revealed something of the potentialities that the new medium offered to the playwright. Modelled, like the main plot of Shakespeare's own *Comedy of Errors*, on the comedies of Plautus and Terence, *Supposes* is a lively and fast-moving play of intrigue. It is about that perennial theme of Latin comedy, the efforts of a young man, aided by a clever servant, to outwit the old men who stand in the way of his obtaining, or rather in this case retaining, the girl of his choice. When it opens, the heroine Polynesta, who appears only in the first scene and takes no part in the subsequent action, is already pregnant by her lover Erostrato, a student at the University of Ferrara. Seeing her in the street on his arrival in the city from his home in Sicily, Erostrato fell in love with her at once, and, in order to gain access to her, changed names and identities with his man Dulipo. For the past two years Erostrato has been a servant in the house of Polynesta's father, Damon, while Dulipo has been taking his place at the University. Polynesta is sought in marriage by Cleander, an old lawyer who wants to beget a son and heir to replace the son whom he lost, years before the action of the play begins, during an attack on Otranto by the Turks. In an attempt to foil Cleander's plans, Dulipo, who is, of course, known throughout Ferrara as Erostrato and held in some esteem, also becomes a suitor for the hand of Polynesta. So far as her father is concerned, the only relevant question in deciding which of the two suitors he shall give his daughter to – her feelings are not considered at all – is which of them can provide her with the greater dowry. The advantage here is very much on the side of Cleander, who is his own master, whereas any promise made by Dulipo will only be valid when it receives the approval and blessing of his supposed father in Sicily. The ingenious Dulipo therefore provides himself with a father. Meeting a Sienese merchant who is just entering Ferrara, he invents a cock-and-bull story to persuade the man that Ferrara is a highly dangerous place for him, because it is almost on the brink of a war with Siena. He then offers to help the Sienese by taking him to his own house and giving out that the man is his own father, come from Sicily to see him. In return for this favour, the Sienese is to guarantee his supposed son's dowry. At this point two things complicate the issue: Damon discovers that Polynesta is pregnant by Erostrato, and casts him into a dungeon; and Erostrato's real father, Philogano, arrives in Ferrara. There is much confusion when the real father and the supposed father meet. Each calls the other an impostor, and Dulipo denies any connexion with his old master Philogano. Philogano enlists the services of the lawyer Cleander to put matters right, and as the two of them talk together it dawns on them that Dulipo is Cleander's long-lost son. Erostrato is then released, his real father is only too glad to provide the dowry, Damon is delighted to get the embarrassment of Polynesta off his hands, and all ends happily.

The value of this play for Shakespeare was threefold. First, it offered him an intrigue plot which would form an excellent contrast to Petruchio's wooing of Katherina, which is direct and open, with Petruchio making a straight-forward proposal to her father Baptista, and telling Katherina herself 'I am he am born to tame you, Kate'. Secondly, it enabled him to treat the whole matter of marriage and its social implications much more fully than he could otherwise have done. Thirdly, it gave him one of the central ideas that he employs to unify the varied elements of which *The Taming of the Shrew* is compounded. As it stood, however, the action of *Supposes* was not sufficiently romantic, even in a surface fashion, which was all Shakespeare required of it, to suit his purposes. Consequently, while retaining the basic structure of this play of mistaken identities, he also modified much of the detail in it, adding some things and suppressing others. In classical style Ariosto had confined his play to the final stages of the action, leaving the story of how Erostrato and Polynesta met, and of its progress through two years, to be briefly recounted in the first scene. But in a romantic play the initial encounter of hero and heroine is a matter of the first importance, and must therefore be enacted, as it is in I.1 of Shakespeare's play, where Lucentio is transported at the sight of Bianca and expresses his feelings in the stock terms and phrases of conventional Elizabethan love-poetry. Nor would Ariosto's heroine do. Pregnancy is too practical a matter to be romantic, and, in any case, Polynesta's part was much too restricted a one for the kind of comedy Shakespeare was writing, where the women always have a substantial role. Bianca, therefore, is given a much larger share in the action and shows far more initiative than her counterpart in *Supposes*, not only for these reasons, but also because her main function is to act as a contrast to the sister, Katherina, with whom Shakespeare endows her.

There are two other significant alterations. The motive of the lost son who is restored to his father is completely suppressed, perhaps because Shakespeare had just handled it at length in *The Comedy of Errors*, but more probably because he realized that it would be out of place in this comedy of wooing and wedding for which he had designed a very different ending from that of *Supposes*. Then there is an addition to the number of Bianca's wooers in the shape of Hortensio. The main reason for his inclusion is clearly to provide yet more 'supposes' when he assumes the disguise of Licio, the music teacher, and to complicate and enrich the lesson scene, III.1, but he also serves as a useful link between Petruchio and Padua, and is essential to the success of the last scene of all, where three sets of husbands and wives are needed to give the right amount of suspense and climax to the business of the wager. He is, in fact, part of the plot mechanism rather than a coherent character, since his various roles are not consistent with one another.

The comedy that results from these changes is still, when viewed apart from the story of Petruchio and Katherina, very much a comedy of situation, culminating in the riotous fun and muddle of V.1, where the real father of Lucentio arrives unexpectedly in Padua and meets his supposed father, the Pedant. Of its very nature, comedy of this sort works through the activities of type figures who remain unchanged throughout, and whose actions and reactions are entirely predictable: the Pedant, the old pantaloon (Gremio), the father (Baptista), the lover (Lucentio), and the clever, scheming servant (Tranio). Except for Bianca, whose position is different from that of the rest and who is therefore developed along rather different lines, the characters involved in this part of the play can be divided into two groups: the old, who are tricked, and the young, who do the tricking, setting their wits to work to outmanoeuvre the old, and one another as well. In such a situation the most successful man is he who knows the most, and the characters can be arranged according to the extent to which they are aware of what is really happening. The one who knows the least is Baptista, who is consistently mistaken about everything and everybody, so that he does not even understand why Bianca asks his pardon in V.1 when she enters after her secret marriage to Lucentio. Too gullible to be interesting, he is merely the butt for all the intrigues that go on. The character who comes closest to Baptista in his unawareness of the extent to which he is being duped is Gremio, especially when he unwittingly introduces his rival Lucentio into Baptista's house. But Gremio is, it must be added, one of the most satisfactory figures in this section of the play. His character, as the aged suitor who is absurd because he is too old, is admirably sustained and consistent. Foolish in his pretensions as a lover, he is not without shrewdness in other matters, and he certainly gives Tranio a jolt when he tells him, near the end of II.1:

> *Sirrah, young gamester, your father were a fool*
> *To give thee all, and in his waning age*
> *Set foot under thy table. Tut, a toy!*
> *An old Italian fox is not so kind, my boy.*

lines 393–6

When he makes this remark, Gremio is drawing on that stock of proverbial wisdom that contributes so much to the creation of the distinct and distinctive idiom he is endowed with; and his experience in the play is substantially summed up in yet another bit of proverbial lore, which he uses twice: first, when he tells Hortensio 'Our cake's dough on both sides' (I.1.108); and then when he says 'My cake is dough' (V.1.128). It is a wry confession of failure in an action where everyone is busy cooking up plots. The direct opposite to these two, in terms of his knowledge of what is going on, is Tranio, the arch-manipulator, who has all the strings in his hands until the moment when Vincentio turns up, by which time Tranio's main purpose of enabling Lucentio to marry Bianca has been achieved. Tranio, in fact, serves as the brains for his love-besotted master, who is incapable of thinking about anything except Bianca, or rather about his romantic and, as it eventually proves, fatuous and mistaken notion of what Bianca is. Lucentio's bookish and extravagant speeches in praise of his beloved reveal him for the shallow and infatuated type that he is. He is obviously meant to contrast with Petruchio, who has a grasp on things as they are and is not led astray by the workings of his own imagination, just as Bianca provides another contrast, of a rather different kind, with her sister Katherina.

At the level of the action the two stories Shakespeare used for the play proper are firmly linked together by Baptista's first words as he enters in I.1, where he tells Gremio and Hortensio, the suitors of Bianca:

> *Gentlemen, importune me no farther,*
> *For how I firmly am resolved you know;*
> *That is, not to bestow my youngest daughter*
> *Before I have a husband for the elder.*

> lines 48–51

To the modern spectator or reader this decision must sound arbitrary and unreasonable. It would not have done so, however, to those who first saw the play, for it was taken for granted in Elizabethan England that it was a parent's duty to arrange a suitable match for his daughters; and the main criteria of suitability were status and income. Marriage was, in fact, very much a business arrangement, with love and compatibility as decidedly subsidiary factors. Girls looked on it as their proper end in life, and, indeed, as their due, with the result that parents who failed to do their duty in the matter were often censured by their children as well as by their neighbours. Katherina's bitter resentment at her unmarried state is plainly voiced by her

31

in II.1, and it is not without its representative quality.
After Baptista has restrained her when she '*flies after
Bianca*', Katherina bursts out with these words:

> *What, will you not suffer me? Nay, now I see*
> *She is your treasure, she must have a husband.*
> *I must dance bare-foot on her wedding-day,*
> *And for your love to her lead apes in hell.*

lines 31–4

She obviously feels that her father has failed her badly in
not finding a husband for her, and that it would be a deep
personal insult if he were to allow her younger sister to
marry before her.

The Taming of the Shrew, unlike most of Shakespeare's
other comedies – the nearest to it in this respect is *All's Well
that Ends Well* – deals with marriage as it really was in the
England that he knew. Whether Baptista is bargaining
with Petruchio about his marriage to Katherina, or with
Gremio and Tranio about which of them shall wed Bianca,
the crucial consideration is the dowry, both in the sense
of the money which a father paid to the man who took a
daughter off his hands, and in the other sense of the money
or property that the bridegroom assured to his wife in case
he predeceased her, so that she would not be left without
provision for her widowhood. And in each case the bargaining ends with the drawing up of a legal agreement or,
in the words of the play, of an 'assurance'. In these circumstances the needy adventurer on the look-out for a profit-
able match was a common phenomenon, and so was the
older man in search of a young wife on whom he might
beget an heir. In fact, middle-aged bridegrooms were
generally popular with Elizabethan parents, since they
were more likely to be settled in life and financially sound
than were younger men. Petruchio begins as a variant on

the first type, making no pretence about the mercenary motives which have brought him to Padua, and saying quite unashamedly on his arrival:

> *Antonio, my father, is deceased,*
> *And I have thrust myself into this maze,*
> *Haply to wive and thrive as best I may.*

I.2.53-5

He is not, however, needy, because his father has left him well-off. Gremio is a variant on the second, differing from his prototype Cleander in *Supposes* in that he never mentions the begetting of an heir as a motive that carries any weight with him.

But while marriage was primarily a business arrangement, in which parents and guardians took the lead – Petruchio, whose father is dead, enjoys an independence of action that is denied to Lucentio, whose father is alive – changes in attitude were coming about. Many divines and moralists opposed arranged marriages (particularly enforced marriages, which were by no means rare), on the grounds that they were manifestations of parental covetousness and that they led not only to misery but also to adultery and crime. At the same time the poets and writers of romances were extolling true love as productive of happiness and therefore far more valuable than any amount of dirty land. As a result, concessions were being made to the wishes of the young people themselves, who were gradually acquiring the right to say no. The old traditional view and the new attitude, expressed in an outspoken and daring manner, are neatly opposed to each other in *Much Ado About Nothing*, when Antonio, thinking that the Prince is about to propose to Hero, tells her: 'Well, niece, I trust you will be ruled by your father.' Thereupon Beatrice, who has a mind and a will of her own, gives Hero a very different piece of advice, saying: 'Yes, faith; it is my cousin's duty to make curtsy and say, "Father, as it please you". But yet for all that, cousin, let him be a handsome fellow, or else make another curtsy and say, "Father, as it please me"' (II.1.44–9). Even Baptista makes a gesture in the new direction, for after reaching his agreement with Petruchio in II.1, he adds a proviso that the documents are only to be prepared

> *when the special thing is well obtained,*
> *That is, her love; for that is all in all.* lines 128–9

On the face of it *The Taming of the Shrew* looks like a play made out of these two contrasting attitudes. The old approach to marriage is represented by Petruchio, who states quite bluntly that he wants to marry for money, makes a bargain with Katherina's father before he has so much as seen her, pays no attention whatever to her wishes, carries her off from her father's house as though she were some newly acquired possession, and then proceeds to tame her in the way he would tame a hawk. The story of Bianca and Lucentio is the obverse of this, for here the woman is dominant, enjoying the pleasure of a complex and protracted wooing, followed by a runaway marriage that receives the approval of both fathers.

The trouble with this interpretation is that it simply does not square with one's experience of the play, where not only are Petruchio and Katherina consistently more vital and more interesting than Lucentio and Bianca, but also by the end they, with their old-fashioned match, look much the more promising and stable couple of the two. Yet it seems inherently improbable that the poet who wrote Sonnet 116 –

> *Let me not to the marriage of true minds*
> *Admit impediments –*

could ever have written a play to commend the *mariage de convenance* at the expense of the love-match. And, of course, Shakespeare has not. The second half of II.1 puts the matter beyond all doubt, for it is a most telling piece of comic satire on the subject of the Elizabethan marriage-market. The match between Petruchio and Katherina has no sooner been agreed on by the two parties most intimately concerned in it – not with any enthusiasm from Katherina, but at least she does not say no – than Gremio and Tranio begin to compete for the hand of Bianca, addressing themselves to her father. Each asserts that he loves her far more than does the other, but Baptista wastes no time in bringing the argument down to the practical terms that he understands by saying:

> *Content you, gentlemen, I will compound this strife.*
> *'Tis deeds must win the prize, and he of both*
> *That can assure my daughter greatest dower*
> *Shall have my Bianca's love.*   lines 334–7

Thereupon something very like an auction ensues in which the two suitors cap each other's bids, until Gremio is 'out-vied'. At this point Baptista settles for Tranio's offer, but takes care to add that the deal will only go through when Tranio's father underwrites his son's promises; otherwise Bianca will be married to Gremio. The mercenary and stupid nature of the whole business has been fully exposed.

How then does the play function, and what is it saying? The plainest indication is to be found in the contrast that it makes between the characters of the sisters, and in the way in which those characters are developed. Each of them at the end of the play produces exactly the opposite impression from that which she made at its beginning. Bianca, who appears at first to be gentle, modest, and submissive, proves to be a difficult and self-willed wife; while Katherina, who begins by being self-willed, shrewish, and intolerable, becomes a model of wifely obedience and duty. But even from the outset there are signs that first impressions may be misleading. Katherina, on her first appearance, plainly resents the manner in which her father offers her to Gremio and Hortensio, and she has nothing but scorn for the dismay with which they recoil from that offer. Her vigorous and outspoken retort to her father:

> *I pray you, sir, is it your will*
> *To make a stale of me amongst these mates?*

shows where she stands. It is an assertion of self-respect by a woman who, much as she wishes for marriage, has no intention of allowing herself to be sold to a man for whom she can feel nothing but contempt. As well as being something of a spoiled girl, Katherina is a girl of spirit in revolt against the society she is living in. As Petruchio says in II.1, 'If she be curst, it is for policy'. Her shrewishness is a role she has adopted in self-defence, and it disappears when she eventually meets a man who can not only stand up to her but also appreciates her for what she is and responds to the challenge she offers.

Bianca is slower to reveal her real nature. Up to the opening of Act III nothing is clear about her except that she is her father's darling and that Katherina detests her. There is no means of knowing whether the detestation springs from mere jealousy or whether it is based on sounder reasons. Are her gentleness and submissiveness genuine, or are they part of an act put on to impress others? Left alone with two young men – Lucentio and Hortensio –

Bianca soon provides the answer. She thoroughly enjoys this opportunity for carrying on a double flirtation, joins with Lucentio in fooling his rival, and generally behaves like the accomplished minx that she is. More important still, the apparent submissiveness completely disappears. When the two 'tutors' start to wrangle about which of them shall give his lesson first, she promptly puts them in their places by telling them:

> *I am no breeching scholar in the schools,*
> *I'll not be tied to hours nor 'pointed times,*
> *But learn my lessons as I please myself.*
>
> lines 18–20

She is in complete command of the situation, and she remains so, because she has realized that in the society she lives in deception is a woman's most effective weapon. It is not surprising that the plot of which she is the centre should be made up of complicated intrigues.

The Taming of the Shrew depicts two ways to marriage. The road followed by Bianca and Lucentio, though it seems romantic and exciting at a first glance, is in fact unreliable, because at the end of it the husband is altogether in the dark about his new wife's real nature, as the wager scene makes abundantly plain. The other road, taken by Petruchio and Katherina, results in each gaining full knowledge of the other, much as Beatrice and Benedick do through their verbal sparrings in *Much Ado About Nothing*, so that at the end of it they have absolute trust in each other.

6

In addition to being woven closely together by their contrapuntal relationship, the two plots that make up the play proper are connected with each other, and with the Induction, in subtler and less obvious ways. The first – a very strong argument for the view that the entire play is the work of a single hand – is the use Shakespeare makes of the idea of 'supposes'. The primary meaning that this word has in Gascoigne's play is that of 'substitutes' or 'counterfeits', but in his prologue he also plays with its other possible connotations, for he tells his audience:

> *I suppose you are assembled here, supposing to reap the fruit of my travails, and to be plain, I mean presently to present you with a comedy called 'Supposes', the very name whereof may peradventure drive into every of your heads a sundry suppose to suppose the meaning of our supposes. Some percase will suppose we mean to occupy your ears with sophistical handling of subtle suppositions. Some other will suppose we go about to decipher unto you some quaint conceits, which hitherto have been only supposed as it were in shadows. And some I see smiling, as though they supposed we would trouble you with the vain suppose of some wanton suppose. But understand this our suppose is nothing else but a mistaking or imagination of one thing for another. For you shall see the master supposed for the servant, the servant for the master; the freeman for a slave, and the bondslave for a freeman; the stranger for a well-known friend, and the familiar for a stranger. But what? I suppose that even already you suppose me very fond, that have so simply disclosed unto you the subtlety of these our supposes, where otherwise indeed I suppose that you should have heard almost the last of our supposes before you could have supposed any of them aright.*

An elaborate, though somewhat too protracted, piece of wordplay such as this cannot but have caught Shakespeare's eye, and there are two direct allusions to the notion of 'supposes' in his play. The first comes in Tranio's final speech in II.1, where after he has out-vied Gremio for the hand of Bianca he says in soliloquy:

> *I see no reason but supposed Lucentio*
> *Must get a father, called supposed Vincentio.*

The second occurs towards the end of the discovery scene, V.1, when Baptista, who is lost in the maze of events, as well he might be, since he has taken every 'suppose' practised on him at its face value, asks, 'Where is Lucentio?' and receives the answer from the right man:

> *Here's Lucentio,*
> *Right son to the right Vincentio,*
> *That have by marriage made thy daughter mine,*
> *While counterfeit supposes bleared thine eyne.*
> lines 103–6

In both these cases the 'suppose' involved has been the assumption of a false identity as a form of disguise and as a means of imposing on others; it has not led to any real change in the person concerned. But Lucentio himself, as he discovers in the final scene, has been the victim of a much subtler 'suppose' than any of those that he has had a hand in, because he has supposed Bianca to be a rather different person from what she really is. In so far as Christopher Sly is concerned, the 'suppose' goes much deeper, for the Lord, with the assistance of his servants and the players, actually succeeds in convincing him that he is not Christopher Sly the tinker at all, but a member of the aristocracy and the husband of a charming and obedient wife. And, since Sly disappears unobtrusively from the action, one is left in a delightful state of uncertainty, not knowing whether he eventually discovers the deception that has been practised on him, whether he comes to think of it all as a dream, or whether he emerges from it a changed man.

Shakespeare is already very much interested, in this play, in the working of the imagination which he was to explore further in *A Midsummer Night's Dream*. The character most affected by it is Katherina, who ultimately becomes the person that Petruchio has deliberately 'supposed' her to be, and, through his clever speeches of admiration for qualities in her that no one else can recognize, has put it in her head that she ought to be and wants to be. The whole process is carried to the limit at which it becomes a parody of itself in IV.5, where Katherina joins in Petruchio's game and addresses old Vincentio as 'Young budding virgin, fair and fresh and sweet'. So profound is the alteration in Katherina's behaviour, though it has been predicted by Petruchio in II.1, when he says that 'For patience she will prove a second Grissel', that her father says in amazement, after the wager has been won, that 'she is changed, as she had never been'.

These words of Baptista's point straight to the other unifying idea that underlies *The Taming of the Shrew*, the notion of metamorphosis. Whether at the elementary and obvious level of a transformation of the outward appearance, such as Lucentio and Tranio undergo, or at the deeper one of a psychological change like Katherina's, this idea runs all through the play, and is closely related to its references to Ovid, which are many. The 'wanton pictures' that the Lord and his servants offer to fetch for Sly's delectation all have mythological subjects drawn from Ovid's *Metamorphoses*. At the opening of the play proper Tranio recommends his master to study Ovid as well as Aristotle. And Lucentio takes his advice. When he reads Latin with Bianca, it is the First Epistle in the poet's *Heroides* that they translate; and in the next lesson scene,

IV.2, Lucentio acknowledges Ovid as his model and his master when he tells Bianca 'I read that I profess, *The Art to Love*'. '*The Art to Love*' is Ovid's witty mock-manual for lovers, the *Ars Amatoria*, in which he describes himself as *praeceptor amoris*, the Professor of Love. Ovid meant much to Shakespeare, not only because he was such a rich storehouse of legends and such a skilled purveyor of 'the odoriferous flowers of fancy, the jerks of invention', as Holofernes calls them in IV.2 of *Love's Labour's Lost*, but also because there was behind the *Metamorphoses* a philosophical conception of change as the law of the universe, for the fact of change was something Shakespeare was continuously and profoundly aware of. Ovid's pervasive presence in this play, which is so concerned with the changes and transformations brought about by the power of love and, still more, of the skilfully stimulated imagination, is therefore fully justified.

But it is not only the way in which the characters in his play are affected by their own imaginings and by the imaginings of others that interests Shakespeare in *The Taming of the Shrew*: he is also concerned with the effect that the imagination can have on his audience. Time after time in this play some of the characters stand aside to watch the actions of others, and become for a space almost a secondary audience, observing what goes on, without being personally involved in it. This is the position of Petruchio and Katherina, for example, in the central section of V.1, where their amusement at what they witness mirrors that of the spectators. But the most significant figure in this connexion is Christopher Sly. Literally transported out of the world he knows into another environment altogether, he surrenders so completely to the pleasures of the new world which is offered to him that he ultimately becomes lost in it, which is what Shakespeare wishes his audience to do, and employs all his skill to ensure that they do.

7

The Taming of the Shrew is, then, at least in its broad out-lines, a significant piece of social comedy that has some-thing to say about marriage in Elizabethan England, and says it in a truly dramatic manner through a contrast of actions and characters. It is also concerned with the inner world of psychological experience, and particularly with the imagination in relation to human behaviour. These two themes, the social and the personal, are intimately connected with each other, so that the total experience becomes a unified whole. The comedy is a complex work of art. The careful reader, however, as distinct from the theatre audience, will also notice that there are some loose ends in it and some bits of detail that do not fit together as they should. Leaving aside for the time being the unex-plained disappearance of Christopher Sly, which can be justified as part of the total effect that the play seeks to achieve, the critic is faced with the fact that the part of Hortensio is far from coherent and satisfactory. When he first appears, early in I.1, it looks as though his role will be an important one. He is Gremio's rival for the hand of Bianca, and it is he who suggests that they bury their differences temporarily and combine together in the task of finding a man to marry Katherina. The next scene con-firms this impression, for it is Hortensio that Petruchio comes to visit, and it is Hortensio who offers to help Petruchio to a wife. He seems to be in control of things, manipulating the other characters much as he wishes. In II.1, however, Petruchio, at Hortensio's own request, presents him to Baptista under the disguise of Licio, the teacher of music; and from this point onwards Hortensio becomes a figure of fun. Katherina breaks the lute over his head, while Lucentio and Bianca use him as their butt. Moreover, he is not present when Gremio and Tranio make their bids for Bianca in the latter part of II.1, though Baptista knows perfectly well that he is a suitor. Odder still, Tranio, who has never seen Petruchio until the play begins, takes over Hortensio's original role as Petruchio's friend, apologizing for the bridegroom's delay at the opening of III.2, offering to provide him with more suitable clothes for his wedding, and entreating him to remain for the wedding breakfast. Oddest of all, Tranio, in IV.2, seems to know all about Petruchio's 'taming-school' and can tell Bianca that Hortensio has gone there, though Hortensio has said nothing whatever about the matter to him. On top of all this, Hortensio's sudden announcement in this same scene that he intends to marry 'a wealthy widow', whose very existence has not been mentioned hitherto, looks extremely suspect.

The conclusion to be drawn from all this evidence is inescapable: in an earlier version of the play Hortensio's part was larger than it is now, and Tranio's was correspondingly smaller. The inconsistencies are the result of a change of plan, made in order to exploit the comic potentialities of having two disguised suitors wooing Bianca at the same time. The necessary tailoring of the part has been done quickly but somewhat carelessly. Confirmation that this is, in fact, what happened is provided by *The Taming of a Shrew*, which was published in 1594 under the following title: *A Pleasant Conceited History, called The Taming of a Shrew. As it was sundry times acted by the Right honourable the Earl of Pembroke his servants*. In this text Polidor (Hortensio) is the friend of both Aurelius (Lucentio) and Ferando (Petruchio). He does not adopt a disguise, and, as a result, the part of Valeria (Tranio) is much slighter than it is in the *The Taming of the Shrew*. There are no inconsistencies in Polidor's part. It is he, not Valeria (Tranio), who apologizes for Ferando's (Petruchio's) delay on the morning of the wedding, and it is he who offers to lend the bridegroom some more suitable clothes for the occasion. Moreover, Polidor announces, shortly after the marriage of Ferando and Kate has taken place:

> *Within this two days I will ride to him,*
> *And see how lovingly they do agree.*
>> scene viii, lines 113–14

Nor is there any sudden and unexpected appearance of 'a wealthy widow' on the scene. In *The Taming of a Shrew* Katherina has two sisters, not one. The elder of them, Philema (Bianca) is beloved by Aurelius (Lucentio), while the youngest, Emelia (the Widow) is beloved by Polidor.

But *The Taming of a Shrew* is, most modern critics, though not all, think, a pirated text, put together from memory by an actor, or several actors, who had once taken part in performances of *The Taming of the Shrew*. To the present editor the evidence for piracy seems quite conclusive. *The Taming of a Shrew* is made up, like *The Taming of the Shrew*, of three elements: the Induction, consisting of two scenes dealing with the 'translation' of Sly; the taming story of Ferando and Kate; and the tale of the intrigues that Aurelius resorts to in order to win the hand of Kate's younger sister. In his handling of the Induction and of that part of the plot that deals with Petruchio and Katherina the reporter does what reporters usually did, though rather less well than most: he remembers the events in rough outline, but he is far from sure about the words. Even when he gets them more or less right, which is rarely, he misses the point of a jest or a quibble; more

44

generally he falls back on something he knows better –
usually a passage from one of Marlowe's plays, and particularly *Dr Faustus* – that can be made to fit the occasion.
But his version of the intrigue story is so different, with its
use of two sisters for Katherina instead of one, from that
which is to be found in *The Taming of the Shrew* as published in the Folio, that it must rest on an earlier and
somewhat different version of the play.

There is no evidence to show that the author of this
earlier version, which was subsequently revised to make
The Taming of the Shrew as we now know it, was anyone
but Shakespeare. In fact, such evidence as there is points
the other way. *The Taming of the Shrew* is much closer in
the relevant part of its plot to Gascoigne's *Supposes* than is
The Taming of a Shrew. It preserves and expands the whole
business of the aged wooer, which is not represented in the
pirated version at all, and it also has some verbal resem-
blances to Gascoigne's play that are not to be found in *The
Taming of a Shrew*. First, there is the use of the word
'supposed' at II.1.400–401 and of 'counterfeit supposes' at
V.1.106. Then the unusual verb 'to *sol-fa*', which Petruchio employs at I.2.17 when he says to Grumio 'I'll try
how you can *sol-fa* and sing it,' appears also in a very
similar context in IV.2 of *Supposes*, where an old gossip,
called Psyteria, says to Crapyno, a servant, 'If I come near
you, hempstring, I will teach you to sing sol-fa.' Thirdly,
at the end of IV.3 of *Supposes*, when Philogano, the father
of Erostrato, arrives in Ferrara and knocks at the door of
Dulipo's house, the stage direction reads: '*Dalio cometh to
the window, and there maketh them answer.*' Here, clearly, is
the origin of Shakespeare's unusual direction at V.1.13,
the corresponding point in his play: '*Pedant looks out of
the window*'.

The other difference between Shakespeare's first draft

of the play, which was pirated as *The Taming of a Shrew*, and the revision of it that was published for the first time in the Folio of 1623, is that in that first draft Sly did not disappear after the first scene of the play. In *The Taming of a Shrew* he remains on stage up to the point corresponding to the end of V.1 in *The Taming of the Shrew*, by which time he is sound asleep. In the meanwhile, however, he has three times commented on the progress of the action. Before the last scene of the play proper begins, the Lord gives orders that Sly, who is now once again in a drunken stupor, should be dressed in his own clothes and carried back to the side of the alehouse where he was found. And when the play is over, and the characters in it have gone off, it is there that Sly is awakened by the Tapster who threw him out of the alehouse at the beginning. Reluctantly concluding that the whole experience has been a dream – 'the best dream that ever I had in my life' – Sly decides to make use of his newly won knowledge by going home to tame his own shrew.

It is an ending that is not without its attractions, because it rounds the play off so neatly; and some producers have found it irresistible on that account. It also lends further support to the theory that the first draft was the work of Shakespeare in its anticipation of Bottom's reactions when he wakes up at the end of IV.1 in *A Midsummer Night's Dream*. But it is not strictly necessary; there is no warrant for it in the Folio; and it can be argued that the play is better without it. Sly's main function is to lead the spectator into the imaginary world of the play; and, once he has done that, he is no longer required.

FURTHER READING

The Taming of the Shrew is a chronically unstable text, mainly because of the fluctuating status of the 1594 edition of *The Taming of a Shrew*, variously thought to be an anonymous play Shakespeare revised, or an early version by him of *The Taming of the Shrew* that he came back to, or, most likely, a memorial reconstruction, a 'bad' quarto, of whatever text lay behind the 1623 Folio edition of *The Shrew*. The complete text of *A Shrew* can be found in Geoffrey Bullough's edition of *The Narrative and Dramatic Sources of Shakespeare*, Volume I (1957). The history of the relationship between the two texts is most thoroughly explored in modern, 'hybrid' editions of *The Shrew*: the Arden by Brian Morris (1982), the Oxford by H. J. Oliver (1982) and the New Cambridge by Ann Thompson (1984). A convenient summary of the textual situation of this, 'the most problematic play in the canon, textually', is in *William Shakespeare: A Textual Companion* (1987) by Stanley Wells and Gary Taylor.

The Taming of the Shrew is a good illustration of the inevitable interpenetration of textual and critical matters. A major difference textually, for example, between *A Shrew* and *The Shrew* is the absence in the latter of Christopher Sly after the Inductions (apart from a brief intervention at the end of the opening scene). In *A Shrew* Sly remains on stage throughout to make the occasional caustic or bored comment on the action and to round off the play. In her New Cambridge edition, Ann Thompson argues persuasively for retaining Sly in any 'final' edition of the play, but only goes as far as to include his interventions after Act I as an Appendix (as do the Arden and Oxford editions). In Graham Holderness's discussion of the play in the Shakespeare in

Performance Series (1989), he makes a forceful argument for the thematic integrity of *A Shrew*'s treatment of Sly, noting that his presence on the stage throughout reflected contemporary practice while serving to remind the audience that they are 'as much a victim of illusion as the tinker'. Holderness's book is one of the better ones in this series, offering thoughtful and provocative discussions of four major productions of *The Shrew*: two in the theatre, by John Barton (1960) and Michael Bogdanov (1978); a film by Franco Zeffirelli (1966); and Jonathan Miller's 1980 production for BBC television.

The Taming of the Shrew, like *The Merchant of Venice*, is one of those plays by Shakespeare that some critics rather wish wasn't by him. Most books on the play record varying degrees of discomfort with what seems to be its rambunctious sexism. Robert Ornstein's *Shakespeare's Comedies: From Roman Farce to Romantic Mystery* (1986) amusingly lists some of the critics' favourite evasive explanations for Shakespeare's gaucherie (farce as insulation, Kate as *really* a subtle husband manager, the indulgence of paradoxicality). What he says we have to face up to, however, is the simple fact that Kate *is* a shrew and the only one in Shakespeare (though one should remember that Lady Macbeth has her moments). Assuming – probably wrongly – that Shakespeare revised an earlier play, Ornstein also points out that the taming story in *The Shrew* is more unpleasant than in *A Shrew*, arguing that Shakespeare may not have enjoyed the task of transforming the earlier play (Ornstein compares the case of *King John*). Calling a shrew a shrew, and the play misogynist, characterizes most feminist criticism of the play. Shirley Nelson Garner, for instance, in her contribution to Maurice Charney's *'Bad' Shakespeare: Revaluations of the Shakespeare Canon* (1988), argues that you have to be a man to be able to enjoy the play's humour – it is acted for the benefit of the male characters of the Inductions. Linda Bamber in *Comic Women, Tragic Men: A Study of Gender and Genre in Shakespeare* (1982) believes that 'Kate's challenge is entirely negative' and that Shakespeare after *Shrew* abandons satire for saturnalia. Penny Gay in *As She Likes It: Shakespeare's Unruly Women* (1994) feels that the play's unpalatable ideology is rarely questioned in twentieth-century productions. This rather pessimistic judgement is not exactly borne out by Tori Haring-Smith's exhaustive history of the play in the theatre, *From Farce to Metadrama: A Stage History of 'The Taming of the Shrew', 1594–1983* (1985), which suggests that the different interpretations of the play in the theatre reflect 'our shifting cultural notions of the relationship between men and women in marriage'.

Some feminist criticism attempts to rescue the play for Shakespeare, if not for the theatre. Irene Dash's *Wooing, Wedding and Power: Women in Shakespeare's Plays* (1981) thinks that the play's misogynistic theatrical history is at the expense of 'Shakespeare's vision'. J. A. Bryant Jr in *Shakespeare & the Uses of Comedy* (1986) believes Shakespeare to be Euripidean in his awareness of women's potential and talks of 'Kate's serenity' at the play's end. Marianne Novy in *Gender Relations in Shakespeare* (1984) is one of those critics who see Petruchio as teaching Kate to play, where play equals power. The most interesting book along these lines is J. Dennis Huston's *Shakespeare's Comedies of Play* (1981), which concentrates on the fairy-tale aspect of *Shrew*, in which the monstrous is won over by human ingenuity. Kate is like an autistic child: fearing, hating and yet seeking isolation. In Petruchio's castle of terrors, so Huston argues, Kate experiences a 'rite of passage which frees her from the tyranny of her infantile self and releases her into the true adulthood of marriage and mutuality'.

Huston's response is not simply wishful thinking. There is much in the play that makes accusations of Shakespeare's (or Petruchio's) misogyny seem heavy-handed. In *Man's Estate: Masculine Identity in Shakespeare* (1981), Coppélia Kahn responds to these ambiguous elements and argues that Kate's dependency 'underlies mastery, the strength behind submission'. Similarly, William Carroll in *The Metamor-*

phoses of Shakespearean Comedy (1985) considers the play's ending to be riddled with ambiguity and sees the *Shrew* as containing 'virtually every mode of metamorphosis found in the later plays'. Noting that *Shrew* has a 'marked resistance to enclosure', Barbara Freedman, in a densely argued book, *Staging the Gaze: Postmodernism, Psychoanalysis and Shakespearean Comedy* (1991), acknowledges the ambiguity of the ending but is chiefly interested in what this says about 'our construction as subjects'. This approach is more accessibly explored in H. R. Coursen's *Shakespearean Performance as Interpretation* (1992). Yet although Coursen claims that there can be no consensus on the question of how Kate rejoins society, that there is no *essential* version of the play, he comes down heavily in favour of the 'send-up' version of Kate's last speech. Hence his distaste for Jonathan Miller's 'patriarchal' interpretation (BBC, 1980) and for Bogdanov's 1978 production at Stratford which left Kate as Petruchio's victim.

Michael Taylor, 1995

THE TAMING OF THE SHREW

THE CHARACTERS IN THE PLAY

INDUCTION

CHRISTOPHER SLY, a drunken tinker
The Hostess of a country alehouse
A Lord
Page, Huntsmen, and Servants attending on the Lord
A company of strolling Players

THE TAMING OF THE SHREW

BAPTISTA MINOLA, a wealthy citizen of Padua

KATHERINA, the Shrew, elder daughter of Baptista
PETRUCHIO, a gentleman of Verona, suitor for the hand of Katherina
GRUMIO, Petruchio's personal lackey
CURTIS, Petruchio's servant, in charge of his country house
A Tailor
A Haberdasher
Five other servants of Petruchio

BIANCA, the Prize, younger daughter of Baptista
GREMIO, a wealthy old citizen of Padua, suitor for the hand of Bianca
HORTENSIO, a gentleman of Padua, suitor for the hand of Bianca
LUCENTIO, a gentleman of Pisa, in love with Bianca

Enter Christopher Sly and the Hostess **1**

SLY I'll pheeze you, in faith.

HOSTESS A pair of stocks, you rogue!

SLY Y'are a baggage, the Slys are no rogues. Look in the Chronicles, we came in with Richard Conqueror. Therefore *paucas pallabris*, let the world slide. Sessa!

HOSTESS You will not pay for the glasses you have burst?

SLY No, not a denier. Go by, Saint Jeronimy, go to thy cold bed and warm thee.

 He lies on the ground

HOSTESS I know my remedy, I must go fetch the third-borough. *Exit* **10**

SLY Third, or fourth, or fifth borough, I'll answer him by law. I'll not budge an inch, boy. Let him come, and kindly.

 He falls asleep
 Wind horns. Enter a Lord from hunting, with his train

LORD

 Huntsman, I charge thee, tender well my hounds.

 Breathe Merriman, the poor cur is embossed,

 And couple Clowder with the deep-mouthed brach.

 Saw'st thou not, boy, how Silver made it good

 At the hedge corner, in the coldest fault?

 I would not lose the dog for twenty pound.

FIRST HUNTSMAN

 Why, Belman is as good as he, my lord. **20**

 He cried upon it at the merest loss,

 And twice today picked out the dullest scent.

Trust me, I take him for the better dog.

LORD

Thou art a fool. If Echo were as fleet,
I would esteem him worth a dozen such.
But sup them well, and look unto them all.
Tomorrow I intend to hunt again.

FIRST HUNTSMAN

I will, my lord.

LORD

What's here? One dead, or drunk? See, doth he
 breathe?

SECOND HUNTSMAN

30 He breathes, my lord. Were he not warmed with ale,
This were a bed but cold to sleep so soundly.

LORD

O monstrous beast, how like a swine he lies!
Grim death, how foul and loathsome is thine image!
Sirs, I will practise on this drunken man.
What think you, if he were conveyed to bed,
Wrapped in sweet clothes, rings put upon his fingers,
A most delicious banquet by his bed,
And brave attendants near him when he wakes,
Would not the beggar then forget himself?

FIRST HUNTSMAN

40 Believe me, lord, I think he cannot choose.

SECOND HUNTSMAN

It would seem strange unto him when he waked.

LORD

Even as a flattering dream or worthless fancy.
Then take him up, and manage well the jest.
Carry him gently to my fairest chamber,
And hang it round with all my wanton pictures.
Balm his foul head in warm distillèd waters,
And burn sweet wood to make the lodging sweet.

Procure me music ready when he wakes,
To make a dulcet and a heavenly sound.
And if he chance to speak, be ready straight   50
And with a low submissive reverence
Say 'What is it your honour will command?'
Let one attend him with a silver basin
Full of rose-water and bestrewed with flowers,
Another bear the ewer, the third a diaper,
And say 'Will't please your lordship cool your hands?'
Some one be ready with a costly suit,
And ask him what apparel he will wear.
Another tell him of his hounds and horse,
And that his lady mourns at his disease.   60
Persuade him that he hath been lunatic,
And when he says he is Sly, say that he dreams,
For he is nothing but a mighty lord.
This do, and do it kindly, gentle sirs.
It will be pastime passing excellent,
If it be husbanded with modesty.

FIRST HUNTSMAN
My lord, I warrant you we will play our part
As he shall think by our true diligence
He is no less than what we say he is.

LORD
Take him up gently and to bed with him,   70
And each one to his office when he wakes.

Sly is carried away

A trumpet sounds
Sirrah, go see what trumpet 'tis that sounds –

Exit Servingman
Belike some noble gentleman that means,
Travelling some journey, to repose him here.

Enter Servingman
How now? Who is it?

57

SERVINGMAN   An't please your honour, players
  That offer service to your lordship.

LORD
  Bid them come near.
     Enter Players
                   Now, fellows, you are welcome.

PLAYERS
  We thank your honour.

LORD
  Do you intend to stay with me tonight?

FIRST PLAYER
80   So please your lordship to accept our duty.

LORD
  With all my heart. This fellow I remember
  Since once he played a farmer's eldest son.
  'Twas where you wooed the gentlewoman so well.
  I have forgot your name; but, sure, that part
  Was aptly fitted and naturally performed.

FIRST PLAYER
  I think 'twas Soto that your honour means.

LORD
  'Tis very true, thou didst it excellent.
  Well, you are come to me in happy time,
  The rather for I have some sport in hand
90   Wherein your cunning can assist me much.
  There is a lord will hear you play tonight;
  But I am doubtful of your modesties,
  Lest over-eyeing of his odd behaviour –
  For yet his honour never heard a play –
  You break into some merry passion
  And so offend him, for I tell you, sirs,
  If you should smile, he grows impatient.

FIRST PLAYER
  Fear not, my lord, we can contain ourselves,

Were he the veriest antic in the world.

LORD

  Go, sirrah, take them to the buttery,   100
  And give them friendly welcome every one.
  Let them want nothing that my house affords.

Exit one with the Players

  Sirrah, go you to Barthol'mew my page,
  And see him dressed in all suits like a lady.
  That done, conduct him to the drunkard's chamber,
  And call him 'madam', do him obeisance.
  Tell him from me – as he will win my love –
  He bear himself with honourable action,
  Such as he hath observed in noble ladies
  Unto their lords, by them accomplishèd.   110
  Such duty to the drunkard let him do,
  With soft low tongue and lowly courtesy,
  And say 'What is't your honour will command,
  Wherein your lady and your humble wife
  May show her duty and make known her love?'
  And then with kind embracements, tempting kisses,
  And with declining head into his bosom,
  Bid him shed tears, as being overjoyed
  To see her noble lord restored to health,
  Who for this seven years hath esteemèd him   120
  No better than a poor and loathsome beggar.
  And if the boy have not a woman's gift
  To rain a shower of commanded tears,
  An onion will do well for such a shift,
  Which in a napkin being close conveyed,
  Shall in despite enforce a watery eye.
  See this dispatched with all the haste thou canst,
  Anon I'll give thee more instructions.

Exit a Servingman

  I know the boy will well usurp the grace,

130 Voice, gait, and action of a gentlewoman.
I long to hear him call the drunkard husband,
And how my men will stay themselves from laughter
When they do homage to this simple peasant.
I'll in to counsel them. Haply my presence
May well abate the over-merry spleen,
Which otherwise would grow into extremes.   *Exeunt*

2   *Enter aloft Sly, with attendants; some with apparel,*
          basin and ewer, and other appurtenances; and Lord

SLY For God's sake, a pot of small ale.

FIRST SERVINGMAN
    Will't please your lordship drink a cup of sack?

SECOND SERVINGMAN
    Will't please your honour taste of these conserves?

THIRD SERVINGMAN
    What raiment will your honour wear today?

SLY I am Christophero Sly, call not me 'honour' nor 'lordship'. I ne'er drank sack in my life. And if you give me
any conserves, give me conserves of beef. Ne'er ask me
what raiment I'll wear, for I have no more doublets than
backs, no more stockings than legs, nor no more shoes
10 than feet – nay, sometimes more feet than shoes, or such
shoes as my toes look through the overleather.

LORD
    Heaven cease this idle humour in your honour!
    O, that a mighty man of such descent,
    Of such possessions, and so high esteem,
    Should be infusèd with so foul a spirit!

SLY What, would you make me mad? Am not I Christopher Sly, old Sly's son of Burton-heath, by birth a ped-
lar, by education a cardmaker, by transmutation a
bear-herd, and now by present profession a tinker? Ask

Marian Hacket, the fat ale-wife of Wincot, if she know 20
me not. If she say I am not fourteen pence on the score
for sheer ale, score me up for the lyingest knave in
Christendom.

A Servingman brings him a pot of ale

What! I am not bestraught. Here's –

He drinks

THIRD SERVINGMAN

O, this it is that makes your lady mourn.

SECOND SERVINGMAN

O, this is it that makes your servants droop.

LORD

Hence comes it that your kindred shuns your house,
As beaten hence by your strange lunacy.
O noble lord, bethink thee of thy birth,
Call home thy ancient thoughts from banishment, 30
And banish hence these abject lowly dreams.
Look how thy servants do attend on thee,
Each in his office ready at thy beck.
Wilt thou have music? Hark, Apollo plays,

Music

And twenty cagèd nightingales do sing.
Or wilt thou sleep? We'll have thee to a couch
Softer and sweeter than the lustful bed
On purpose trimmed up for Semiramis.
Say thou wilt walk; we will bestrew the ground.
Or wilt thou ride? Thy horses shall be trapped, 40
Their harness studded all with gold and pearl.
Dost thou love hawking? Thou hast hawks will soar
Above the morning lark. Or wilt thou hunt?
Thy hounds shall make the welkin answer them
And fetch shrill echoes from the hollow earth.

FIRST SERVINGMAN

Say thou wilt course, thy greyhounds are as swift

As breathèd stags, ay, fleeter than the roe.

SECOND SERVINGMAN

Dost thou love pictures? We will fetch thee straight
Adonis painted by a running brook,

50 And Cytherea all in sedges hid,
Which seem to move and wanton with her breath
Even as the waving sedges play wi'th'wind.

LORD

We'll show thee Io as she was a maid,
And how she was beguilèd and surprised,
As lively painted as the deed was done.

THIRD SERVINGMAN

Or Daphne roaming through a thorny wood,
Scratching her legs that one shall swear she bleeds,
And at that sight shall sad Apollo weep,
So workmanly the blood and tears are drawn.

LORD

60 Thou art a lord, and nothing but a lord.
Thou hast a lady far more beautiful
Than any woman in this waning age.

FIRST SERVINGMAN

And till the tears that she hath shed for thee
Like envious floods o'errun her lovely face,
She was the fairest creature in the world –
And yet she is inferior to none.

SLY

Am I a lord and have I such a lady?
Or do I dream? Or have I dreamed till now?
I do not sleep. I see, I hear, I speak.

70 I smell sweet savours and I feel soft things.
Upon my life, I am a lord indeed,
And not a tinker nor Christophero Sly.
Well, bring our lady hither to our sight,
And once again a pot o'th'smallest ale.

SECOND SERVINGMAN
  Will't please your mightiness to wash your hands?
  O, how we joy to see your wit restored!
  O, that once more you knew but what you are!
  These fifteen years you have been in a dream,
  Or when you waked, so waked as if you slept.

SLY
  These fifteen years! By my fay, a goodly nap.　　　80
  But did I never speak of all that time?

FIRST SERVINGMAN
  O, yes, my lord, but very idle words,
  For though you lay here in this goodly chamber,
  Yet would you say ye were beaten out of door,
  And rail upon the hostess of the house,
  And say you would present her at the leet,
  Because she brought stone jugs and no sealed quarts.
  Sometimes you would call out for Cicely Hacket.

SLY
  Ay, the woman's maid of the house.

THIRD SERVINGMAN
  Why, sir, you know no house, nor no such maid,　　　90
  Nor no such men as you have reckoned up,
  As Stephen Sly, and old John Naps of Greece,
  And Peter Turph, and Henry Pimpernell,
  And twenty more such names and men as these,
  Which never were nor no man ever saw.

SLY
  Now Lord be thankèd for my good amends.

ALL Amen.

         *Enter Page as a lady, with attendants. One gives Sly
         a pot of ale*

SLY I thank thee, thou shalt not lose by it.

PAGE How fares my noble lord?

SLY Marry, I fare well, for here is cheer enough.　　　100

63

He drinks

Where is my wife?

PAGE

  Here, noble lord, what is thy will with her?

SLY

  Are you my wife, and will not call me husband?
  My men should call me 'lord', I am your goodman.

PAGE

  My husband and my lord, my lord and husband,
  I am your wife in all obedience.

SLY I know it well. What must I call her?

LORD Madam.

SLY Al'ce madam, or Joan madam?

LORD

110 Madam and nothing else, so lords call ladies.

SLY

  Madam wife, they say that I have dreamed
  And slept above some fifteen year or more.

PAGE

  Ay, and the time seems thirty unto me,
  Being all this time abandoned from your bed.

SLY

  'Tis much. Servants, leave me and her alone.

                     Exeunt Lord and Servingmen

  Madam, undress you and come now to bed.

PAGE

  Thrice-noble lord, let me entreat of you
  To pardon me yet for a night or two,
  Or, if not so, until the sun be set.

120 For your physicians have expressly charged,
  In peril to incur your former malady,
  That I should yet absent me from your bed.
  I hope this reason stands for my excuse.

SLY Ay, it stands so that I may hardly tarry so long. But I

would be loath to fall into my dreams again. I will therefore tarry in despite of the flesh and the blood.

Enter the Lord as a Messenger

LORD

Your honour's players, hearing your amendment,
Are come to play a pleasant comedy;
For so your doctors hold it very meet,
Seeing too much sadness hath congealed your blood,   130
And melancholy is the nurse of frenzy.
Therefore they thought it good you hear a play
And frame your mind to mirth and merriment,
Which bars a thousand harms and lengthens life.

SLY Marry, I will. Let them play it. Is not a comonty a
Christmas gambold or a tumbling-trick?

PAGE

No, my good lord, it is more pleasing stuff.

SLY What, household stuff?

PAGE It is a kind of history.

SLY Well, we'll see't. Come, madam wife, sit by my side   140
and let the world slip, we shall ne'er be younger.

They sit
A flourish of trumpets to announce the play

Enter Lucentio and his man Tranio   I.1

LUCENTIO

Tranio, since for the great desire I had
To see fair Padua, nursery of arts,
I am arrived for fruitful Lombardy,
The pleasant garden of great Italy,
And by my father's love and leave am armed
With his good will and thy good company,

My trusty servant well approved in all,
Here let us breathe and haply institute
A course of learning and ingenious studies.
10 Pisa renownèd for grave citizens
Gave me my being and my father first,
A merchant of great traffic through the world,
Vincentio come of the Bentivolii.
Vincentio's son, brought up in Florence,
It shall become to serve all hopes conceived
To deck his fortune with his virtuous deeds.
And therefore, Tranio, for the time I study
Virtue, and that part of philosophy
Will I apply that treats of happiness
20 By virtue specially to be achieved.
Tell me thy mind, for I have Pisa left
And am to Padua come as he that leaves
A shallow plash to plunge him in the deep,
And with satiety seeks to quench his thirst.

TRANIO

Mi perdonato, gentle master mine.
I am in all affected as yourself,
Glad that you thus continue your resolve
To suck the sweets of sweet philosophy.
Only, good master, while we do admire
30 This virtue and this moral discipline,
Let's be no stoics nor no stocks, I pray,
Or so devote to Aristotle's checks
As Ovid be an outcast quite abjured.
Balk logic with acquaintance that you have,
And practise rhetoric in your common talk,
Music and poesy use to quicken you,
The mathematics and the metaphysics
Fall to them as you find your stomach serves you.
No profit grows where is no pleasure ta'en.

In brief, sir, study what you most affect.   40
LUCENTIO
Gramercies, Tranio, well dost thou advise.
If, Biondello, thou wert come ashore,
We could at once put us in readiness,
And take a lodging fit to entertain
Such friends as time in Padua shall beget.

> *Enter Baptista with his two daughters Katherina and*
> *Bianca; Gremio, a pantaloon, and Hortensio, suitor*
> *to Bianca. Lucentio and Tranio stand by*

But stay awhile, what company is this?
TRANIO
Master, some show to welcome us to town.
BAPTISTA
Gentlemen, importune me no farther,
For how I firmly am resolved you know;
That is, not to bestow my youngest daughter   50
Before I have a husband for the elder.
If either of you both love Katherina,
Because I know you well and love you well,
Leave shall you have to court her at your pleasure.
GREMIO
To cart her rather. She's too rough for me.
There, there, Hortensio, will you any wife?
KATHERINA (*to Baptista*)
I pray you, sir, is it your will
To make a stale of me amongst these mates?
HORTENSIO
Mates, maid, how mean you that? No mates for you
Unless you were of gentler, milder mould.   60
KATHERINA
I'faith, sir, you shall never need to fear.
Iwis it is not halfway to her heart.
But if it were, doubt not her care should be

To comb your noddle with a three-legged stool,
And paint your face, and use you like a fool.

HORTENSIO

From all such devils, good Lord deliver us!

GREMIO

And me too, good Lord!

TRANIO (*aside to Lucentio*)

Husht, master, here's some good pastime toward.
That wench is stark mad or wonderful froward.

LUCENTIO (*aside to Tranio*)

70 But in the other's silence do I see
Maid's mild behaviour and sobriety.
Peace, Tranio.

TRANIO (*aside to Lucentio*)

Well said, master. Mum! And gaze your fill.

BAPTISTA

Gentlemen, that I may soon make good
What I have said – Bianca, get you in.
And let it not displease thee, good Bianca,
For I will love thee ne'er the less, my girl.

KATHERINA

A pretty peat! It is best
Put finger in the eye, an she knew why.

BIANCA

80 Sister, content you in my discontent.
Sir, to your pleasure humbly I subscribe.
My books and instruments shall be my company,
On them to look and practise by myself.

LUCENTIO (*aside*)

Hark, Tranio, thou mayst hear Minerva speak.

HORTENSIO

Signor Baptista, will you be so strange?
Sorry am I that our good will effects
Bianca's grief.

68

GREMIO   Why will you mew her up,
Signor Baptista, for this fiend of hell,
And make her bear the penance of her tongue?

BAPTISTA
Gentlemen, content ye. I am resolved.   90
Go in, Bianca.   *Exit Bianca*
And for I know she taketh most delight
In music, instruments, and poetry,
Schoolmasters will I keep within my house
Fit to instruct her youth. If you, Hortensio,
Or Signor Gremio, you, know any such,
Prefer them hither; for to cunning men
I will be very kind, and liberal
To mine own children in good bringing-up.
And so farewell. Katherina, you may stay,   100
For I have more to commune with Bianca.   *Exit*

KATHERINA
Why, and I trust I may go too, may I not?
What, shall I be appointed hours, as though, belike,
I knew not what to take and what to leave? Ha? *Exit*

GREMIO You may go to the devil's dam. Your gifts are so
good here's none will hold you. There! Love is not so
great, Hortensio, but we may blow our nails together,
and fast it fairly out. Our cake's dough on both sides.
Farewell. Yet, for the love I bear my sweet Bianca, if I
can by any means light on a fit man to teach her that 110
wherein she delights, I will wish him to her father.

HORTENSIO So will I, Signor Gremio. But a word, I
pray. Though the nature of our quarrel yet never
brooked parle, know now, upon advice, it toucheth us
both – that we may yet again have access to our fair
mistress and be happy rivals in Bianca's love – to
labour and effect one thing specially.

GREMIO What's that, I pray?

HORTENSIO Marry, sir, to get a husband for her sister.
120 GREMIO A husband? A devil.

HORTENSIO I say a husband.

GREMIO I say a devil. Think'st thou, Hortensio, though
her father be very rich, any man is so very a fool to be
married to hell?

HORTENSIO Tush, Gremio. Though it pass your patience
and mine to endure her loud alarums, why, man, there be
good fellows in the world, an a man could light on them,
would take her with all faults, and money enough.

GREMIO I cannot tell. But I had as lief take her dowry
130 with this condition – to be whipped at the high-cross
every morning.

HORTENSIO Faith, as you say, there's small choice in
rotten apples. But come, since this bar in law makes us
friends, it shall be so far forth friendly maintained till by
helping Baptista's eldest daughter to a husband we set
his youngest free for a husband, and then have to't
afresh. Sweet Bianca! Happy man be his dole. He that
runs fastest gets the ring. How say you, Signor Gremio?

GREMIO I am agreed, and would I had given him the best
140 horse in Padua to begin his wooing that would thoroughly woo her, wed her, and bed her, and rid the house
of her. Come on.   *Exeunt Gremio and Hortensio*

TRANIO
  I pray, sir, tell me, is it possible
  That love should of a sudden take such hold?

LUCENTIO
  O Tranio, till I found it to be true,
  I never thought it possible or likely.
  But see, while idly I stood looking on,
  I found the effect of love in idleness,
  And now in plainness do confess to thee,
150 That art to me as secret and as dear

As Anna to the Queen of Carthage was –
Tranio, I burn, I pine, I perish, Tranio,
If I achieve not this young modest girl.
Counsel me, Tranio, for I know thou canst.
Assist me, Tranio, for I know thou wilt.

TRANIO

Master, it is no time to chide you now;
Affection is not rated from the heart.
If love have touched you, naught remains but so –
Redime te captum quam queas minimo.

LUCENTIO

Gramercies, lad. Go forward, this contents.　　　　160
The rest will comfort, for thy counsel's sound.

TRANIO

Master, you looked so longly on the maid,
Perhaps you marked not what's the pith of all.

LUCENTIO

O yes, I saw sweet beauty in her face,
Such as the daughter of Agenor had,
That made great Jove to humble him to her hand,
When with his knees he kissed the Cretan strand.

TRANIO

Saw you no more? Marked you not how her sister
Began to scold and raise up such a storm
That mortal ears might hardly endure the din?　　　170

LUCENTIO

Tranio, I saw her coral lips to move,
And with her breath she did perfume the air.
Sacred and sweet was all I saw in her.

TRANIO

Nay, then 'tis time to stir him from his trance.
I pray, awake, sir. If you love the maid,
Bend thoughts and wits to achieve her. Thus it stands:
Her elder sister is so curst and shrewd

That till the father rid his hands of her,
Master, your love must live a maid at home,
180 And therefore has he closely mewed her up,
Because she will not be annoyed with suitors.

LUCENTIO
Ah, Tranio, what a cruel father's he!
But art thou not advised he took some care
To get her cunning schoolmasters to instruct her?

TRANIO
Ay, marry, am I, sir – and now 'tis plotted.

LUCENTIO
I have it, Tranio.

TRANIO   Master, for my hand,
Both our inventions meet and jump in one.

LUCENTIO
Tell me thine first.

TRANIO   You will be schoolmaster,
And undertake the teaching of the maid –
190 That's your device.

LUCENTIO   It is. May it be done?

TRANIO
Not possible. For who shall bear your part
And be in Padua here Vincentio's son,
Keep house and ply his book, welcome his friends,
Visit his countrymen and banquet them?

LUCENTIO
Basta, content thee, for I have it full.
We have not yet been seen in any house,
Nor can we be distinguished by our faces
For man or master. Then it follows thus –
Thou shalt be master, Tranio, in my stead,
200 Keep house, and port, and servants, as I should.
I will some other be – some Florentine,
Some Neapolitan, or meaner man of Pisa.

'Tis hatched, and shall be so. Tranio, at once
Uncase thee, take my coloured hat and cloak.
When Biondello comes, he waits on thee,
But I will charm him first to keep his tongue.

TRANIO
So had you need.
  They exchange garments
In brief, sir, sith it your pleasure is,
And I am tied to be obedient –
For so your father charged me at our parting: 210
'Be serviceable to my son', quoth he,
Although I think 'twas in another sense –
I am content to be Lucentio,
Because so well I love Lucentio.

LUCENTIO
Tranio, be so, because Lucentio loves.
And let me be a slave t'achieve that maid
Whose sudden sight hath thralled my wounded eye.
  Enter Biondello
Here comes the rogue. Sirrah, where have you been?

BIONDELLO Where have I been? Nay, how now, where
are you? Master, has my fellow Tranio stolen your 220
clothes, or you stolen his, or both? Pray, what's the
news?

LUCENTIO
Sirrah, come hither. 'Tis no time to jest,
And therefore frame your manners to the time.
Your fellow Tranio here, to save my life,
Puts my apparel and my countenance on,
And I for my escape have put on his.
For in a quarrel since I came ashore
I killed a man, and fear I was descried.
Wait you on him, I charge you, as becomes, 230
While I make way from hence to save my life.

73

You understand me?

BIONDELLO   I, sir? Ne'er a whit.

LUCENTIO

And not a jot of Tranio in your mouth.
Tranio is changed into Lucentio.

BIONDELLO

The better for him, would I were so too!

TRANIO

So could I, faith, boy, to have the next wish after,
That Lucentio indeed had Baptista's youngest daughter.
But, sirrah, not for my sake but your master's, I advise
You use your manners discreetly in all kind of com-
      panies.
240   When I am alone, why then I am Tranio,
But in all places else your master Lucentio.

LUCENTIO

Tranio, let's go.
One thing more rests, that thyself execute –
To make one among these wooers. If thou ask me why,
Sufficeth, my reasons are both good and weighty. *Exeunt*
      The Presenters above speak

LORD

My lord, you nod, you do not mind the play.

SLY (*coming to with a start*) Yes, by Saint Anne, do I. A
good matter, surely. Comes there any more of it?

PAGE My lord, 'tis but begun.

250   SLY 'Tis a very excellent piece of work, madam lady.
Would 'twere done!

      They sit and mark

I.2   *Enter Petruchio and his man Grumio*

PETRUCHIO

Verona, for a while I take my leave,
To see my friends in Padua, but of all

My best belovèd and approvèd friend,
Hortensio; and I trow this is his house.
Here, sirrah Grumio, knock, I say.

GRUMIO Knock, sir? Whom should I knock? Is there any
man has rebused your worship?

PETRUCHIO Villain, I say, knock me here soundly.

GRUMIO Knock you here, sir? Why, sir, what am I, sir,
that I should knock you here, sir?   10

PETRUCHIO
Villain, I say, knock me at this gate,
And rap me well, or I'll knock your knave's pate.

GRUMIO
My master is grown quarrelsome. I should knock you
      first,
And then I know after who comes by the worst.

PETRUCHIO
Will it not be?
Faith, sirrah, an you'll not knock, I'll ring it.
I'll try how you can *sol-fa* and sing it.
      He wrings him by the ears

GRUMIO
Help, masters, help! My master is mad.

PETRUCHIO
Now knock when I bid you, sirrah villain.
      Enter Hortensio

HORTENSIO How now, what's the matter? My old friend   20
Grumio and my good friend Petruchio! How do you all
at Verona?

PETRUCHIO
Signor Hortensio, come you to part the fray?
Con tutto il cuore ben trovato, may I say.

HORTENSIO
Alla nostra casa ben venuto,
Molto honorato signor mio Petruchio.

75

Rise, Grumio, rise. We will compound this quarrel.

GRUMIO Nay, 'tis no matter, sir, what he 'leges in Latin. If
this be not a lawful cause for me to leave his service,
30 look you, sir. He bid me knock him and rap him
soundly, sir. Well, was it fit for a servant to use his
master so, being perhaps, for aught I see, two and thirty,
a pip out?

Whom would to God I had well knocked at first,
Then had not Grumio come by the worst.

PETRUCHIO
A senseless villain. Good Hortensio,
I bade the rascal knock upon your gate,
And could not get him for my heart to do it.

GRUMIO Knock at the gate? O heavens! Spake you not
40 these words plain, 'Sirrah, knock me here, rap me here,
knock me well, and knock me soundly'? And come you
now with 'knocking at the gate'?

PETRUCHIO
Sirrah, be gone, or talk not, I advise you.

HORTENSIO
Petruchio, patience, I am Grumio's pledge.
Why, this's a heavy chance 'twixt him and you,
Your ancient, trusty, pleasant servant Grumio.
And tell me now, sweet friend, what happy gale
Blows you to Padua here from old Verona?

PETRUCHIO
Such wind as scatters young men through the world
50 To seek their fortunes farther than at home,
Where small experience grows. But in a few,
Signor Hortensio, thus it stands with me:
Antonio, my father, is deceased,
And I have thrust myself into this maze,
Haply to wive and thrive as best I may.
Crowns in my purse I have, and goods at home,

And so am come abroad to see the world.

HORTENSIO

Petruchio, shall I then come roundly to thee
And wish thee to a shrewd ill-favoured wife?
Thou'dst thank me but a little for my counsel,   60
And yet I'll promise thee she shall be rich,
And very rich. But th' art too much my friend,
And I'll not wish thee to her.

PETRUCHIO

Signor Hortensio, 'twixt such friends as we
Few words suffice; and therefore, if thou know
One rich enough to be Petruchio's wife –
As wealth is burden of my wooing dance –
Be she as foul as was Florentius' love,
As old as Sibyl, and as curst and shrewd
As Socrates' Xanthippe, or a worse,   70
She moves me not, or not removes at least
Affection's edge in me, were she as rough
As are the swelling Adriatic seas.
I come to wive it wealthily in Padua;
If wealthily, then happily in Padua.

GRUMIO Nay, look you, sir, he tells you flatly what his
mind is. Why, give him gold enough and marry him to
a puppet or an aglet-baby, or an old trot with ne'er a
tooth in her head, though she have as many diseases
as two and fifty horses. Why, nothing comes amiss, so 80
money comes withal.

HORTENSIO

Petruchio, since we are stepped thus far in,
I will continue that I broached in jest.
I can, Petruchio, help thee to a wife
With wealth enough, and young and beauteous,
Brought up as best becomes a gentlewoman.
Her only fault – and that is faults enough –

Is that she is intolerable curst,
And shrewd and froward so beyond all measure
90 That, were my state far worser than it is,
I would not wed her for a mine of gold.

PETRUCHIO

Hortensio, peace. Thou know'st not gold's effect.
Tell me her father's name and 'tis enough.
For I will board her though she chide as loud
As thunder when the clouds in autumn crack.

HORTENSIO

Her father is Baptista Minola,
An affable and courteous gentleman.
Her name is Katherina Minola,
Renowned in Padua for her scolding tongue.

PETRUCHIO

100 I know her father, though I know not her,
And he knew my deceasèd father well.
I will not sleep, Hortensio, till I see her,
And therefore let me be thus bold with you
To give you over at this first encounter,
Unless you will accompany me thither.

GRUMIO I pray you, sir, let him go while the humour lasts.
O' my word, an she knew him as well as I do, she would
think scolding would do little good upon him. She may
perhaps call him half a score knaves or so. Why, that's
110 nothing; an he begin once, he'll rail in his rope-tricks.
I'll tell you what, sir, an she stand him but a little, he
will throw a figure in her face, and so disfigure her with
it that she shall have no more eyes to see withal than a
cat. You know him not, sir.

HORTENSIO

Tarry, Petruchio, I must go with thee,
For in Baptista's keep my treasure is.
He hath the jewel of my life in hold,

His youngest daughter, beautiful Bianca,
And her withholds from me and other more,
Suitors to her and rivals in my love, 120
Supposing it a thing impossible,
For those defects I have before rehearsed,
That ever Katherina will be wooed.
Therefore this order hath Baptista ta'en,
That none shall have access unto Bianca
Till Katherine the curst have got a husband.

GRUMIO
Katherine the curst,
A title for a maid of all titles the worst.

HORTENSIO
Now shall my friend Petruchio do me grace,
And offer me disguised in sober robes 130
To old Baptista as a schoolmaster
Well seen in music, to instruct Bianca,
That so I may by this device at least
Have leave and leisure to make love to her,
And unsuspected court her by herself.

GRUMIO Here's no knavery! See, to beguile the old folks,
how the young folks lay their heads together.

*Enter Gremio, and Lucentio disguised as Cambio, a
schoolmaster*

Master, master, look about you. Who goes there, ha?

HORTENSIO
Peace, Grumio. It is the rival of my love.
Petruchio, stand by a while. 140

GRUMIO
A proper stripling and an amorous!
They stand aside

GREMIO
O, very well – I have perused the note.
Hark you, sir, I'll have them very fairly bound –

All books of love, see that at any hand –
And see you read no other lectures to her.
You understand me. Over and beside
Signor Baptista's liberality,
I'll mend it with a largess. Take your paper too.
And let me have them very well perfumed,
150 For she is sweeter than perfume itself
To whom they go to. What will you read to her?

LUCENTIO
Whate'er I read to her, I'll plead for you
As for my patron, stand you so assured,
As firmly as yourself were still in place,
Yea, and perhaps with more successful words
Than you, unless you were a scholar, sir.

GREMIO
O this learning, what a thing it is!

GRUMIO (aside)
O this woodcock, what an ass it is!

PETRUCHIO (aside)
Peace, sirrah.

HORTENSIO (aside)
160 Grumio, mum! (Coming forward) God save you, Signor
Gremio.

GREMIO
And you are well met, Signor Hortensio.
Trow you whither I am going? To Baptista Minola.
I promised to enquire carefully
About a schoolmaster for the fair Bianca,
And by good fortune I have lighted well
On this young man, for learning and behaviour
Fit for her turn, well read in poetry
And other books – good ones, I warrant ye.

HORTENSIO
'Tis well. And I have met a gentleman

Hath promised me to help me to another,   170
A fine musician to instruct our mistress.
So shall I no whit be behind in duty
To fair Bianca, so beloved of me.

GREMIO
Beloved of me, and that my deeds shall prove.

GRUMIO (*aside*)
And that his bags shall prove.

HORTENSIO
Gremio, 'tis now no time to vent our love.
Listen to me, and if you speak me fair,
I'll tell you news indifferent good for either.
Here is a gentleman whom by chance I met,
Upon agreement from us to his liking,   180
Will undertake to woo curst Katherine,
Yea, and to marry her, if her dowry please.

GREMIO
So said, so done, is well.
Hortensio, have you told him all her faults?

PETRUCHIO
I know she is an irksome brawling scold.
If that be all, masters, I hear no harm.

GREMIO
No, say'st me so, friend? What countryman?

PETRUCHIO
Born in Verona, old Antonio's son.
My father dead, my fortune lives for me,
And I do hope good days and long to see.   190

GREMIO
O sir, such a life with such a wife were strange.
But if you have a stomach, to't a God's name –
You shall have me assisting you in all.
But will you woo this wildcat?

PETRUCHIO   Will I live?

GRUMIO

Will he woo her? Ay, or I'll hang her.

PETRUCHIO

Why came I hither but to that intent?
Think you a little din can daunt mine ears?
Have I not in my time heard lions roar?
Have I not heard the sea, puffed up with winds,
200 Rage like an angry boar chafèd with sweat?
Have I not heard great ordnance in the field,
And heaven's artillery thunder in the skies?
Have I not in a pitchèd battle heard
Loud 'larums, neighing steeds, and trumpets' clang?
And do you tell me of a woman's tongue,
That gives not half so great a blow to hear
As will a chestnut in a farmer's fire?
Tush, tush, fear boys with bugs!

GRUMIO   For he fears none.

GREMIO

210 This gentleman is happily arrived,
My mind presumes, for his own good and yours.

HORTENSIO

I promised we would be contributors
And bear his charge of wooing, whatsoe'er.

GREMIO

And so we will – provided that he win her.

GRUMIO

I would I were as sure of a good dinner.

> *Enter Tranio, bravely dressed as Lucentio, and Biondello*

TRANIO

Gentlemen, God save you. If I may be bold,
Tell me, I beseech you, which is the readiest way
To the house of Signor Baptista Minola?

BIONDELLO He that has the two fair daughters – is't he
  you mean? 220

TRANIO Even he, Biondello.

GREMIO
  Hark you, sir, you mean not her too?

TRANIO
  Perhaps him and her, sir. What have you to do?

PETRUCHIO
  Not her that chides, sir, at any hand, I pray.

TRANIO
  I love no chiders, sir. Biondello, let's away.

LUCENTIO (*aside*)
  Well begun, Tranio.

HORTENSIO   Sir, a word ere you go.
  Are you a suitor to the maid you talk of, yea or no?

TRANIO
  And if I be, sir, is it any offence?

GREMIO
  No, if without more words you will get you hence.

TRANIO
  Why, sir, I pray, are not the streets as free 230
  For me as for you?

GREMIO   But so is not she.

TRANIO
  For what reason, I beseech you?

GREMIO   For this reason, if you'll know,
  That she's the choice love of Signor Gremio.

HORTENSIO
  That she's the chosen of Signor Hortensio.

TRANIO
  Softly, my masters! If you be gentlemen,
  Do me this right – hear me with patience.
  Baptista is a noble gentleman,
  To whom my father is not all unknown,

And were his daughter fairer than she is,
240 She may more suitors have and me for one.
Fair Leda's daughter had a thousand wooers,
Then well one more may fair Bianca have.
And so she shall. Lucentio shall make one,
Though Paris came, in hope to speed alone.

GREMIO
What, this gentleman will out-talk us all!

LUCENTIO
Sir, give him head, I know he'll prove a jade.

PETRUCHIO
Hortensio, to what end are all these words?

HORTENSIO
Sir, let me be so bold as ask you,
Did you yet ever see Baptista's daughter?

TRANIO
250 No, sir, but hear I do that he hath two;
The one as famous for a scolding tongue
As is the other for beauteous modesty.

PETRUCHIO
Sir, sir, the first's for me, let her go by.

GREMIO
Yea, leave that labour to great Hercules,
And let it be more than Alcides' twelve.

PETRUCHIO
Sir, understand you this of me in sooth,
The youngest daughter whom you hearken for
Her father keeps from all access of suitors,
And will not promise her to any man
260 Until the elder sister first be wed.
The younger then is free, and not before.

TRANIO
If it be so, sir, that you are the man
Must stead us all – and me amongst the rest –

And if you break the ice and do this feat,
Achieve the elder, set the younger free
For our access – whose hap shall be to have her
Will not so graceless be to be ingrate.

HORTENSIO
Sir, you say well, and well you do conceive.
And since you do profess to be a suitor,
You must, as we do, gratify this gentleman, 270
To whom we all rest generally beholding.

TRANIO
Sir, I shall not be slack. In sign whereof,
Please ye we may contrive this afternoon,
And quaff carouses to our mistress' health,
And do as adversaries do in law,
Strive mightily, but eat and drink as friends.

GRUMIO *and* BIONDELLO
O excellent motion! Fellows, let's be gone.

HORTENSIO
The motion's good indeed, and be it so.
Petruchio, I shall be your *ben venuto*.   *Exeunt*

*

Enter Katherina, and Bianca with her hands tied   II.1

BIANCA
Good sister, wrong me not, nor wrong yourself,
To make a bondmaid and a slave of me.
That I disdain. But for these other gauds,
Unbind my hands, I'll pull them off myself,
Yea, all my raiment, to my petticoat,
Or what you will command me will I do,
So well I know my duty to my elders.

KATHERINA

   Of all thy suitors here I charge thee tell
   Whom thou lov'st best. See thou dissemble not.

BIANCA

10   Believe me, sister, of all men alive
   I never yet beheld that special face
   Which I could fancy more than any other.

KATHERINA

   Minion, thou liest. Is't not Hortensio?

BIANCA

   If you affect him, sister, here I swear
   I'll plead for you myself but you shall have him.

KATHERINA

   O then, belike, you fancy riches more.
   You will have Gremio to keep you fair.

BIANCA

   Is it for him you do envy me so?
   Nay then you jest, and now I well perceive
20   You have but jested with me all this while.
   I prithee, sister Kate, untie my hands.

KATHERINA

   Strikes her
   If that be jest, then all the rest was so.
   Enter Baptista

BAPTISTA

   Why, how now, dame, whence grows this insolence?
   Bianca, stand aside. Poor girl, she weeps.
   He unties her hands
   Go ply thy needle, meddle not with her.
   (*to Katherina*) For shame, thou hilding of a devilish spirit,
   Why dost thou wrong her that did ne'er wrong thee?
   When did she cross thee with a bitter word?

KATHERINA

   Her silence flouts me, and I'll be revenged.

She flies after Bianca

BAPTISTA

What, in my sight? Bianca, get thee in.　　*Exit Bianca* 30

KATHERINA

What, will you not suffer me? Nay, now I see
She is your treasure, she must have a husband.
I must dance bare-foot on her wedding-day,
And for your love to her lead apes in hell.
Talk not to me, I will go sit and weep,
Till I can find occasion of revenge.　　*Exit Katherina*

BAPTISTA

Was ever gentleman thus grieved as I?
But who comes here?

>　*Enter Gremio, with Lucentio, disguised as Cambio, in*
>　*the habit of a mean man; Petruchio, with Hortensio,*
>　*disguised as Licio; and Tranio, disguised as Lucentio,*
>　*with his boy, Biondello, bearing a lute and books*

GREMIO　Good morrow, neighbour Baptista.

BAPTISTA　Good morrow, neighbour Gremio. God save 40
you, gentlemen.

PETRUCHIO

And you, good sir. Pray have you not a daughter
Called Katherina, fair and virtuous?

BAPTISTA

I have a daughter, sir, called Katherina.

GREMIO

You are too blunt, go to it orderly.

PETRUCHIO

You wrong me, Signor Gremio, give me leave.
I am a gentleman of Verona, sir,
That hearing of her beauty and her wit,
Her affability and bashful modesty,
Her wondrous qualities and mild behaviour,　　50
Am bold to show myself a forward guest

87

Within your house, to make mine eye the witness
Of that report which I so oft have heard.
And for an entrance to my entertainment
I do present you with a man of mine,
    (*presenting Hortensio*)
Cunning in music and the mathematics,
To instruct her fully in those sciences,
Whereof I know she is not ignorant.
Accept of him, or else you do me wrong.

60 His name is Licio, born in Mantua.

BAPTISTA

Y'are welcome, sir, and he for your good sake.
But for my daughter Katherine, this I know,
She is not for your turn, the more my grief.

PETRUCHIO

I see you do not mean to part with her,
Or else you like not of my company.

BAPTISTA

Mistake me not, I speak but as I find.
Whence are you, sir? What may I call your name?

PETRUCHIO

Petruchio is my name, Antonio's son,
A man well known throughout all Italy.

BAPTISTA

70 I know him well. You are welcome for his sake.

GREMIO

Saving your tale, Petruchio, I pray
Let us that are poor petitioners speak too.
Baccare! You are marvellous forward.

PETRUCHIO

O pardon me, Signor Gremio, I would fain be doing.

GREMIO

I doubt it not, sir, but you will curse your wooing.
(*to Baptista*) Neighbour, this is a gift very grateful, I am

sure of it. To express the like kindness, myself, that have been more kindly beholding to you than any, freely give unto you this young scholar (*presenting Lucentio*) that hath been long studying at Rheims, as cunning in Greek, 80 Latin, and other languages, as the other in music and mathematics. His name is Cambio. Pray accept his service.

BAPTISTA A thousand thanks, Signor Gremio. Welcome, good Cambio. (*To Tranio*) But, gentle sir, methinks you walk like a stranger. May I be so bold to know the cause of your coming?

TRANIO

Pardon me, sir, the boldness is mine own
That, being a stranger in this city here,
Do make myself a suitor to your daughter, 90
Unto Bianca, fair and virtuous.
Nor is your firm resolve unknown to me
In the preferment of the eldest sister.
This liberty is all that I request –
That, upon knowledge of my parentage,
I may have welcome 'mongst the rest that woo,
And free access and favour as the rest.
And toward the education of your daughters
I here bestow a simple instrument,
And this small packet of Greek and Latin books. 100
    Biondello steps forward with the lute and the books
If you accept them, then their worth is great.

BAPTISTA (*opening one of the books*)
Lucentio is your name? Of whence, I pray?

TRANIO

Of Pisa, sir, son to Vincentio.

BAPTISTA

A mighty man of Pisa. By report
I know him well. You are very welcome, sir.

(*to Hortensio*) Take you the lute, (*to Lucentio*) and you
    the set of books.
You shall go see your pupils presently.
Holla, within!

Enter a Servant

               Sirrah, lead these gentlemen
To my daughters, and tell them both
These are their tutors. Bid them use them well.

*Exit Servant, conducting Hortensio
and Lucentio, followed by Biondello*

We will go walk a little in the orchard,
And then to dinner. You are passing welcome,
And so I pray you all to think yourselves.

PETRUCHIO

Signor Baptista, my business asketh haste,
And every day I cannot come to woo.
You knew my father well, and in him me,
Left solely heir to all his lands and goods,
Which I have bettered rather than decreased.
Then tell me, if I get your daughter's love,
What dowry shall I have with her to wife?

BAPTISTA

After my death the one half of my lands,
And in possession twenty thousand crowns.

PETRUCHIO

And for that dowry I'll assure her of
Her widowhood – be it that she survive me –
In all my lands and leases whatsoever.
Let specialties be therefore drawn between us,
That covenants may be kept on either hand.

BAPTISTA

Ay, when the special thing is well obtained,
That is, her love; for that is all in all.

90

PETRUCHIO

  Why, that is nothing. For I tell you, father,   130
  I am as peremptory as she proud-minded;
  And where two raging fires meet together,
  They do consume the thing that feeds their fury.
  Though little fire grows great with little wind,
  Yet extreme gusts will blow out fire and all.
  So I to her, and so she yields to me,
  For I am rough and woo not like a babe.

BAPTISTA

  Well mayst thou woo, and happy be thy speed.
  But be thou armed for some unhappy words.

PETRUCHIO

  Ay, to the proof, as mountains are for winds,   140
  That shakes not though they blow perpetually.

    Enter Hortensio with his head broke

BAPTISTA

  How now, my friend, why dost thou look so pale?

HORTENSIO

  For fear, I promise you, if I look pale.

BAPTISTA

  What, will my daughter prove a good musician?

HORTENSIO

  I think she'll sooner prove a soldier.
  Iron may hold with her, but never lutes.

BAPTISTA

  Why then, thou canst not break her to the lute?

HORTENSIO

  Why no, for she hath broke the lute to me.
  I did but tell her she mistook her frets,
  And bowed her hand to teach her fingering,   150
  When, with a most impatient devilish spirit,
  'Frets, call you these?' quoth she, 'I'll fume with them.'
  And with that word she struck me on the head,

And through the instrument my pate made way,
And there I stood amazèd for a while,
As on a pillory, looking through the lute,
While she did call me rascal fiddler
And twangling Jack, with twenty such vile terms,
As had she studied to misuse me so.

PETRUCHIO

160 Now, by the world, it is a lusty wench.
I love her ten times more than e'er I did.
O, how I long to have some chat with her!

BAPTISTA

Well, go with me, and be not so discomfited.
Proceed in practice with my younger daughter,
She's apt to learn and thankful for good turns.
Signor Petruchio, will you go with us,
Or shall I send my daughter Kate to you?

PETRUCHIO

I pray you do.   *Exeunt all but Petruchio*
                I'll attend her here,
And woo her with some spirit when she comes.
170 Say that she rail, why then I'll tell her plain
She sings as sweetly as a nightingale.
Say that she frown, I'll say she looks as clear
As morning roses newly washed with dew.
Say she be mute and will not speak a word,
Then I'll commend her volubility,
And say she uttereth piercing eloquence.
If she do bid me pack, I'll give her thanks,
As though she bid me stay by her a week.
If she deny to wed, I'll crave the day
180 When I shall ask the banns, and when be married.
But here she comes, and now, Petruchio, speak.
    Enter Katherina
Good morrow, Kate – for that's your name, I hear.

KATHERINA
 Well have you heard, but something hard of hearing;
 They call me Katherine that do talk of me.

PETRUCHIO
 You lie, in faith, for you are called plain Kate,
 And bonny Kate, and sometimes Kate the curst.
 But Kate, the prettiest Kate in Christendom,
 Kate of Kate Hall, my super-dainty Kate,
 For dainties are all Kates, and therefore, Kate,
 Take this of me, Kate of my consolation –   190
 Hearing thy mildness praised in every town,
 Thy virtues spoke of, and thy beauty sounded,
 Yet not so deeply as to thee belongs,
 Myself am moved to woo thee for my wife.

KATHERINA
 Moved, in good time! Let him that moved you hither
 Remove you hence. I knew you at the first
 You were a movable.

PETRUCHIO   Why, what's a movable?

KATHERINA
 A joint-stool.

PETRUCHIO   Thou hast hit it. Come, sit on me.

KATHERINA
 Asses are made to bear, and so are you.

PETRUCHIO
 Women are made to bear, and so are you.   200

KATHERINA
 No such jade as you, if me you mean.

PETRUCHIO
 Alas, good Kate, I will not burden thee!
 For knowing thee to be but young and light –

KATHERINA
 Too light for such a swain as you to catch,
 And yet as heavy as my weight should be.

PETRUCHIO
Should be? Should – buzz!

KATHERINA   Well ta'en, and like a buzzard.

PETRUCHIO
O slow-winged turtle, shall a buzzard take thee?

KATHERINA
Ay, for a turtle, as he takes a buzzard.

PETRUCHIO
Come, come, you wasp, i'faith, you are too angry.

KATHERINA
210   If I be waspish, best beware my sting.

PETRUCHIO
My remedy is then to pluck it out.

KATHERINA
Ay, if the fool could find it where it lies.

PETRUCHIO
Who knows not where a wasp does wear his sting?
In his tail.

KATHERINA   In his tongue.

PETRUCHIO   Whose tongue?

KATHERINA
Yours, if you talk of tales, and so farewell.
    She turns to go

PETRUCHIO
What, with my tongue in your tail? Nay, come again.
    He takes her in his arms
Good Kate, I am a gentleman –

KATHERINA   That I'll try.
    She strikes him

PETRUCHIO
I swear I'll cuff you, if you strike again.

KATHERINA
So may you loose your arms.

220   If you strike me, you are no gentleman,

94

And if no gentleman, why then no arms.

PETRUCHIO

A herald, Kate? O, put me in thy books!

KATHERINA

What is your crest – a coxcomb?

PETRUCHIO

A combless cock, so Kate will be my hen.

KATHERINA

No cock of mine, you crow too like a craven.

PETRUCHIO

Nay, come, Kate, come, you must not look so sour.

KATHERINA

It is my fashion when I see a crab.

PETRUCHIO

Why, here's no crab, and therefore look not sour.

KATHERINA

There is, there is.

PETRUCHIO

Then show it me

KATHERINA   Had I a glass, I would.   230

PETRUCHIO

What, you mean my face?

KATHERINA   Well aimed of such a young one.

PETRUCHIO

Now, by Saint George, I am too young for you.

KATHERINA

Yet you are withered.

PETRUCHIO   'Tis with cares.

KATHERINA   I care not.

PETRUCHIO

Nay, hear you, Kate –
      She struggles

                    In sooth, you scape not so.

KATHERINA

   I chafe you, if I tarry. Let me go.

PETRUCHIO

   No, not a whit. I find you passing gentle.

   'Twas told me you were rough, and coy, and sullen,

   And now I find report a very liar.

   For thou art pleasant, gamesome, passing courteous,

240   But slow in speech, yet sweet as spring-time flowers.

   Thou canst not frown, thou canst not look askance,

   Nor bite the lip, as angry wenches will,

   Nor hast thou pleasure to be cross in talk.

   But thou with mildness entertain'st thy wooers,

   With gentle conference, soft and affable.

     He lets her go

   Why does the world report that Kate doth limp?

   O slanderous world! Kate like the hazel-twig

   Is straight and slender, and as brown in hue

   As hazel-nuts and sweeter than the kernels.

250   O, let me see thee walk. Thou dost not halt.

KATHERINA

   Go, fool, and whom thou keep'st command.

PETRUCHIO

   Did ever Dian so become a grove

   As Kate this chamber with her princely gait?

   O, be thou Dian, and let her be Kate,

   And then let Kate be chaste and Dian sportful.

KATHERINA

   Where did you study all this goodly speech?

PETRUCHIO

   It is extempore, from my mother-wit.

KATHERINA

   A witty mother, witless else her son.

PETRUCHIO

   Am I not wise?

KATHERINA   Yes, keep you warm.

PETRUCHIO

Marry, so I mean, sweet Katherine, in thy bed.   260
And therefore, setting all this chat aside,
Thus in plain terms – your father hath consented
That you shall be my wife; your dowry 'greed on;
And will you, nill you, I will marry you.
Now, Kate, I am a husband for your turn,
For by this light whereby I see thy beauty,
Thy beauty that doth make me like thee well,
Thou must be married to no man but me.
For I am he am born to tame you, Kate,
And bring you from a wild Kate to a Kate   270
Conformable as other household Kates.

Enter Baptista, Gremio, and Tranio

Here comes your father. Never make denial;
I must and will have Katherine to my wife.

BAPTISTA

Now, Signor Petruchio, how speed you with my daughter?

PETRUCHIO

How but well, sir? How but well?
It were impossible I should speed amiss.

BAPTISTA

Why, how now, daughter Katherine? In your dumps?

KATHERINA

Call you me daughter? Now I promise you
You have showed a tender fatherly regard
To wish me wed to one half lunatic,   280
A madcap ruffian and a swearing Jack,
That thinks with oaths to face the matter out.

PETRUCHIO

Father, 'tis thus – yourself and all the world
That talked of her have talked amiss of her.
If she be curst, it is for policy,

97

For she's not froward, but modest as the dove.
She is not hot, but temperate as the morn.
For patience she will prove a second Grissel,
And Roman Lucrece for her chastity.
290 And to conclude, we have 'greed so well together
That upon Sunday is the wedding-day.

KATHERINA
I'll see thee hanged on Sunday first.

GREMIO
Hark, Petruchio, she says she'll see thee hanged first.

TRANIO
Is this your speeding? Nay then, good night our part.

PETRUCHIO
Be patient, gentlemen, I choose her for myself.
If she and I be pleased, what's that to you?
'Tis bargained 'twixt us twain, being alone,
That she shall still be curst in company.
I tell you 'tis incredible to believe
300 How much she loves me – O, the kindest Kate!
She hung about my neck, and kiss on kiss
She vied so fast, protesting oath on oath,
That in a twink she won me to her love.
O, you are novices! 'Tis a world to see
How tame, when men and women are alone,
A meacock wretch can make the curstest shrew.
Give me thy hand, Kate, I will unto Venice,
To buy apparel 'gainst the wedding-day.
Provide the feast, father, and bid the guests.
310 I will be sure my Katherine shall be fine.

BAPTISTA
I know not what to say – but give me your hands.
God send you joy! Petruchio, 'tis a match.

GREMIO *and* TRANIO
Amen, say we. We will be witnesses.

PETRUCHIO

  Father, and wife, and gentlemen, adieu,

  I will to Venice – Sunday comes apace.

  We will have rings, and things, and fine array,

  And kiss me, Kate, we will be married o' Sunday.

                Exeunt Petruchio and Katherina

GREMIO

  Was ever match clapped up so suddenly?

BAPTISTA

  Faith, gentlemen, now I play a merchant's part,

  And venture madly on a desperate mart.   320

TRANIO

  'Twas a commodity lay fretting by you,

  'Twill bring you gain, or perish on the seas.

BAPTISTA

  The gain I seek is quiet in the match.

GREMIO

  No doubt but he hath got a quiet catch.

  But now, Baptista, to your younger daughter –

  Now is the day we long have lookèd for.

  I am your neighbour, and was suitor first.

TRANIO

  And I am one that love Bianca more

  Than words can witness or your thoughts can guess.

GREMIO

  Youngling, thou canst not love so dear as I.   330

TRANIO

  Greybeard, thy love doth freeze.

GREMIO   But thine doth fry.

  Skipper, stand back, 'tis age that nourisheth.

TRANIO

  But youth in ladies' eyes that flourisheth.

BAPTISTA

  Content you, gentlemen, I will compound this strife.

'Tis deeds must win the prize, and he of both
That can assure my daughter greatest dower
Shall have my Bianca's love.
Say, Signor Gremio, what can you assure her?

GREMIO

First, as you know, my house within the city
340   Is richly furnishèd with plate and gold,
Basins and ewers to lave her dainty hands –
My hangings all of Tyrian tapestry.
In ivory coffers I have stuffed my crowns,
In cypress chests my arras counterpoints,
Costly apparel, tents, and canopies,
Fine linen, Turkey cushions bossed with pearl,
Valance of Venice gold in needlework,
Pewter and brass, and all things that belongs
To house or housekeeping. Then at my farm
350   I have a hundred milch-kine to the pail,
Six score fat oxen standing in my stalls,
And all things answerable to this portion.
Myself am struck in years, I must confess,
And if I die tomorrow this is hers,
If whilst I live she will be only mine.

TRANIO

That 'only' came well in. Sir, list to me.
I am my father's heir and only son.
If I may have your daughter to my wife,
I'll leave her houses three or four as good,
360   Within rich Pisa walls, as any one
Old Signor Gremio has in Padua,
Besides two thousand ducats by the year
Of fruitful land, all which shall be her jointure.
What, have I pinched you, Signor Gremio?

GREMIO

Two thousand ducats by the year of land!

(*aside*) My land amounts not to so much in all.
(*to them*) That she shall have, besides an argosy
That now is lying in Marseilles road.
What, have I choked you with an argosy?

TRANIO

Gremio, 'tis known my father hath no less   370
Than three great argosies, besides two galliasses
And twelve tight galleys. These I will assure her,
And twice as much whate'er thou off'rest next.

GREMIO

Nay, I have offered all, I have no more,
And she can have no more than all I have.
If you like me, she shall have me and mine.

TRANIO

Why, then the maid is mine from all the world
By your firm promise. Gremio is out-vied.

BAPTISTA

I must confess your offer is the best,
And let your father make her the assurance,   380
She is your own. Else, you must pardon me,
If you should die before him, where's her dower?

TRANIO

That's but a cavil. He is old, I young.

GREMIO

And may not young men die as well as old?

BAPTISTA

Well, gentlemen,
I am thus resolved. On Sunday next you know
My daughter Katherine is to be married.
Now, on the Sunday following shall Bianca
Be bride to you, if you make this assurance;
If not, to Signor Gremio.   390
And so I take my leave, and thank you both.

GREMIO

Adieu, good neighbour. *Exit Baptista*

Now I fear thee not.

Sirrah, young gamester, your father were a fool

To give thee all, and in his waning age

Set foot under thy table. Tut, a toy!

An old Italian fox is not so kind, my boy. *Exit*

TRANIO

A vengeance on your crafty withered hide!

Yet I have faced it with a card of ten.

'Tis in my head to do my master good.

400   I see no reason but supposed Lucentio

Must get a father, called supposed Vincentio.

And that's a wonder. Fathers commonly

Do get their children; but in this case of wooing

A child shall get a sire, if I fail not of my cunning. *Exit*

*

III.1   *Enter Lucentio as Cambio, Hortensio as Licio,*
          and Bianca

LUCENTIO

Fiddler, forbear, you grow too forward, sir.

Have you so soon forgot the entertainment

Her sister Katherine welcomed you withal?

HORTENSIO

But, wrangling pedant, this is

The patroness of heavenly harmony.

Then give me leave to have prerogative,

And when in music we have spent an hour,

Your lecture shall have leisure for as much.

LUCENTIO

Preposterous ass, that never read so far

To know the cause why music was ordained!   10
Was it not to refresh the mind of man
After his studies or his usual pain?
Then give me leave to read philosophy,
And while I pause serve in your harmony.

HORTENSIO
Sirrah, I will not bear these braves of thine.

BIANCA
Why, gentlemen, you do me double wrong
To strive for that which resteth in my choice.
I am no breeching scholar in the schools,
I'll not be tied to hours nor 'pointed times,
But learn my lessons as I please myself.   20
And, to cut off all strife, here sit we down.
Take you your instrument, play you the whiles –
His lecture will be done ere you have tuned.

HORTENSIO
You'll leave his lecture when I am in tune?

LUCENTIO
That will be never. Tune your instrument.

BIANCA Where left we last?

LUCENTIO Here, madam.
    (He reads)
   '*Hic ibat Simois, hic est Sigeia tellus,*
   Hic steterat Priami regia celsa senis.'

BIANCA Construe them.   30

LUCENTIO '*Hic ibat*', as I told you before – '*Simois*', I am
Lucentio – '*hic est*', son unto Vincentio of Pisa – '*Sigeia
tellus*', disguised thus to get your love – '*Hic steterat*',
and that Lucentio that comes a-wooing – '*Priami*', is my
man Tranio – '*regia*', bearing my port – '*celsa senis*',
that we might beguile the old pantaloon.

HORTENSIO Madam, my instrument's in tune.

BIANCA Let's hear. *(He plays)* O fie! The treble jars.

LUCENTIO Spit in the hole, man, and tune again.

40 BIANCA Now let me see if I can construe it. '*Hic ibat Simois*', I know you not – '*hic est Sigeia tellus*', I trust you not – '*Hic steterat Priami*', take heed he hear us not – '*regia*', presume not – '*celsa senis*', despair not.

HORTENSIO
Madam, 'tis now in tune.

LUCENTIO   All but the bass.

HORTENSIO
The bass is right, 'tis the base knave that jars.
(*aside*) How fiery and forward our pedant is.
Now, for my life, the knave doth court my love.
Pedascule, I'll watch you better yet.

BIANCA
In time I may believe, yet I mistrust.

LUCENTIO
50 Mistrust it not – for, sure, Aeacides
Was Ajax, called so from his grandfather.

BIANCA
I must believe my master, else, I promise you,
I should be arguing still upon that doubt.
But let it rest. Now, Licio, to you.
Good master, take it not unkindly, pray,
That I have been thus pleasant with you both.

HORTENSIO (*to Lucentio*)
You may go walk, and give me leave awhile.
My lessons make no music in three parts.

LUCENTIO
Are you so formal, sir? Well, I must wait –
60 (*aside*) And watch withal, for, but I be deceived,
Our fine musician groweth amorous.

HORTENSIO
Madam, before you touch the instrument
To learn the order of my fingering,

I must begin with rudiments of art,
To teach you gamut in a briefer sort,
More pleasant, pithy, and effectual,
Than hath been taught by any of my trade.
And there it is in writing fairly drawn.

BIANCA
Why, I am past my gamut long ago.

HORTENSIO
Yet read the gamut of Hortensio.   70

BIANCA (*reads*)
'Gamut *I am, the ground of all accord* –
A re, *to plead Hortensio's passion* –
B mi, *Bianca, take him for thy lord* –
C fa ut, *that loves with all affection* –
D sol re, *one clef, two notes have I* –
E la mi, *show pity or I die.*'
Call you this gamut? Tut, I like it not!
Old fashions please me best. I am not so nice
To change true rules for odd inventions.

        Enter a Servant

SERVANT
Mistress, your father prays you leave your books,   80
And help to dress your sister's chamber up.
You know tomorrow is the wedding-day.

BIANCA
Farewell, sweet masters both, I must be gone.

                        Exeunt Bianca and Servant

LUCENTIO
Faith, mistress, then I have no cause to stay.   *Exit*

HORTENSIO
But I have cause to pry into this pedant,
Methinks he looks as though he were in love.
Yet if thy thoughts, Bianca, be so humble
To cast thy wandering eyes on every stale,

Seize thee that list. If once I find thee ranging,
90   Hortensio will be quit with thee by changing.   *Exit*

III.2   *Enter Baptista, Gremio, Tranio as Lucentio, Kather-*
          ina, Bianca, Lucentio as Cambio, and attendants on
          Katherina

BAPTISTA (*to Tranio*)
   Signor Lucentio, this is the 'pointed day
   That Katherine and Petruchio should be married,
   And yet we hear not of our son-in-law.
   What will be said? What mockery will it be
   To want the bridegroom when the priest attends
   To speak the ceremonial rites of marriage!
   What says Lucentio to this shame of ours?

KATHERINA
   No shame but mine. I must forsooth be forced
   To give my hand, opposed against my heart,
10   Unto a mad-brain rudesby, full of spleen,
   Who wooed in haste and means to wed at leisure.
   I told you, I, he was a frantic fool,
   Hiding his bitter jests in blunt behaviour.
   And to be noted for a merry man,
   He'll woo a thousand, 'point the day of marriage,
   Make feast, invite friends, and proclaim the banns,
   Yet never means to wed where he hath wooed.
   Now must the world point at poor Katherine,
   And say 'Lo, there is mad Petruchio's wife,
20   If it would please him come and marry her.'

TRANIO
   Patience, good Katherine, and Baptista too.
   Upon my life, Petruchio means but well,
   Whatever fortune stays him from his word.
   Though he be blunt, I know him passing wise,

Though he be merry, yet withal he's honest.

KATHERINA

Would Katherine had never seen him though.

Exit weeping, followed by Bianca and the other women

BAPTISTA

Go, girl, I cannot blame thee now to weep,

For such an injury would vex a saint,

Much more a shrew of thy impatient humour.

Enter Biondello

BIONDELLO Master, master, news! And such old news as you never heard of. 30

BAPTISTA Is it new and old too? How may that be?

BIONDELLO Why, is it not news to hear of Petruchio's coming?

BAPTISTA Is he come?

BIONDELLO Why, no, sir.

BAPTISTA What then?

BIONDELLO He is coming.

BAPTISTA When will he be here?

BIONDELLO When he stands where I am and sees you there. 40

TRANIO But say, what to thine old news?

BIONDELLO Why, Petruchio is coming in a new hat and an old jerkin; a pair of old breeches thrice turned; a pair of boots that have been candle-cases, one buckled, another laced; an old rusty sword ta'en out of the town armoury, with a broken hilt, and chapeless; with two broken points; his horse hipped – with an old mothy saddle and stirrups of no kindred – besides, possessed with the glanders and like to mose in the chine, troubled with the lampass, infected with the fashions, full of windgalls, sped with spavins, rayed with the yellows, past cure of the fives, stark spoiled with the staggers, begnawn with the bots, swayed in the back and shoulder- 50

shotten, near-legged before, and with a half-cheeked
bit and a headstall of sheep's leather, which, being
restrained to keep him from stumbling, hath been often
burst and new-repaired with knots; one girth six times
pieced, and a woman's crupper of velure, which hath
60 two letters for her name fairly set down in studs, and
here and there pieced with pack-thread.

BAPTISTA Who comes with him?

BIONDELLO O sir, his lackey, for all the world caparisoned
like the horse; with a linen stock on one leg and a kersey
boot-hose on the other, gartered with a red and blue
list; an old hat, and the humour of forty fancies pricked
in't for a feather; a monster, a very monster in apparel,
and not like a Christian footboy or a gentleman's lackey.

TRANIO
'Tis some odd humour pricks him to this fashion.
70 Yet oftentimes he goes but mean-apparelled.

BAPTISTA I am glad he's come, howsoe'er he comes.

BIONDELLO Why, sir, he comes not.

BAPTISTA Didst thou not say he comes?

BIONDELLO Who? That Petruchio came?

BAPTISTA Ay, that Petruchio came.

BIONDELLO No, sir. I say his horse comes with him on
his back.

BAPTISTA Why, that's all one.

BIONDELLO

Nay, by Saint Jamy,
80 I hold you a penny,
A horse and a man
Is more than one,
And yet not many.

Enter Petruchio and Grumio

PETRUCHIO Come, where be these gallants? Who's at
home?

BAPTISTA You are welcome, sir.

PETRUCHIO And yet I come not well?

BAPTISTA And yet you halt not.

TRANIO Not so well apparelled as I wish you were.

PETRUCHIO

Were it not better I should rush in thus?   90
But where is Kate? Where is my lovely bride?
How does my father? Gentles, methinks you frown.
And wherefore gaze this goodly company
As if they saw some wondrous monument,
Some comet, or unusual prodigy?

BAPTISTA

Why, sir, you kn w this is your wedding-day.
First were we sad, fearing you would not come,
Now sadder that you come so unprovided.
Fie, doff this habit, shame to your estate,
An eye-sore to our solemn festival.   100

TRANIO

And tell us what occasion of import
Hath all so long detained you from your wife
And sent you hither so unlike yourself?

PETRUCPIO

Tedious it were to tell, and harsh to hear –
Sufficeth I am come to keep my word,
Though in some part enforcèd to digress,
Which at more leisure I will so excuse
As you shall well be satisfied withal.
But where is Kate? I stay too long from her.
The morning wears, 'tis time we were at church.   110

TRANIO

See not your bride in these unreverent robes,
Go to my chamber, put on clothes of mine.

PETRUCHIO

Not I, believe me. Thus I'll visit her.

BAPTISTA

But thus, I trust, you will not marry her.

PETRUCHIO

Good sooth, even thus. Therefore ha' done with words;
To me she's married, not unto my clothes.
Could I repair what she will wear in me
As I can change these poor accoutrements,
'Twere well for Kate and better for myself.
But what a fool am I to chat with you,
When I should bid good morrow to my bride,
And seal the title with a lovely kiss.

Exit with Grumio

TRANIO

He hath some meaning in his mad attire.
We will persuade him, be it possible,
To put on better ere he go to church.

BAPTISTA

I'll after him and see the event of this.

Exit followed by Gremio, Biondello, and attendants

TRANIO

But, sir, to love concerneth us to add
Her father's liking, which to bring to pass,
As I before imparted to your worship,
I am to get a man – whate'er he be
It skills not much, we'll fit him to our turn –
And he shall be Vincentio of Pisa,
And make assurance here in Padua
Of greater sums than I have promisèd.
So shall you quietly enjoy your hope
And marry sweet Bianca with consent.

LUCENTIO

Were it not that my fellow schoolmaster
Doth watch Bianca's steps so narrowly,
'Twere good methinks to steal our marriage,

Which once performed, let all the world say no,   140
I'll keep mine own despite of all the world.

TRANIO

That by degrees we mean to look into
And watch our vantage in this business.
We'll overreach the greybeard Gremio,
The narrow-prying father Minola,
The quaint musician, amorous Licio –
All for my master's sake, Lucentio.
  Enter Gremio
Signor Gremio, came you from the church?

GREMIO

As willingly as e'er I came from school.

TRANIO

And is the bride and bridegroom coming home?   150

GREMIO

A bridegroom, say you? 'Tis a groom indeed,
A grumbling groom, and that the girl shall find.

TRANIO

Curster than she? Why, 'tis impossible.

GREMIO

Why, he's a devil, a devil, a very fiend.

TRANIO

Why, she's a devil, a devil, the devil's dam.

GREMIO

Tut, she's a lamb, a dove, a fool to him.
I'll tell you, Sir Lucentio – when the priest
Should ask if Katherine should be his wife,
'Ay, by gogs-wouns', quoth he, and swore so loud
That all-amazed the priest let fall the book,   160
And as he stooped again to take it up,
This mad-brained bridegroom took him such a cuff
That down fell priest and book, and book and priest.

'Now take them up', quoth he, 'if any list.'

TRANIO

What said the wench when he rose up again?

GREMIO

Trembled and shook. For why, he stamped and swore
As if the vicar meant to cozen him.
But after many ceremonies done
He calls for wine. 'A health!' quoth he, as if
170 He had been aboard, carousing to his mates
After a storm; quaffed off the muscadel,
And threw the sops all in the sexton's face,
Having no other reason
But that his beard grew thin and hungerly
And seemed to ask him sops as he was drinking.
This done, he took the bride about the neck,
And kissed her lips with such a clamorous smack
That at the parting all the church did echo.
And I seeing this came thence for very shame,
180 And after me, I know, the rout is coming.
Such a mad marriage never was before.
Hark, hark! I hear the minstrels play.
> *Music plays*
> *Enter Petruchio, Katherina, Bianca, Baptista, Hortensio, Grumio, and attendants*

PETRUCHIO

Gentlemen and friends, I thank you for your pains.
I know you think to dine with me today,
And have prepared great store of wedding cheer,
But so it is, my haste doth call me hence,
And therefore here I mean to take my leave.

BAPTISTA

Is't possible you will away tonight?

PETRUCHIO

I must away today before night come.

Make it no wonder. If you knew my business, 190
You would entreat me rather go than stay.
And, honest company, I thank you all
That have beheld me give away myself
To this most patient, sweet, and virtuous wife.
Dine with my father, drink a health to me,
For I must hence, and farewell to you all.

TRANIO
Let us entreat you stay till after dinner.

PETRUCHIO
It may not be.

GREMIO   Let me entreat you.

PETRUCHIO
It cannot be.

KATHERINA   Let me entreat you.

PETRUCHIO
I am content.

KATHERINA   Are you content to stay? 200

PETRUCHIO
I am content you shall entreat me stay –
But yet not stay, entreat me how you can.

KATHERINA
Now if you love me stay.

PETRUCHIO   Grumio, my horse.

GRUMIO Ay, sir, they be ready – the oats have eaten the
horses.

KATHERINA
Nay then,
Do what thou canst, I will not go today,
No, nor tomorrow – not till I please myself.
The door is open, sir, there lies your way,
You may be jogging whiles your boots are green. 210
For me, I'll not be gone till I please myself.
'Tis like you'll prove a jolly surly groom

That take it on you at the first so roundly.

PETRUCHIO

O Kate, content thee, prithee be not angry.

KATHERINA

I will be angry – what hast thou to do?
Father, be quiet – he shall stay my leisure.

GREMIO

Ay marry, sir, now it begins to work.

KATHERINA

Gentlemen, forward to the bridal dinner.
I see a woman may be made a fool
220 If she had not a spirit to resist.

PETRUCHIO

They shall go forward, Kate, at thy command.
Obey the bride, you that attend on her.
Go to the feast, revel and domineer,
Carouse full measure to her maidenhead,
Be mad and merry, or go hang yourselves.
But for my bonny Kate, she must with me.

*He seizes her, as though to protect her from the rest of
the company, to whom he speaks*

Nay, look not big, nor stamp, nor stare, nor fret,
I will be master of what is mine own.
She is my goods, my chattels, she is my house,
230 My household stuff, my field, my barn,
My horse, my ox, my ass, my any thing,
And here she stands. Touch her whoever dare!
I'll bring mine action on the proudest he
That stops my way in Padua. Grumio,
Draw forth thy weapon, we are beset with thieves,
Rescue thy mistress if thou be a man.
Fear not, sweet wench, they shall not touch thee, Kate.
I'll buckler thee against a million.

Exeunt Petruchio, Katherina, and Grumio

BAPTISTA
Nay, let them go, a couple of quiet ones.

GREMIO
Went they not quickly, I should die with laughing. 240

TRANIO
Of all mad matches never was the like.

LUCENTIO
Mistress, what's your opinion of your sister?

BIANCA
That being mad herself, she's madly mated.

GREMIO
I warrant him, Petruchio is Kated.

BAPTISTA
Neighbours and friends, though bride and bridegroom
        wants
For to supply the places at the table,
You know there wants no junkets at the feast.
Lucentio, you shall supply the bridegroom's place,
And let Bianca take her sister's room.

TRANIO
Shall sweet Bianca practise how to bride it? 250

BAPTISTA
She shall, Lucentio. Come, gentlemen, let's go. *Exeunt*

*

Enter Grumio IV.1

GRUMIO Fie, fie on all tired jades, on all mad masters, and
all foul ways! Was ever man so beaten? Was ever man so
rayed? Was ever man so weary? I am sent before to make
a fire, and they are coming after to warm them. Now
were not I a little pot and soon hot, my very lips might
freeze to my teeth, my tongue to the roof of my mouth, my

heart in my belly, ere I should come by a fire to thaw me.
But I with blowing the fire shall warm myself, for, con-
sidering the weather, a taller man than I will take cold.
10 Holla, ho! Curtis!

Enter Curtis

CURTIS Who is that calls so coldly?

GRUMIO A piece of ice. If thou doubt it, thou mayst slide
from my shoulder to my heel with no greater a run but
my head and my neck. A fire, good Curtis.

CURTIS Is my master and his wife coming, Grumio?

GRUMIO O ay, Curtis, ay – and therefore fire, fire, cast on
no water.

CURTIS Is she so hot a shrew as she's reported?

GRUMIO She was, good Curtis, before this frost. But thou
20 know'st winter tames man, woman, and beast; for it
hath tamed my old master, and my new mistress, and
myself, fellow Curtis.

CURTIS Away, you three-inch fool! I am no beast.

GRUMIO Am I but three inches? Why, thy horn is a foot,
and so long am I at the least. But wilt thou make a fire,
or shall I complain on thee to our mistress, whose hand
– she being now at hand – thou shalt soon feel, to thy
cold comfort, for being slow in thy hot office?

CURTIS I prithee, good Grumio, tell me how goes the
30 world?

He kindles a fire

GRUMIO A cold world, Curtis, in every office but thine –
and therefore fire. Do thy duty, and have thy duty, for
my master and mistress are almost frozen to death.

CURTIS There's fire ready – and therefore, good Grumio,
the news.

GRUMIO Why, 'Jack boy, ho boy!' and as much news as
wilt thou.

CURTIS Come, you are so full of cony-catching.

GRUMIO Why therefore fire, for I have caught extreme
cold. Where's the cook? Is supper ready, the house 40
trimmed, rushes strewed, cobwebs swept, the servingmen in their new fustian, their white stockings, and
every officer his wedding-garment on? Be the Jacks
fair within, the Jills fair without, the carpets laid, and
everything in order?

CURTIS All ready – and therefore, I pray thee, news.

GRUMIO First know my horse is tired, my master and
mistress fallen out.

CURTIS How?

GRUMIO Out of their saddles into the dirt, and thereby 50
hangs a tale.

CURTIS Let's ha't, good Grumio.

GRUMIO Lend thine ear.

CURTIS Here.

GRUMIO There.

He boxes Curtis's ear

CURTIS This 'tis to feel a tale, not to hear a tale.

GRUMIO And therefore 'tis called a sensible tale; and this
cuff was but to knock at your ear and beseech listening.
Now I begin. *Imprimis,* we came down a foul hill, my
master riding behind my mistress – 60

CURTIS Both of one horse?

GRUMIO What's that to thee?

CURTIS Why, a horse.

GRUMIO Tell thou the tale. But hadst thou not crossed
me, thou shouldst have heard how her horse fell, and
she under her horse; thou shouldst have heard in how
miry a place, how she was bemoiled, how he left her
with the horse upon her, how he beat me because her
horse stumbled, how she waded through the dirt to
pluck him off me, how he swore, how she prayed that 70
never prayed before, how I cried, how the horses ran

away, how her bridle was burst, how I lost my crupper – with many things of worthy memory, which now shall die in oblivion, and thou return unexperienced to thy grave.

CURTIS By this reckoning he is more shrew than she.

GRUMIO Ay, and that thou and the proudest of you all shall find when he comes home. But what talk I of this? Call forth Nathaniel, Joseph, Nicholas, Philip, Walter,
80   Sugarsop, and the rest. Let their heads be slickly combed, their blue coats brushed, and their garters of an indifferent knit. Let them curtsy with their left legs, and not presume to touch a hair of my master's horse-tail till they kiss their hands. Are they all ready?

CURTIS They are.

GRUMIO Call them forth.

CURTIS Do you hear, ho? You must meet my master to countenance my mistress.

GRUMIO Why, she hath a face of her own.

90 CURTIS Who knows not that?

GRUMIO Thou, it seems, that calls for company to countenance her.

CURTIS I call them forth to credit her.

GRUMIO Why, she comes to borrow nothing of them.

Enter four or five Servingmen

NATHANIEL Welcome home, Grumio.

PHILIP How now, Grumio.

JOSEPH What, Grumio.

NICHOLAS Fellow Grumio.

NATHANIEL How now, old lad.

100 GRUMIO Welcome, you. How now, you. What, you. Fellow, you. And thus much for greeting. Now, my spruce companions, is all ready, and all things neat?

NATHANIEL All things is ready. How near is our master?

GRUMIO E'en at hand, alighted by this. And therefore be

not – Cock's passion, silence! I hear my master.
    Enter Petruchio and Katherina

PETRUCHIO

Where be these knaves? What, no man at door
To hold my stirrup nor to take my horse?
Where is Nathaniel, Gregory, Philip?

ALL SERVINGMEN Here, here sir, here sir.

PETRUCHIO

Here sir, here sir, here sir, here sir!   110
You logger-headed and unpolished grooms!
What, no attendance? No regard? No duty?
Where is the foolish knave I sent before?

GRUMIO

Here sir, as foolish as I was before.

PETRUCHIO

You peasant swain, you whoreson malt-horse drudge!
Did I not bid thee meet me in the park
And bring along these rascal knaves with thee?

GRUMIO

Nathaniel's coat, sir, was not fully made,
And Gabriel's pumps were all unpinked i'th'heel.
There was no link to colour Peter's hat,   120
And Walter's dagger was not come from sheathing.
There were none fine but Adam, Rafe, and Gregory –
The rest were ragged, old, and beggarly.
Yet, as they are, here are they come to meet you.

PETRUCHIO

Go, rascals, go and fetch my supper in.
                  Exeunt Servingmen

    He sings
        Where is the life that late I led?
        Where are those –
Sit down, Kate, and welcome. Food, food, food, food!
    Enter Servants with supper

Why, when, I say? Nay, good sweet Kate, be merry.
130 Off with my boots, you rogues! You villains, when?

He sings

> It was the friar of orders grey,
> As he forth walkèd on his way –

Out, you rogue! You pluck my foot awry.

He strikes the Servant

Take that, and mend the plucking off the other.
Be merry, Kate. Some water here. What ho!

Enter one with water

Where's my spaniel Troilus? Sirrah, get you hence,
And bid my cousin Ferdinand come hither.

Exit another Servingman

One, Kate, that you must kiss and be acquainted with.
Where are my slippers? Shall I have some water?
140 Come, Kate, and wash, and welcome heartily.

He knocks the basin out of the Servant's hands

You whoreson villain, will you let it fall?

He strikes the Servant

KATHERINA
Patience, I pray you, 'twas a fault unwilling.

PETRUCHIO
A whoreson, beetle-headed, flap-eared knave!
Come, Kate, sit down, I know you have a stomach.
Will you give thanks, sweet Kate, or else shall I?
What's this? Mutton?

FIRST SERVINGMAN   Ay.

PETRUCHIO   Who brought it?

PETER   I.

PETRUCHIO
'Tis burnt, and so is all the meat.
What dogs are these! Where is the rascal cook?
How durst you, villains, bring it from the dresser
150 And serve it thus to me that love it not?

There, take it to you, trenchers, cups, and all.
> *He throws the food and dishes at them*

You heedless joltheads and unmannered slaves!
What, do you grumble? I'll be with you straight.
> *Exeunt Servants hurriedly*

KATHERINA

I pray you, husband, be not so disquiet.
The meat was well, if you were so contented.

PETRUCHIO

I tell thee, Kate, 'twas burnt and dried away,
And I expressly am forbid to touch it,
For it engenders choler, planteth anger;
And better 'twere that both of us did fast,
Since, of ourselves, ourselves are choleric,   160
Than feed it with such over-roasted flesh.
Be patient, tomorrow't shall be mended,
And for this night we'll fast for company.
Come, I will bring thee to thy bridal chamber. *Exeunt*
> *Enter Servants severally*

NATHANIEL Peter, didst ever see the like?

PETER He kills her in her own humour.
> *Enter Curtis*

GRUMIO Where is he?

CURTIS

In her chamber,
Making a sermon of continency to her,
And rails, and swears, and rates, that she, poor soul,   170
Knows not which way to stand, to look, to speak,
And sits as one new-risen from a dream.
Away, away, for he is coming hither.   *Exeunt*
> *Enter Petruchio*

PETRUCHIO

Thus have I politicly begun my reign,
And 'tis my hope to end successfully.

My falcon now is sharp and passing empty,
And till she stoop she must not be full-gorged,
For then she never looks upon her lure.
Another way I have to man my haggard,
180 To make her come and know her keeper's call,
That is, to watch her, as we watch these kites
That bate and beat and will not be obedient.
She eat no meat today, nor none shall eat.
Last night she slept not, nor tonight she shall not.
As with the meat, some undeservèd fault
I'll find about the making of the bed,
And here I'll fling the pillow, there the bolster,
This way the coverlet, another way the sheets.
Ay, and amid this hurly I intend
190 That all is done in reverend care of her.
And, in conclusion, she shall watch all night,
And if she chance to nod I'll rail and brawl,
And with the clamour keep her still awake.
This is a way to kill a wife with kindness,
And thus I'll curb her mad and headstrong humour.
He that knows better how to tame a shrew,
Now let him speak – 'tis charity to show.   *Exit*

IV.2   *Enter Tranio as Lucentio, and Hortensio as Licio*
TRANIO
   Is't possible, friend Licio, that Mistress Bianca
   Doth fancy any other but Lucentio?
   I tell you, sir, she bears me fair in hand.
HORTENSIO
   Sir, to satisfy you in what I have said,
   Stand by and mark the manner of his teaching.
          They stand aside
          Enter Bianca, and Lucentio as Cambio

122

LUCENTIO
  Now, mistress, profit you in what you read?
BIANCA
  What, master, read you? First resolve me that.
LUCENTIO
  I read that I profess, *The Art to Love*.
BIANCA
  And may you prove, sir, master of your art.
LUCENTIO
  While you, sweet dear, prove mistress of my heart.   10
    They court each other
HORTENSIO
  Quick proceeders, marry! Now tell me, I pray,
  You that durst swear that your mistress Bianca
  Loved none in the world so well as Lucentio.
TRANIO
  O despiteful love, unconstant womankind!
  I tell thee, Licio, this is wonderful.
HORTENSIO
  Mistake no more, I am not Licio,
  Nor a musician as I seem to be,
  But one that scorn to live in this disguise
  For such a one as leaves a gentleman
  And makes a god of such a cullion.   20
  Know, sir, that I am called Hortensio.
TRANIO
  Signor Hortensio, I have often heard
  Of your entire affection to Bianca,
  And since mine eyes are witness of her lightness,
  I will with you, if you be so contented,
  Forswear Bianca and her love for ever.
HORTENSIO
  See how they kiss and court! Signor Lucentio,
  Here is my hand, and here I firmly vow

Never to woo her more, but do forswear her,
30　As one unworthy all the former favours
That I have fondly flattered her withal.

TRANIO

And here I take the like unfeignèd oath,
Never to marry with her though she would entreat.
Fie on her! See how beastly she doth court him.

HORTENSIO

Would all the world but he had quite forsworn!
For me, that I may surely keep mine oath,
I will be married to a wealthy widow
Ere three days pass, which hath as long loved me
As I have loved this proud disdainful haggard.
40　And so farewell, Signor Lucentio.
Kindness in women, not their beauteous looks,
Shall win my love – and so I take my leave,
In resolution as I swore before.　　　　　　*Exit*

　　　Tranio joins Lucentio and Bianca

TRANIO

Mistress Bianca, bless you with such grace
As 'longeth to a lover's blessèd case!
Nay, I have ta'en you napping, gentle love,
And have forsworn you with Hortensio.

BIANCA

Tranio, you jest – but have you both forsworn me?

TRANIO

Mistress, we have.

LUCENTIO　　　　　　Then we are rid of Licio.

TRANIO

50　I'faith, he'll have a lusty widow now,
That shall be wooed and wedded in a day.

BIANCA

God give him joy!

124

TRANIO

Ay, and he'll tame her.

BIANCA   He says so, Tranio.

TRANIO

Faith, he is gone unto the taming-school.

BIANCA

The taming-school? What, is there such a place?

TRANIO

Ay, mistress, and Petruchio is the master,

That teacheth tricks eleven and twenty long,

To tame a shrew and charm her chattering tongue.

  Enter Biondello

BIONDELLO

O master, master, I have watched so long

That I'm dog-weary, but at last I spied   60

An ancient angel coming down the hill

Will serve the turn.

TRANIO   What is he, Biondello?

BIONDELLO

Master, a marcantant or a pedant,

I know not what – but formal in apparel,

In gait and countenance surely like a father.

LUCENTIO

And what of him, Tranio?

TRANIO

If he be credulous and trust my tale,

I'll make him glad to seem Vincentio,

And give assurance to Baptista Minola

As if he were the right Vincentio.   70

Take in your love, and then let me alone.

      Exeunt Lucentio and Bianca

  Enter a Pedant

PEDANT

God save you, sir.

TRANIO   And you, sir. You are welcome.
Travel you farrer on, or are you at the farthest?

PEDANT
Sir, at the farthest for a week or two,
But then up farther, and as far as Rome,
And so to Tripoli, if God lend me life.

TRANIO
What countryman, I pray?

PEDANT   Of Mantua.

TRANIO
Of Mantua? Sir, marry, God forbid!
And come to Padua, careless of your life?

PEDANT
80   My life, sir? How, I pray? For that goes hard.

TRANIO
'Tis death for any one in Mantua
To come to Padua. Know you not the cause?
Your ships are stayed at Venice, and the Duke,
For private quarrel 'twixt your Duke and him,
Hath published and proclaimed it openly.
'Tis marvel – but that you are newly come,
You might have heard it else proclaimed about.

PEDANT
Alas, sir, it is worse for me than so!
For I have bills for money by exchange
90   From Florence, and must here deliver them.

TRANIO
Well, sir, to do you courtesy,
This will I do, and this I will advise you –
First tell me, have you ever been at Pisa?

PEDANT
Ay, sir, in Pisa have I often been,
Pisa renownèd for grave citizens.

TRANIO
Among them know you one Vincentio?

PEDANT

  I know him not, but I have heard of him,
  A merchant of incomparable wealth.

TRANIO

  He is my father, sir, and sooth to say,
  In countenance somewhat doth resemble you.   100

BIONDELLO (*aside*) As much as an apple doth an oyster,
  and all one.

TRANIO

  To save your life in this extremity,
  This favour will I do you for his sake –
  And think it not the worst of all your fortunes
  That you are like to Sir Vincentio –
  His name and credit shall you undertake,
  And in my house you shall be friendly lodged.
  Look that you take upon you as you should.
  You understand me, sir. So shall you stay   110
  Till you have done your business in the city.
  If this be courtesy, sir, accept of it.

PEDANT

  O, sir, I do, and will repute you ever
  The patron of my life and liberty.

TRANIO

  Then go with me to make the matter good.
  This, by the way, I let you understand –
  My father is here looked for every day
  To pass assurance of a dower in marriage
  'Twixt me and one Baptista's daughter here.
  In all these circumstances I'll instruct you.   120
  Go with me, sir, to clothe you as becomes you.

                                      Exeunt

GRUMIO

No, no, forsooth, I dare not for my life.

KATHERINA

The more my wrong, the more his spite appears.
What, did he marry me to famish me?
Beggars that come unto my father's door
Upon entreaty have a present alms,
If not, elsewhere they meet with charity.
But I, who never knew how to entreat,
Nor never needed that I should entreat,
Am starved for meat, giddy for lack of sleep,
With oaths kept waking, and with brawling fed.
And that which spites me more than all these wants,
He does it under name of perfect love,
As who should say, if I should sleep or eat,
'Twere deadly sickness or else present death.
I prithee go and get me some repast,
I care not what, so it be wholesome food.

GRUMIO

What say you to a neat's foot?

KATHERINA

'Tis passing good, I prithee let me have it.

GRUMIO

I fear it is too choleric a meat.
How say you to a fat tripe finely broiled?

KATHERINA

I like it well. Good Grumio, fetch it me.

GRUMIO

I cannot tell, I fear 'tis choleric.
What say you to a piece of beef and mustard?

KATHERINA

A dish that I do love to feed upon.

GRUMIO

Ay, but the mustard is too hot a little.

KATHERINA

Why then, the beef, and let the mustard rest.

GRUMIO

Nay then, I will not. You shall have the mustard,
Or else you get no beef of Grumio.

KATHERINA

Then both, or one, or anything thou wilt.

GRUMIO

Why then, the mustard without the beef.　30

KATHERINA

Go, get thee gone, thou false deluding slave,
She beats him
That feed'st me with the very name of meat.
Sorrow on thee and all the pack of you
That triumph thus upon my misery!
Go, get thee gone, I say.
Enter Petruchio and Hortensio with meat

PETRUCHIO

How fares my Kate? What, sweeting, all amort?

HORTENSIO

Mistress, what cheer?

KATHERINA　　　　　　　　Faith, as cold as can be.

PETRUCHIO

Pluck up thy spirits, look cheerfully upon me.
Here, love, thou seest how diligent I am,
To dress thy meat myself, and bring it thee.　40
He sets the dish down
I am sure, sweet Kate, this kindness merits thanks.
What, not a word? Nay then, thou lov'st it not,
And all my pains is sorted to no proof.
Here, take away this dish.

KATHERINA　　　　　　　　I pray you, let it stand.

PETRUCHIO

 The poorest service is repaid with thanks,
 And so shall mine before you touch the meat.

KATHERINA

 I thank you, sir.

HORTENSIO

 Signor Petruchio, fie, you are to blame.
 Come, Mistress Kate, I'll bear you company.

PETRUCHIO (*aside to Hortensio*)

50 Eat it up all, Hortensio, if thou lovest me.
 (*to Katherina*) Much good do it unto thy gentle heart!
 Kate, eat apace. And now, my honey love,
 Will we return unto thy father's house
 And revel it as bravely as the best,
 With silken coats and caps, and golden rings,
 With ruffs and cuffs and farthingales and things,
 With scarfs and fans and double change of bravery,
 With amber bracelets, beads, and all this knavery.
 What, hast thou dined? The tailor stays thy leisure,
60 To deck thy body with his ruffling treasure.

                Enter Tailor

 Come, tailor, let us see these ornaments.
 Lay forth the gown.

                Enter Haberdasher

                    What news with you, sir?

HABERDASHER

 Here is the cap your worship did bespeak.

PETRUCHIO

 Why, this was moulded on a porringer –
 A velvet dish. Fie, fie, 'tis lewd and filthy!
 Why, 'tis a cockle or a walnut-shell,
 A knack, a toy, a trick, a baby's cap.
 Away with it! Come, let me have a bigger.

KATHERINA

 I'll have no bigger. This doth fit the time,

And gentlewomen wear such caps as these.   70

PETRUCHIO

When you are gentle, you shall have one too,
And not till then.

HORTENSIO (*aside*) That will not be in haste.

KATHERINA

Why sir, I trust I may have leave to speak,
And speak I will. I am no child, no babe.
Your betters have endured me say my mind,
And if you cannot, best you stop your ears.
My tongue will tell the anger of my heart,
Or else my heart concealing it will break,
And rather than it shall, I will be free
Even to the uttermost, as I please, in words.   80

PETRUCHIO

Why, thou say'st true – it is a paltry cap,
A custard-coffin, a bauble, a silken pie.
I love thee well in that thou lik'st it not.

KATHERINA

Love me or love me not, I like the cap,
And it I will have, or I will have none.

PETRUCHIO

Thy gown? Why, ay. Come, tailor, let us see't.
                                        Exit Haberdasher

O mercy, God! What masquing stuff is here?
What's this? A sleeve? 'Tis like a demi-cannon.
What, up and down carved like an apple-tart?
Here's snip and nip and cut and slish and slash,   90
Like to a censer in a barber's shop.
Why, what a devil's name, tailor, call'st thou this?

HORTENSIO (*aside*)

I see she's like to have neither cap nor gown.

TAILOR

You bid me make it orderly and well,
According to the fashion and the time.

PETRUCHIO

Marry, and did. But if you be remembered,
I did not bid you mar it to the time.
Go, hop me over every kennel home,
For you shall hop without my custom, sir.
100 I'll none of it. Hence, make your best of it.

KATHERINA

I never saw a better-fashioned gown,
More quaint, more pleasing, nor more commendable.
Belike you mean to make a puppet of me.

PETRUCHIO

Why, true, he means to make a puppet of thee.

TAILOR

She says your worship means to make a puppet of her.

PETRUCHIO

O monstrous arrogance! Thou liest, thou thread, thou
        thimble,
Thou yard, three-quarters, half-yard, quarter, nail,
Thou flea, thou nit, thou winter-cricket thou!
Braved in mine own house with a skein of thread?
110 Away, thou rag, thou quantity, thou remnant,
Or I shall so bemete thee with thy yard
As thou shalt think on prating whilst thou liv'st.
I tell thee, I, that thou hast marred her gown.

TAILOR

Your worship is deceived – the gown is made
Just as my master had direction.
Grumio gave order how it should be done.

GRUMIO I gave him no order, I gave him the stuff.

TAILOR

But how did you desire it should be made?

GRUMIO Marry, sir, with needle and thread.

TAILOR

120 But did you not request to have it cut?

GRUMIO Thou hast faced many things.

TAILOR I have.

GRUMIO Face not me. Thou hast braved many men, brave
not me. I will neither be faced nor braved. I say unto
thee, I bid thy master cut out the gown, but I did not
bid him cut it to pieces. Ergo, thou liest.

TAILOR Why, here is the note of the fashion to testify.

PETRUCHIO Read it.

GRUMIO The note lies in's throat, if he say I said so.

TAILOR (*reads*) '*Imprimis*, a loose-bodied gown.'   130

GRUMIO Master, if ever I said loose-bodied gown, sew me
in the skirts of it and beat me to death with a bottom of
brown thread. I said a gown.

PETRUCHIO Proceed.

TAILOR 'With a small compassed cape.'

GRUMIO I confess the cape.

TAILOR 'With a trunk sleeve.'

GRUMIO I confess two sleeves.

TAILOR 'The sleeves curiously cut.'

PETRUCHIO Ay, there's the villainy.   140

GRUMIO Error i'th'bill, sir, error i'th'bill! I commanded
the sleeves should be cut out, and sewed up again; and
that I'll prove upon thee, though thy little finger be
armed in a thimble.

TAILOR This is true that I say; an I had thee in place
where, thou shouldst know it.

GRUMIO I am for thee straight. Take thou the bill, give
me thy mete-yard, and spare not me.

HORTENSIO God-a-mercy, Grumio, then he shall have no
odds.   150

PETRUCHIO Well sir, in brief, the gown is not for me.

GRUMIO You are i'th'right, sir, 'tis for my mistress.

PETRUCHIO Go, take it up unto thy master's use.

GRUMIO Villain, not for thy life! Take up my mistress'

gown for thy master's use!

PETRUCHIO Why sir, what's your conceit in that?

GRUMIO

O sir, the conceit is deeper than you think for.

Take up my mistress' gown to his master's use!

O fie, fie, fie!

PETRUCHIO (*aside*)

160 Hortensio, say thou wilt see the tailor paid.

(*to the Tailor*) Go take it hence, be gone, and say no more.

HORTENSIO (*aside*)

Tailor, I'll pay thee for thy gown tomorrow.

Take no unkindness of his hasty words.

Away, I say, commend me to thy master. *Exit Tailor*

PETRUCHIO

Well, come my Kate, we will unto your father's

Even in these honest mean habiliments.

Our purses shall be proud, our garments poor,

For 'tis the mind that makes the body rich,

And as the sun breaks through the darkest clouds,

170 So honour peereth in the meanest habit.

What, is the jay more precious than the lark

Because his feathers are more beautiful?

Or is the adder better than the eel

Because his painted skin contents the eye?

O no, good Kate, neither art thou the worse

For this poor furniture and mean array.

If thou account'st it shame, lay it on me.

And therefore frolic. We will hence forthwith

To feast and sport us at thy father's house.

180 (*to Grumio*) Go call my men, and let us straight to him,

And bring our horses unto Long-lane end,

There will we mount, and thither walk on foot.

Let's see, I think 'tis now some seven o'clock,

And well we may come there by dinner-time.

KATHERINA

   I dare assure you, sir, 'tis almost two,

   And 'twill be supper-time ere you come there.

PETRUCHIO

   It shall be seven ere I go to horse.

   Look what I speak, or do, or think to do,

   You are still crossing it. Sirs, let't alone,

   I will not go today, and ere I do,   190

   It shall be what o'clock I say it is.

HORTENSIO

   Why, so this gallant will command the sun.

                                   Exeunt

   Enter Tranio as Lucentio, and the Pedant, booted, and **IV.4**
   dressed like Vincentio

TRANIO

   Sir, this is the house – please it you that I call?

PEDANT

   Ay, what else? And but I be deceived

   Signor Baptista may remember me

   Near twenty years ago in Genoa,

   Where we were lodgers at the Pegasus.

TRANIO

   'Tis well, and hold your own, in any case,

   With such austerity as 'longeth to a father.

   Enter Biondello

PEDANT

   I warrant you. But sir, here comes your boy.

   'Twere good he were schooled.

TRANIO

   Fear you not him. Sirrah Biondello,   10

   Now do your duty throughly, I advise you.

   Imagine 'twere the right Vincentio.

BIONDELLO

Tut, fear not me.

TRANIO

But hast thou done thy errand to Baptista?

BIONDELLO

I told him that your father was at Venice,
And that you looked for him this day in Padua.

TRANIO

Th' art a tall fellow, hold thee that to drink.

Enter Baptista, and Lucentio as Cambio

Here comes Baptista. Set your countenance, sir.
Signor Baptista, you are happily met.

20   (*to the Pedant*) Sir, this is the gentleman I told you of.
I pray you stand good father to me now,
Give me Bianca for my patrimony.

PEDANT

Soft, son!
Sir, by your leave, having come to Padua
To gather in some debts, my son Lucentio
Made me acquainted with a weighty cause
Of love between your daughter and himself.
And – for the good report I hear of you,
And for the love he beareth to your daughter,
30   And she to him – to stay him not too long,
I am content, in a good father's care,
To have him matched; and, if you please to like
No worse than I, upon some agreement
Me shall you find ready and willing
With one consent to have her so bestowed.
For curious I cannot be with you,
Signor Baptista, of whom I hear so well.

BAPTISTA

Sir, pardon me in what I have to say.
Your plainness and your shortness please me well.

Right true it is your son Lucentio here 40
Doth love my daughter, and she loveth him,
Or both dissemble deeply their affections.
And therefore if you say no more than this,
That like a father you will deal with him,
And pass my daughter a sufficient dower,
The match is made, and all is done –
Your son shall have my daughter with consent.

TRANIO

I thank you, sir. Where then do you know best
We be affied and such assurance ta'en
As shall with either part's agreement stand? 50

BAPTISTA

Not in my house, Lucentio, for you know
Pitchers have ears, and I have many servants.
Besides, old Gremio is hearkening still,
And happily we might be interrupted.

TRANIO

Then at my lodging, an it like you.
There doth my father lie; and there this night
We'll pass the business privately and well.
Send for your daughter by your servant here.
        He winks at Lucentio
My boy shall fetch the scrivener presently.
The worst is this, that at so slender warning 60
You are like to have a thin and slender pittance.

BAPTISTA

It likes me well. Cambio, hie you home,
And bid Bianca make her ready straight.
And, if you will, tell what hath happenèd –
Lucentio's father is arrived in Padua,
And how she's like to be Lucentio's wife. *Exit Lucentio*

BIONDELLO

I pray the gods she may, with all my heart.

TRANIO
Dally not with the gods, but get thee gone.

Exit Biondello

Enter Peter, a Servingman

Signor Baptista, shall I lead the way?
70 Welcome! One mess is like to be your cheer.
Come sir, we will better it in Pisa.

BAPTISTA
I follow you.   *Exeunt*

Enter Lucentio and Biondello

BIONDELLO
Cambio.

LUCENTIO What say'st thou, Biondello?

BIONDELLO
You saw my master wink and laugh upon you?

LUCENTIO Biondello, what of that?

BIONDELLO Faith, nothing – but 'has left me here behind
to expound the meaning or moral of his signs and tokens.

LUCENTIO I pray thee moralize them.

BIONDELLO Then thus – Baptista is safe, talking with the
80 deceiving father of a deceitful son.

LUCENTIO And what of him?

BIONDELLO His daughter is to be brought by you to the
supper.

LUCENTIO And then?

BIONDELLO The old priest at Saint Luke's church is at
your command at all hours.

LUCENTIO And what of all this?

BIONDELLO I cannot tell, except they are busied about a
counterfeit assurance. Take you assurance of her, *cum*
90 *privilegio ad imprimendum solum.* To th'church! Take
the priest, clerk, and some sufficient honest witnesses.
If this be not that you look for, I have no more to say,
But bid Bianca farewell for ever and a day.

He turns to go

LUCENTIO Hear'st thou, Biondello?

BIONDELLO I cannot tarry. I knew a wench married in an
afternoon as she went to the garden for parsley to stuff a
rabbit. And so may you, sir; and so adieu, sir. My master
hath appointed me to go to Saint Luke's to bid the
priest be ready to come against you come with your
appendix.   *Exit* 100

LUCENTIO

I may and will, if she be so contented.
She will be pleased, then wherefore should I doubt?
Hap what hap may, I'll roundly go about her.
It shall go hard if Cambio go without her.

Exit

Enter Petruchio, Katherina, Hortensio and Servants IV.5

PETRUCHIO

Come on, a God's name, once more toward our father's.
Good Lord, how bright and goodly shines the moon!

KATHERINA

The moon? The sun! It is not moonlight now.

PETRUCHIO

I say it is the moon that shines so bright.

KATHERINA

I know it is the sun that shines so bright.

PETRUCHIO

Now by my mother's son, and that's myself,
It shall be moon, or star, or what I list,
Or e'er I journey to your father's house.
(*to the Servants*) Go on and fetch our horses back again.
Evermore crossed and crossed, nothing but crossed!   10

HORTENSIO

Say as he says, or we shall never go.

KATHERINA

    Forward, I pray, since we have come so far,
    And be it moon, or sun, or what you please.
    And if you please to call it a rush-candle,
    Henceforth I vow it shall be so for me.

PETRUCHIO

    I say it is the moon.

KATHERINA   I know it is the moon.

PETRUCHIO

    Nay, then you lie. It is the blessèd sun.

KATHERINA

    Then, God be blessed, it is the blessèd sun.
    But sun it is not, when you say it is not,
20   And the moon changes even as your mind.
    What you will have it named, even that it is,
    And so it shall be so for Katherine.

HORTENSIO (aside)

    Petruchio, go thy ways, the field is won.

PETRUCHIO

    Well, forward, forward! Thus the bowl should run,
    And not unluckily against the bias.
    But soft, company is coming here.

        Enter Vincentio

    (*to Vincentio*) Good morrow, gentle mistress, where
        away?
    Tell me, sweet Kate, and tell me truly too,
    Hast thou beheld a fresher gentlewoman?
30   Such war of white and red within her cheeks!
    What stars do spangle heaven with such beauty
    As those two eyes become that heavenly face?
    Fair lovely maid, once more good day to thee.
    Sweet Kate, embrace her for her beauty's sake.

HORTENSIO (aside) 'A will make the man mad, to make
    the woman of him.

KATHERINA
  Young budding virgin, fair and fresh and sweet,
  Whither away, or where is thy abode?
  Happy the parents of so fair a child,
  Happier the man whom favourable stars   40
  Allots thee for his lovely bedfellow.

PETRUCHIO
  Why, how now, Kate, I hope thou art not mad!
  This is a man, old, wrinkled, faded, withered,
  And not a maiden, as thou say'st he is.

KATHERINA
  Pardon, old father, my mistaking eyes,
  That have been so bedazzled with the sun
  That everything I look on seemeth green.
  Now I perceive thou art a reverend father.
  Pardon, I pray thee, for my mad mistaking.

PETRUCHIO
  Do, good old grandsire, and withal make known   50
  Which way thou travellest – if along with us,
  We shall be joyful of thy company.

VINCENTIO
  Fair sir, and you my merry mistress,
  That with your strange encounter much amazed me,
  My name is called Vincentio, my dwelling Pisa,
  And bound I am to Padua, there to visit
  A son of mine, which long I have not seen.

PETRUCHIO
  What is his name?

VINCENTIO   Lucentio, gentle sir.

PETRUCHIO
  Happily met – the happier for thy son.
  And now by law, as well as reverend age,   60
  I may entitle thee my loving father.
  The sister to my wife, this gentlewoman,

Thy son by this hath married. Wonder not,
Nor be not grieved – she is of good esteem,
Her dowry wealthy, and of worthy birth,
Beside, so qualified as may beseem
The spouse of any noble gentleman.
Let me embrace with old Vincentio,
And wander we to see thy honest son,
70 Who will of thy arrival be full joyous.

VINCENTIO
But is this true, or is it else your pleasure,
Like pleasant travellers, to break a jest
Upon the company you overtake?

HORTENSIO
I do assure thee, father, so it is.

PETRUCHIO
Come, go along and see the truth hereof,
For our first merriment hath made thee jealous.
Exeunt all but Hortensio

HORTENSIO
Well, Petruchio, this has put me in heart.
Have to my widow! And if she be froward,
Then hast thou taught Hortensio to be untoward.
Exit

*

V.1   *Enter Biondello, Lucentio as himself, and Bianca.*
Gremio is out before

BIONDELLO Softly and swiftly, sir, for the priest is ready.

LUCENTIO I fly, Biondello. But they may chance to need
thee at home, therefore leave us.
Exeunt Lucentio and Bianca

BIONDELLO Nay, faith, I'll see the church a your back,

and then come back to my master's as soon as I can.

Exit

GREMIO

I marvel Cambio comes not all this while.

Enter Petruchio, Katherina, Vincentio and Grumio,
with attendants

PETRUCHIO

Sir, here's the door, this is Lucentio's house.
My father's bears more toward the market-place.
Thither must I, and here I leave you, sir.

VINCENTIO

You shall not choose but drink before you go.   10
I think I shall command your welcome here,
And by all likelihood some cheer is toward.

He knocks

GREMIO They're busy within. You were best knock louder.

More knocking
Pedant looks out of the window

PEDANT What's he that knocks as he would beat down the
gate?

VINCENTIO Is Signor Lucentio within, sir?

PEDANT He's within, sir, but not to be spoken withal.

VINCENTIO What if a man bring him a hundred pound or
two to make merry withal?

PEDANT Keep your hundred pounds to yourself. He shall   20
need none so long as I live.

PETRUCHIO Nay, I told you your son was well beloved
in Padua. Do you hear, sir? To leave frivolous circumstances, I pray you tell Signor Lucentio that his father is
come from Pisa, and is here at the door to speak with
him.

PEDANT Thou liest. His father is come from Mantua, and
here looking out at the window.

VINCENTIO Art thou his father?

30 PEDANT Ay sir, so his mother says, if I may believe her.

PETRUCHIO (*to Vincentio*) Why how now, gentleman! Why, this is flat knavery, to take upon you another man's name.

PEDANT Lay hands on the villain. I believe 'a means to cozen somebody in this city under my countenance.

Enter Biondello

BIONDELLO (*aside*) I have seen them in the church together. God send 'em good shipping! But who is here? Mine old master Vincentio! Now we are undone and brought to nothing.

40 VINCENTIO (*seeing Biondello*) Come hither, crack-hemp.

BIONDELLO I hope I may choose, sir.

VINCENTIO Come hither, you rogue. What, have you forgot me?

BIONDELLO Forgot you? No, sir. I could not forget you, for I never saw you before in all my life.

VINCENTIO What, you notorious villain, didst thou never see thy master's father, Vincentio?

BIONDELLO What, my old worshipful old master? Yes, marry, sir – see where he looks out of the window.

50 VINCENTIO Is't so, indeed?

He beats Biondello

BIONDELLO Help, help, help! Here's a madman will murder me. *Exit*

PEDANT Help, son! Help, Signor Baptista!

Exit from the window

PETRUCHIO Prithee, Kate, let's stand aside and see the end of this controversy.

They stand aside

Enter Pedant below, with Servants, Baptista, and Tranio

TRANIO Sir, what are you that offer to beat my servant?

VINCENTIO What am I, sir? Nay, what are you, sir? O immortal gods! O fine villain! A silken doublet, a velvet hose, a scarlet cloak, and a copatain hat! O, I am undone, I am undone! While I play the good husband at home, 60 my son and my servant spend all at the university.

TRANIO How now, what's the matter?

BAPTISTA What, is the man lunatic?

TRANIO Sir, you seem a sober ancient gentleman by your habit, but your words show you a madman. Why, sir, what 'cerns it you if I wear pearl and gold? I thank my good father, I am able to maintain it.

VINCENTIO Thy father? O villain, he is a sail-maker in Bergamo.

BAPTISTA You mistake, sir, you mistake, sir. Pray, what 70 do you think is his name?

VINCENTIO His name? As if I knew not his name! I have brought him up ever since he was three years old, and his name is Tranio.

PEDANT Away, away, mad ass! His name is Lucentio, and he is mine only son, and heir to the lands of me, Signor Vincentio.

VINCENTIO Lucentio? O, he hath murdered his master! Lay hold on him, I charge you, in the Duke's name. O, my son, my son! Tell me, thou villain, where is my son 80 Lucentio?

TRANIO Call forth an officer.

Enter an Officer

Carry this mad knave to the gaol. Father Baptista, I charge you see that he be forthcoming.

VINCENTIO Carry me to the gaol?

GREMIO Stay, officer. He shall not go to prison.

BAPTISTA Talk not, Signor Gremio. I say he shall go to prison.

GREMIO Take heed, Signor Baptista, lest you be cony-catched in this business. I dare swear this is the right 90 Vincentio.

PEDANT Swear if thou dar'st.

GREMIO Nay, I dare not swear it.

TRANIO Then thou wert best say that I am not Lucentio.

GREMIO Yes, I know thee to be Signor Lucentio.

BAPTISTA Away with the dotard, to the gaol with him!

VINCENTIO Thus strangers may be haled and abused. O
    monstrous villain!

    Enter Biondello, with Lucentio and Bianca

BIONDELLO O, we are spoiled, and yonder he is! Deny
100 him, forswear him, or else we are all undone.

LUCENTIO (*kneeling*)
    Pardon, sweet father.

VINCENTIO   Lives my sweet son?

    Exeunt Biondello, Tranio and Pedant, as fast as may be

BIANCA
    Pardon, dear father.

BAPTISTA   How hast thou offended?
    Where is Lucentio?

LUCENTIO   Here's Lucentio,
    Right son to the right Vincentio,
    That have by marriage made thy daughter mine,
    While counterfeit supposes bleared thine eyne.

GREMIO
    Here's packing, with a witness, to deceive us all.

VINCENTIO
    Where is that damnèd villain, Tranio,
    That faced and braved me in this matter so?

BAPTISTA
110 Why, tell me, is not this my Cambio?

BIANCA
    Cambio is changed into Lucentio.

LUCENTIO
    Love wrought these miracles. Bianca's love
    Made me exchange my state with Tranio,
    While he did bear my countenance in the town,

And happily I have arrivèd at last
Unto the wishèd haven of my bliss.
What Tranio did, myself enforced him to;
Then pardon him, sweet father, for my sake.

VINCENTIO I'll slit the villain's nose that would have sent
me to the gaol.   120

BAPTISTA (*to Lucentio*) But do you hear, sir? Have you
married my daughter without asking my good will?

VINCENTIO Fear not, Baptista, we will content you, go to.
But I will in to be revenged for this villainy.   *Exit*

BAPTISTA And I to sound the depth of this knavery. *Exit*

LUCENTIO Look not pale, Bianca – thy father will not
frown.   *Exeunt Lucentio and Bianca*

GREMIO
My cake is dough, but I'll in among the rest,
Out of hope of all but my share of the feast.   *Exit*

KATHERINA Husband, let's follow to see the end of this   130
ado.

PETRUCHIO First kiss me, Kate, and we will.

KATHERINA What, in the midst of the street?

PETRUCHIO What, art thou ashamed of me?

KATHERINA No, sir, God forbid – but ashamed to kiss.

PETRUCHIO
Why then, let's home again.
(*to Grumio*) Come, sirrah, let's away.

KATHERINA
Nay, I will give thee a kiss.
    She kisses him
Now pray thee, love, stay.

PETRUCHIO
Is not this well? Come, my sweet Kate.   140
Better once than never, for never too late.   *Exeunt*

Enter Baptista with Vincentio, Gremio with the
Pedant, Lucentio with Bianca, Petruchio with
Katherina, Hortensio with the Widow; followed by
Tranio, Biondello, and Grumio, with the Servingmen
bringing in a banquet

LUCENTIO
At last, though long, our jarring notes agree,
And time it is when raging war is done
To smile at scapes and perils overblown.
My fair Bianca, bid my father welcome,
While I with self-same kindness welcome thine.
Brother Petruchio, sister Katherina,
And thou, Hortensio, with thy loving widow,
Feast with the best, and welcome to my house.
My banquet is to close our stomachs up
After our great good cheer. Pray you, sit down, 10
For now we sit to chat as well as eat.
They sit

PETRUCHIO
Nothing but sit and sit, and eat and eat!

BAPTISTA
Padua affords this kindness, son Petruchio

PETRUCHIO
Padua affords nothing but what is kind.

HORTENSIO
For both our sakes I would that word were true.

PETRUCHIO
Now, for my life, Hortensio fears his widow.

WIDOW
Then never trust me if I be afeard.

PETRUCHIO
You are very sensible, and yet you miss my sense:
I mean Hortensio is afeard of you.

WIDOW
He that is giddy thinks the world turns round. 20

PETRUCHIO
Roundly replied.

KATHERINA   Mistress, how mean you that?

WIDOW
Thus I conceive by him.

PETRUCHIO
Conceives by me! How likes Hortensio that?

HORTENSIO
My widow says thus she conceives her tale.

PETRUCHIO
Very well mended. Kiss him for that, good widow.

KATHERINA
'He that is giddy thinks the world turns round' –
I pray you tell me what you meant by that.

WIDOW
Your husband, being troubled with a shrew,
Measures my husband's sorrow by his woe.
And now you know my meaning.   30

KATHERINA
A very mean meaning.

WIDOW   Right, I mean you.

KATHERINA
And I am mean, indeed, respecting you.

PETRUCHIO
To her, Kate!

HORTENSIO
To her, widow!

PETRUCHIO
A hundred marks, my Kate does put her down.

HORTENSIO
That's my office.

PETRUCHIO
Spoke like an officer – ha' to thee, lad.
    He drinks to Hortensio

149

BAPTISTA

How likes Gremio these quick-witted folks?

GREMIO

Believe me, sir, they butt together well.

BIANCA

40 Head and butt! An hasty-witted body

Would say your head and butt were head and horn.

VINCENTIO

Ay, mistress bride, hath that awakened you?

BIANCA

Ay, but not frighted me, therefore I'll sleep again.

PETRUCHIO

Nay, that you shall not. Since you have begun,

Have at you for a bitter jest or two.

BIANCA

Am I your bird? I mean to shift my bush,

And then pursue me as you draw your bow.

You are welcome all.

Exeunt Bianca, Katherina, and Widow

PETRUCHIO

She hath prevented me. Here, Signor Tranio,

50 This bird you aimed at, though you hit her not –

Therefore a health to all that shot and missed.

TRANIO

O sir, Lucentio slipped me like his greyhound,

Which runs himself, and catches for his master.

PETRUCHIO

A good swift simile, but something currish.

TRANIO

'Tis well, sir, that you hunted for yourself.

'Tis thought your deer does hold you at a bay.

BAPTISTA

O, O, Petruchio! Tranio hits you now.

LUCENTIO

I thank thee for that gird, good Tranio.

HORTENSIO
Confess, confess, hath he not hit you here?

PETRUCHIO
'A has a little galled me, I confess;   60
And as the jest did glance away from me,
'Tis ten to one it maimed you two outright.

BAPTISTA
Now, in good sadness, son Petruchio,
I think thou hast the veriest shrew of all.

PETRUCHIO
Well, I say no. And therefore for assurance
Let's each one send unto his wife,
And he whose wife is most obedient,
To come at first when he doth send for her,
Shall win the wager which we will propose.

HORTENSIO
Content. What's the wager?

LUCENTIO   Twenty crowns.   70

PETRUCHIO
Twenty crowns?
I'll venture so much of my hawk or hound,
But twenty times so much upon my wife.

LUCENTIO
A hundred then.

HORTENSIO   Content.

PETRUCHIO   A match! 'Tis done.

HORTENSIO
Who shall begin?

LUCENTIO   That will I. Biondello,
Go bid your mistress come to me.

BIONDELLO   I go.   *Exit*

BAPTISTA
Son, I'll be your half Bianca comes.

LUCENTIO
I'll have no halves. I'll bear it all myself.

151

Enter Biondello

How now, what news?

BIONDELLO   Sir, my mistress sends you word

80   That she is busy and she cannot come.

PETRUCHIO

How? She's busy, and she cannot come!
Is that an answer?

GREMIO   Ay, and a kind one too.

Pray God, sir, your wife send you not a worse.

PETRUCHIO

I hope better.

HORTENSIO

Sirrah Biondello, go and entreat my wife
To come to me forthwith.   *Exit Biondello*

PETRUCHIO   O ho, entreat her!

Nay, then she must needs come.

HORTENSIO   I am afraid, sir,

Do what you can, yours will not be entreated.

Enter Biondello

Now, where's my wife?

BIONDELLO

90   She says you have some goodly jest in hand.
She will not come. She bids you come to her.

PETRUCHIO

Worse and worse, she will not come! O vile,
Intolerable, not to be endured!
Sirrah Grumio, go to your mistress,
Say I command her come to me.   *Exit Grumio*

HORTENSIO

I know her answer.

PETRUCHIO   What?

HORTENSIO   She will not.

PETRUCHIO

The fouler fortune mine, and there an end.

Enter Katherina

BAPTISTA

Now, by my holidame, here comes Katherina.

KATHERINA

What is your will, sir, that you send for me?

PETRUCHIO

Where is your sister, and Hortensio's wife?   100

KATHERINA

They sit conferring by the parlour fire.

PETRUCHIO

Go fetch them hither. If they deny to come,
Swinge me them soundly forth unto their husbands.
Away, I say, and bring them hither straight.

Exit Katherina

LUCENTIO

Here is a wonder, if you talk of a wonder.

HORTENSIO

And so it is. I wonder what it bodes.

PETRUCHIO

Marry, peace it bodes, and love, and quiet life,
An awful rule, and right supremacy,
And, to be short, what not that's sweet and happy.

BAPTISTA

Now fair befall thee, good Petruchio!   110
The wager thou hast won, and I will add
Unto their losses twenty thousand crowns –
Another dowry to another daughter,
For she is changed, as she had never been.

PETRUCHIO

Nay, I will win my wager better yet,
And show more sign of her obedience,
Her new-built virtue and obedience.

Enter Katherina with Bianca and Widow

See where she comes, and brings your froward wives

As prisoners to her womanly persuasion.
120   Katherine, that cap of yours becomes you not.
Off with that bauble, throw it under foot.
    She obeys

WIDOW
Lord, let me never have a cause to sigh
Till I be brought to such a silly pass!

BIANCA
Fie, what a foolish duty call you this?

LUCENTIO
I would your duty were as foolish too!
The wisdom of your duty, fair Bianca,
Hath cost me a hundred crowns since supper-time.

BIANCA
The more fool you for laying on my duty.

PETRUCHIO
Katherine, I charge thee, tell these headstrong women
130   What duty they do owe their lords and husbands.

WIDOW
Come, come, you're mocking. We will have no telling.

PETRUCHIO
Come on, I say, and first begin with her.

WIDOW
She shall not.

PETRUCHIO
I say she shall. And first begin with her.

KATHERINA
Fie, fie, unknit that threatening unkind brow,
And dart not scornful glances from those eyes
To wound thy lord, thy king, thy governor.
It blots thy beauty as frosts do bite the meads,
Confounds thy fame as whirlwinds shake fair buds,
140   And in no sense is meet or amiable.
A woman moved is like a fountain troubled,

Muddy, ill-seeming, thick, bereft of beauty,
And while it is so, none so dry or thirsty
Will deign to sip or touch one drop of it.
Thy husband is thy lord, thy life, thy keeper,
Thy head, thy sovereign; one that cares for thee,
And for thy maintenance; commits his body
To painful labour both by sea and land,
To watch the night in storms, the day in cold,
Whilst thou liest warm at home, secure and safe;   150
And craves no other tribute at thy hands
But love, fair looks, and true obedience –
Too little payment for so great a debt.
Such duty as the subject owes the prince,
Even such a woman oweth to her husband.
And when she is froward, peevish, sullen, sour,
And not obedient to his honest will,
What is she but a foul contending rebel
And graceless traitor to her loving lord?
I am ashamed that women are so simple   160
To offer war where they should kneel for peace,
Or seek for rule, supremacy, and sway,
When they are bound to serve, love, and obey.
Why are our bodies soft, and weak, and smooth,
Unapt to toil and trouble in the world,
But that our soft conditions and our hearts
Should well agree with our external parts?
Come, come, you froward and unable worms,
My mind hath been as big as one of yours,
My heart as great, my reason haply more,   170
To bandy word for word and frown for frown.
But now I see our lances are but straws,
Our strength as weak, our weakness past compare,
That seeming to be most which we indeed least are.
Then vail your stomachs, for it is no boot,

And place your hands below your husband's foot.
In token of which duty, if he please,
My hand is ready, may it do him ease.

PETRUCHIO

Why, there's a wench! Come on, and kiss me, Kate.

LUCENTIO

180 Well, go thy ways, old lad, for thou shalt ha't.

VINCENTIO

'Tis a good hearing when children are toward.

LUCENTIO

But a harsh hearing when women are froward.

PETRUCHIO

Come, Kate, we'll to bed.
We three are married, but you two are sped.
(*to Lucentio*) 'Twas I won the wager, though you hit the
　　　　white,
And being a winner, God give you good night!

　　　　　　　　　　　　　　Exeunt Petruchio and Katherina

HORTENSIO

Now go thy ways, thou hast tamed a curst shrew.

LUCENTIO

'Tis a wonder, by your leave, she will be tamed so.

　　　　　　　　　　　　　　　　　　　Exeunt

THE SLY SCENES IN 'A SHREW'

IN *The Taming of a Shrew* Christopher Sly is involved in the action, after the Induction is over, on five subsequent occasions. Pope inserted these passages into his edition of Shakespeare's play, and many producers have found them irresistible. They are, therefore, given here.

(i) Occurring at a point for which there is no precise equivalent in *The Taming of the Shrew*, this intervention by Sly would, if used in a modern production of Shakespeare's play, best come at the end of II.1.

SLY Sim, when will the fool [Sander, the equivalent of Grumio] come again?

LORD He'll come again, my lord, anon.

SLY Gi's some more drink here. Zounds, where's the tapster? Here, Sim, eat some of these things.

LORD So I do, my lord.

SLY Here, Sim, I drink to thee.

LORD My lord, here comes the players again.

SLY O brave! Here's two fine gentlewomen.

(ii) Sly's next intervention comes between the end of IV.4 and the beginning of IV.5, the scene in which Petruchio and Katherina dispute about the sun and the moon. Polidor and Aurelius have just gone off to marry Emelia and Phylema.

SLY Sim, must they be married now?

LORD Ay, my lord.

Enter Ferando and Kate and Sander

SLY Look, Sim, the fool is come again now.

(iii) Sly is at his most lordly on the final occasion that he intrudes on the play that is being performed for his benefit. This happens at V.I.IOI of Shakespeare's play, the stage direction with which the passage opens coinciding exactly with his direction *Exeunt Biondello, Tranio and Pedant, as fast as may be.* The Duke of Cestus has just given orders that the impostors, Phylotus and Valeria, should be sent to prison.

Phylotus and Valeria runs away

Then Sly speaks

SLY I say we'll have no sending to prison.

LORD My lord, this is but the play, they're but in jest.

SLY I tell thee, Sim, we'll have no sending to prison, that's flat. Why, Sim, am I not Don Christo Vary? Therefore I say they shall not go to prison.

LORD No more they shall not, my lord. They be run away.

SLY Are they run away, Sim? That's well. Then gi's some more drink, and let them play again.

LORD Here, my lord.

Sly drinks and then falls asleep

(iv) Between the end of V.I and the beginning of V.2 Sly is removed.

Exeunt omnes

Sly sleeps

LORD

Who's within there? Come hither, sirs.

Enter Servants

My lord's

Asleep again. Go take him easily up,
And put him in his own apparel again,
And lay him in the place where we did find him,
Just underneath the alehouse side below,
But see you wake him not in any case.

BOY It shall be done, my lord. Come help to bear him
hence.

(v) When the play proper is over, and all the characters
have left the stage, this follows:

> *Then enter two bearing of Sly in his own apparel again,
> and leaves him where they found him, and then goes out.
> Then enter the Tapster*

TAPSTER
Now that the darksome night is overpast,
And dawning day appears in crystal sky,
Now must I haste abroad. But soft, who's this?
What, Sly? O wondrous! Hath he lain here all night?
I'll wake him. I think he's starved by this,
But that his belly was so stuffed with ale.
What ho, Sly! Awake for shame.

SLY Sim, gi's some more wine. What's all the players gone?
Am not I a lord?

TAPSTER A lord, with a murrain. Come, art thou drunken
still?

SLY Who's this? Tapster! O Lord, sirrah, I have had the
bravest dream tonight that ever thou heardest in all
thy life.

TAPSTER Ay, marry, but you had best get you home, for
your wife will course [thrash] you for dreaming here
tonight.

SLY Will she? I know now how to tame a shrew. I dreamt
upon it all this night till now, and thou hast waked me

out of the best dream that ever I had in my life. But I'll
to my wife presently, and tame her too an if she anger
me.

TAPSTER
Nay tarry, Sly, for I'll go home with thee,
And hear the rest that thou hast dreamt tonight.

Exeunt omnes

COMMENTARY

THE Act and scene divisions are those of Peter Alexander's edition of the Complete Works, London, 1951. All references to other plays by Shakespeare not yet available in the New Penguin Shakespeare edition are to Alexander.

The Characters in the Play

No list of the Characters is given in the Folio. An alternative way of arranging the characters in the play proper, so as to bring out the extent to which they fall into groups, would be to put the three old men (Baptista, Gremio, and Vincentio) together; then the three young men (Petruchio, Lucentio, and Hortensio); then the three young women (Katherina, Bianca, and the Widow); and finally, the rest, who are all servants and tradesmen, or, in the case of the Pedant, a sort of employee.

1. Induction

The opening of this play is of peculiar interest, because in no other of his works does Shakespeare make use of an Induction (see Introduction, pages 14–15). The setting, it soon becomes plain, is outside an alehouse in the playwright's native Warwickshire, and then, for the second scene, in a large country house. Shakespeare is clearly drawing on direct personal experience in his depiction of country people and their activities. The tang and raciness of the altercation between Sly and the Hostess has the stamp of observed reality about it, making their brief but lively dialogue a fitting prelude to the fuller evocation of life in Elizabethan England that is to follow.

Although it is obviously a separate part of the play, the Induction is not distinguished from the rest of it in the Folio, where the text, like many others, is simply headed '*Actus primus. Scæna Prima.*'

1.   (stage direction) *Enter Christopher Sly and the Hostess.*
The Folio reads: '*Enter Begger and Hostes, Christophero
Sly.*' Sly's speeches are consistently headed *Beg.*,
and the Lord refers to him as 'the beggar' at line
39, though according to Sly himself he is in fact
a tinker. The distinction between beggars and tinkers
was not a very sharp one, and both were proverbially
noted for their fondness for ale. The name Christophero
Sly in this initial direction is evidently an afterthought,
derived from the text (Induction.2.5), and may well
be an addition made by the prompter. The implications
of the neutral word *Enter* are well brought out by the
corresponding stage direction in *The Taming of a Shrew*,
which reads: 'Enter a Tapster, beating out of his
doores *Slie Droonken*.'

1   *pheeze you* settle your hash, fix you. Given in the
Oxford English Dictionary under the commoner spelling
feeze, this word originally meant 'to drive away or
frighten off', but by Shakespeare's time it seems to have
taken on an abusive connotation and to have become
part of the language of the tavern. It occurs again in
Troilus and Cressida (II.3.200), where Ajax says of
Achilles: 'An 'a be proud with me I'll pheeze his pride',
and, with a punning reference to 'vizier', in *The Merry
Wives of Windsor* (I.3.10), where the Host calls Falstaff
his 'Pheazar'.

3   *Y'are* you are (colloquial)
    baggage good-for-nothing woman, strumpet

4   *Richard Conqueror.* Sly's knowledge of history, like his
knowledge of hagiology, is rather shaky. He has confused Richard Cœur-de-Lion with William the Conqueror. But his pretensions to aristocratic descent,
though intended primarily to impress the Hostess, also
prepare the way for his assumption of a lordly role in
the second scene.

5   *paucas pallabris.* This phrase, which was something of
a cant term in Shakespeare's England, is a corruption

of the Spanish *pocas palabras* (few words). Its use here may well be a reminiscence of, or a jesting allusion to, Thomas Kyd's *The Spanish Tragedy* (III.14.118), where Hieronimo, the hero of the play, cautions himself against revealing too much of what he knows by saying: '*Pocas Palabras*, mild as the Lamb.'

let the world slide let the world go by, don't worry. The phrase, which was a proverbial one, was recorded by John Heywood in 1546 in the following form: 'To let the world wag, and take mine ease in mine inn.' It sums up Sly's general attitude to life very well, and is substantially repeated by him at Induction.2.141 when he tells his 'wife' to 'let the world slip'.

Sessa! The precise meaning of this exclamation, which is also used twice by Edgar in *King Lear* (III.4.99 and III.6.73), is uncertain. In all three cases it appears to be an incitement to haste, roughly equivalent to 'Off you go!' or 'Be off with you!'

6   *burst* broken, smashed

7   *denier* pronounced to rhyme with 'many a'. It was a very small French coin worth one twelfth of a sou.

     Go by, Saint Jeronimy. Sly is misquoting from *The Spanish Tragedy* (III.12.31), where Hieronimo warns himself against over-hasty action by saying, '*Hieronimo* beware; go by, go by.' The words became a popular catch-phrase. Kyd's editor comments: 'Perhaps no single passage in Elizabethan drama became so notorious as this. It is quoted over and over again as the stock phrase to imply impatience of anything disagreeable, inconvenient, or old-fashioned' (*The Works of Thomas Kyd*, ed. F. S. Boas, Oxford, 1901, p. 406). Sly characteristically mixes Hieronimo up with Saint Jerome, as well he might, since *The Spanish Tragedy* seems to be his Bible.

7–8   *go to thy cold bed and warm thee.* Precisely these words, which may have had some proverbial association with beggars whose 'cold bed' frequently was the ground, are used by Edgar, disguised as Poor Tom, in *King Lear* (III.4.47).

9–10   *thirdborough* petty constable of a township or manor. The Folio reads: 'Headborough' (another name for the same officer), but Sly's rejoinder demands the emendation.

11–12   *by law* with judicial proceedings, in court. Sly is still trying to give the impression that he is a man of importance.

12   *budge an inch.* Sly is quibbling on the literal sense of the phrase and on its metaphorical sense of giving way on a matter of principle.

boy servant, inferior (used here as a term of abuse). Compare *Coriolanus*, V.6.101–17.

12–13   *and kindly* naturally, of course, by all means. Sly is being ironical.

13   (stage direction) *Wind horns.* This command is intended, of course, for those in charge of the effects in Shakespeare's theatre.

train retinue, followers

14   *tender well* take good care of

15   *Breathe Merriman* give Merriman a breathing space. 'Breathe' is C. J. Sisson's emendation of the Folio reading 'Brach' which does not make very good sense. A 'brach' is a bitch-hound, whereas Merriman looks like the name of a dog-hound; the sentence requires a verb at this point to go with 'couple' in the next line; and the repetition of 'brach' at the end of the sentence is ugly and unconvincing. 'Breathing' would be the right treatment for a hound that was dead beat. Dover Wilson reads 'Broach', meaning 'bleed'.

embossed foaming at the mouth (with exhaustion)

16   *couple* leash together. The Elizabethans took their hounds to and from the hunt in couples.

17   *made it good* put matters right (by picking up the scent)

18   *in the coldest fault* at the point where the scent was most completely lost. A 'fault' is a break in the scent.

21   *cried upon it at the merest loss* yelped out on the right
scent when it was totally lost

26   *sup them well* give them a good supper
look unto take care of

31   *a bed but cold* but a cold bed in which

33   *image* likeness. Sly, in his drunken stupor, looks like a
dead man.

34   *practise* play a trick

38   *brave* fine, handsomely dressed

39   *forget himself* lose consciousness of his own identity

40   *he cannot choose* he must, he is bound to

41   *strange* incredible, wonderful

46   *Balm* anoint, bathe
distillèd waters (fragrant liquids, such as rose-water,
made from flowers and herbs)

47   *burn sweet wood* to make the lodging sweet. It was a common Elizabethan practice to burn sweet-scented wood,
such as juniper, in a musty room. Compare *Much Ado
About Nothing*, I.3.54–5 where Borachio says, 'as I was
smoking a musty room'.

48   *Procure me music.* 'Me' is the dative, meaning 'for
me'.

49   *dulcet* melodious

51   *reverence* bow, obeisance

55   *ewer* (pitcher with a wide spout, to bring water for
washing the hands)
diaper towel

60   *disease* disorder of the mind

62   *And when he says he is Sly, say that he dreams.* The Folio
reads: 'And when he sayes he is, say that he dreames',
which does not make very good sense, since there is no
point in getting Sly to admit that he is mad and then
telling him that he is merely dreaming. Dr Johnson's
suggestion, that the word 'Sly' was omitted by the
printer because of its similarity to the word 'say', has
been adopted in this edition. It receives strong support
from Sly's reaction in the next scene (lines 16–19) to the

statement that he is deranged: 'What, would you make me mad? Am not I Christopher Sly . . .?'

64   *kindly* naturally, convincingly
    gentle kind

65   *passing* surpassingly, extremely

66   *husbanded with modesty* managed with moderation, not carried too far

68   *As* so that
    by as a result of
    true fitting, proper

70   *to bed with him* put him to bed

71   *to his office* go about his duty
    (stage direction) *Sly is carried away.* There is no direction for the removal of Sly in the Folio, but *The Taming of a Shrew* reads: '*Exeunt* two with *Slie.*'
    (stage direction) *A trumpet sounds.* The Folio reads: '*Sound trumpets*', but the following line shows that only one is required.

75   *An't* if it

77–102   *Now, fellows, you are welcome . . . nothing that my house affords.* This little episode shows the kind of reception that an acting company, on tour in the provinces, would hope for at a great house, even if they did not always receive it. It has the further interest of anticipating the similar but more extended scene (*Hamlet*, II.2.416–540), in which Hamlet welcomes the actors to Elsinore. Moreover, there are parallels between the Prince's views on acting (III.2.1–44) and the Lord's praise of a part that was 'naturally performed'.

80   *So please* if it so please. The Folio allots this speech to '*2. Player*', though there has been no mention of a First Player.

86   *I think 'twas Soto that your honour means.* The Folio assigns this speech to '*Sincklo*', and so provides the name of the actor for whom the part was written. John Sincklo or Sincler was a performer of minor roles in Shakespeare's company, and his name turns up on

several other occasions. He is first mentioned as a member of the cast that played *The Second Part of the Seven Deadly Sins*, which was probably staged about 1591 and of which only the 'plot' or outline survives. His name appears again in the Folio text of *3 Henry VI* (III.1.1), where he plays a forester; then in the Quarto version of *2 Henry IV* (V.4.0), where he takes the part of the Beadle; and, finally, in the Induction to John Marston's play *The Malcontent*, which was published in 1604. The remarks made about him by Doll Tearsheet and the Hostess in *2 Henry IV* suggest that he was abnormally thin. Doll calls him 'you thin man in a Censor', 'Goodman death, goodman Bones', and 'you thinne thing'; while the Hostess addresses him as 'you starv'd Blood-hound' and as 'Thou Anatomy, thou'. Other parts which may well have been written with Sincklo's peculiar appearance in mind are those of the Apothecary in *Romeo and Juliet*, Robert Faulconbridge in *King John*, and Starveling in *A Midsummer Night's Dream*. Since Shakespeare thought of the pantaloon as 'lean' (*As You Like It*, II.7.159), it seems likely that Sincklo took the part of Gremio in the main action of *The Taming of the Shrew*.

A character called Soto, who is a farmer's son, appears in John Fletcher's play, *Women Pleased*. It is unlikely, however, that Shakespeare is alluding to this particular play here, since it dates from somewhere between 1619 and 1623 – almost thirty years after the composition of *The Taming of the Shrew*, and nearly twenty after the last recorded reference to Sincklo – and since his description of Soto's role does not tally with what happens in *Women Pleased*. Most modern critics are of the opinion that Fletcher's play, which is, for him, rather old-fashioned and not at all well constructed, is probably a revision of a much older play that is no longer extant, and that it is to the part of Soto in this lost play that Shakespeare is referring here. (See G. E.

Bentley, *The Jacobean and Caroline Stage*, volume III, Oxford, 1956, pages 431–2.)

88   *in happy time* just at the right time

89   *The rather for* the more so because

90   *cunning* art, professional skill

92   *doubtful of your modesties* unsure about your ability to control yourselves

93   *over-eyeing of* observing

95   *merry passion* irresistible burst of merriment. Compare 'idle merriment, | A passion hateful to my purposes' (*King John*, III.3.46–7).

97   *impatient* angry, annoyed

98   *contain* restrain

99   *the veriest antic* the most complete buffoon, the oddest and most fantastical fellow

102   *affords* has to offer

103–4   *Sirrah, go you to Barthol'mew my page . . . a lady.* The Lord is cleverly adapting the Elizabethan stage convention that all female parts were played by boys to the purposes of a practical joke in everyday life. The same trick becomes the central motif of an entire play in Ben Jonson's *The Silent Woman* (1609).

104   *in all suits* in all respects (with a pun on 'suits' in the sense of dress)

106   *do him obeisance* show him the respect due to a superior

108   *honourable action* decent behaviour befitting one of high rank

110   *accomplishèd* performed

112   *lowly courtesy* humble curtsy

117   *with declining head into his bosom* with his head drooping on his chest

120   *esteemèd him* thought himself

123   *commanded* forced, feigned

124   *for such a shift* as an expedient, to serve the turn

125   *close* secretly, covertly

126   *in despite* notwithstanding

128   *Anon* soon, immediately afterwards

129   *usurp* counterfeit, assume

130   *action* bodily movements

133   *simple* mere

134   *I'll in* I'll go in. In Elizabethan English the verb of motion was frequently omitted after words implying purpose, such as 'will', 'shall', and 'must'.

       Haply perhaps

135   *spleen* impulse to uncontrollable laughter. In Shakespeare's day the spleen was regarded as the seat of any sudden outburst of feeling, whether of mirth or of anger. Laughter and melancholy both came under its control.

136   *grow into extremes* become quite excessive, get out of hand

       (stage direction) *Exeunt*. This direction, though it does not appear in the Folio, is clearly implied by the Lord's remark 'I'll in' (line 134) and by the massed entry, in which he takes part, that follows. *The Taming of a Shrew*, at the corresponding point in its action, has '*Exeunt omnes*'.

2. This scene, in which Sly's attitude changes from one of complete incredulity to an assured assumption of the lordly role that has been thrust upon him, is not only one of the richest and subtlest pieces of comedy that Shakespeare ever wrote, but also one of the most important documents about the Elizabethan stage that we have. The stage direction with which it opens reads as follows in the Folio: '*Enter aloft the drunkard with attendants, some with apparel, Bason and Ewer, & other appurtenances, & Lord.*' The word 'aloft' clearly indicates that the entire scene was played on some kind of upper stage. Where and how was it done? There are 141 lines of dialogue; at least six characters – and probably more, since the Page is accompanied by attendants when he enters as Sly's wife – must be on the stage at the same time; and somewhere, either on the stage or just off it, there must be a bed or some indication of one. It seems improbable that a scene of this length and complexity

could have been properly or satisfactorily portrayed on the kind of upper stage that is usually thought of as a balustraded gallery, forming part of the façade of the tiring-house. An audience would surely have found difficulty in sustaining its interest in a scene of this length when separated from the actors by railings and by the large expanse of unoccupied main stage. An attractive solution to the problem is suggested by C. Walter Hodges, who thinks that for extended scenes 'aloft', such as this, a temporary structure was employed, jutting out from the façade of the tiring-house and in front of the stage gallery. Consisting essentially of a platform, raised about seven feet above the floor of the main stage, this acting area would have needed nothing more than a single rail around it, so that there would have been no real obstacle to vision, and it would have served to bring the action well forward from the rear wall of the theatre. Attempting to visualize how this particular scene might have been produced effectively, yet with a minimum of properties and without taking up too much space, Mr Hodges writes:

'I will allow myself to imagine the porch-like booth [the temporary structure] hung with its arras, standing between the two tiring-house doors [the two large doors, one on either side of the main stage at the rear of it, that provided the chief means of access to it]. It backs up to the gallery floor, where, behind closed curtains, Sly lies snoring. A light stairway leads up one side, and up this from below come the servants with apparel, basin and ewer. They are now standing on top of the porch-booth in front of the curtain which represents the bed. They draw the curtain. Sly emerges. "For God's sake," he groans, "a pot of small ale." And so it begins.'

C. Walter Hodges, *The Globe Restored*, London, 1953,
pages 64–5.
See also pages 56–64.

1   *small ale* (the weakest and therefore the cheapest form of the beverage)
2   *lordship*. This reading, essential both for sense and

metre, comes from the Second Folio (1632). The First
Folio reads: 'Lord'.

sack (a general name for a class of white wines formerly
imported from Spain and the Canaries)

3   *conserves* candied fruits

7   *conserves of beef* salt beef

8   *doublets* (close-fitting body-garments, with or without
sleeves, worn by men in Shakespeare's day)

11   *as* that

12   *idle humour* empty fancy, foolish aberration of mind

15   *infusèd with so foul a spirit* inspired by such mad ideas,
filled with such diseased notions

16–23   *Am not I . . . in Christendom.* This passage is full of
references to Warwickshire, and gives the impression that
Shakespeare is drawing on direct personal experience.

17   *old Sly's son of Burton-heath* old Sly of Burton-heath's
son. Burton-heath has been identified with Barton-on-
the-Heath, a village about sixteen miles from Stratford,
where Shakespeare's aunt Joan Lambert lived.

18   *cardmaker* one who made cards – instruments with iron
teeth, used for combing out the fibres of wool by hand.
This occupation might well be taken up by a boy living
at Barton-on-the-Heath on the edge of the Cotswolds,
which were one of the chief wool- and cloth-producing
areas of the country in Shakespeare's time.

19   *bear-herd* (man who led a performing bear about the
country)

20   *Marian Hacket, the fat ale-wife of Wincot.* The woman
referred to here may well have been a real person, since
Sara, the daughter of Robert Hacket, was baptized in
Quinton church on 21 November 1591. The hamlet of
Wincot, four miles south of Stratford, lay partly in the
parish of Quinton and partly in that of Clifford
Chambers.

21   *on the score* in debt. The score was originally an account
kept by making notches in a piece of wood; later chalk
marks were used for the purpose.

22   *sheer ale* ale taken alone without solid food to accompany it. Compare Hal's remark about the bill found in Falstaff's pocket: 'O monstrous! but one halfpennyworth of bread to this intolerable deal of sack!' (*1 Henry IV*, II.4.522–3).

      score me up chalk me up

22–3   *the lyingest knave in Christendom.* Humphrey, Duke of Gloucester, addresses the impostor Saunder Simpcox with precisely these words (*2 Henry VI*, II.1.125–6).

23   (stage direction) *A Servingman brings him a pot of ale.* This direction, like the *He drinks* that follows it, is not to be found in the Folio. It seems to be called for, however, for three reasons: first, Sly has asked for a pot of ale (line 1); secondly, he is going to demand a pot of ale 'once again' (line 74); and, thirdly, nothing is more likely to convince him that he is 'not bestraught' than the appearance of what is to him the most important thing in life.

24   *bestraught* distracted, out of my mind

      Here's –. This sentence, had Sly ever finished it, might possibly have run 'Here's proof.'

26   *droop* feel despondent

28   *As beaten* as if driven, feeling themselves driven

29   *bethink thee of* remember, recollect

30   *ancient thoughts* former manner of thinking

33   *office* place of duty

      beck nod (or other mute signal, indicating a command)

34   *Apollo* (god of music and song in classical mythology)

37   *lustful* provocative of lust

38   *trimmed up* luxuriously prepared

      Semiramis (legendary queen of Assyria, proverbial for her voluptuousness and promiscuity)

39   *bestrew* scatter or cover (presumably with rushes)

40   *trapped* caparisoned, decked with an ornamented covering

41   *studded all with* adorned all over with studs of

44–5   *Thy hounds ... hollow earth.* The Elizabethans took

much pleasure in the noise their hounds made, and
went to some pains to ensure that the cry of the pack
was a tunable one. Compare the dialogue between
Theseus and Hippolyta (*A Midsummer Night's Dream*,
IV.1.104–26).

44   *welkin* sky

46   *course* (the technical word for hunting the hare with
      greyhounds)

47   *breathèd* long-winded, strong of wind

48–59 *Dost thou love pictures ... are drawn.* The paintings
      described here are examples of the 'wanton pictures'
      referred to by the Lord in the previous scene (Induc-
      tion.1.45). It is not easy to decide whether Shakespeare
      had actual paintings in mind when he wrote this pas-
      sage. The subjects, all of them mythological, were fre-
      quently handled by the Italian masters of the late
      Renaissance, such as Correggio and Giulio Romano,
      the only Italian artist Shakespeare ever mentions by
      name (*The Winter's Tale*, V.2.92–3). But there seem to
      have been very few Italian pictures in this country in
      the sixteenth century; and there is no reliable evidence
      that Shakespeare ever visited Italy. He may, of course,
      have heard something about Italian art from men who
      had been to that country; but the most likely explana-
      tion for the similarity between these descriptions and
      actual paintings is that the Italian painters, like Shake-
      speare himself, especially in his early work, were deeply
      influenced by Ovid. (For fuller discussion of the whole
      topic than is possible here, see A. Lytton Sells, *The
      Italian Influence in English Poetry*, London, 1955, pages
      188–209; and Mario Praz, *The Flaming Heart*, New
      York, 1958, pages 162–4.)

49–50 *Adonis ... | And Cytherea.* According to Ovid (*Meta-
      morphoses*, x.520–739) Cytherea, more commonly known
      as Venus the goddess of love, became enamoured of
      Adonis, a youth who returned her love. Ultimately,
      however, Adonis, who was even fonder of hunting than

he was of Venus, was killed by a boar. Finding his body, Venus changed his blood into a flower – the anemone. Both in this passage and in his elaborate poem on the subject, *Venus and Adonis*, published in 1593, Shakespeare depicts a reluctant and uncooperative Adonis, pursued by a demanding and exigent Venus. His version of the story here was probably influenced by Spenser, who, in *The Faerie Queene* (III.i.34–8), describes a tapestry portraying it in which Venus watches Adonis bathing,

> *And whilst he bath'd, with her two crafty spies,*
> *She secretly would search each dainty limb.*

Indeed, Spenser's imagined tapestry may well be the 'picture' Shakespeare was thinking of.

51   *wanton* behave in an amorous fashion

52   *wi'th'* with the (abbreviated colloquial form)

53   *Io.* Ovid relates (*Metamorphoses*, i.588–600) how Jupiter saw Io, the daughter of the river-god Inachus, and fell in love with her. Io fled from him, but Jupiter pursued her, and raped her under cover of a dense mist, which he created in order to hide his activities from the eyes of Juno.

55   *As lively painted as the deed was done.* Whenever Shakespeare describes a work of art it is verisimilitude that he looks for and praises. Compare lines 49–52 and lines 56–9. Similar views, all stemming probably from the Renaissance commonplace that poetry was a speaking picture and painting a dumb poem, are to be found in *The Rape of Lucrece* (1371–1442), *Timon of Athens* (I.1.33–41), *Cymbeline* (II.4.68–85), and *The Winter's Tale* (V.2.92–9).

56   *Daphne.* As Ovid tells the story (*Metamorphoses*, i. 452–567), Daphne was the daughter of the river-god Peneus. Cupid, in order to demonstrate his power to the scornful Apollo, caused the god to fall in love with her, but filled her with an aversion for him. As a result, when

Apollo wooed her she fled from him, and, as he was
about to overtake her, she prayed to her father for help.
Thereupon she was changed into a laurel.

57 *that one shall swear* so that one must swear, so that one is
forced to swear

59 *So workmanly* with such art, so skilfully

62 *this waning age.* The belief that the whole history of man
had been a steady degeneration from the state of physical and intellectual perfection that had existed in the
Garden of Eden was widely held in the sixteenth and
seventeenth centuries. See Spenser, *The Faerie Queene*,
V. Proem. 1–9.

64 *o'errun* ran over, flowed over. 'Run' as the form of the
past tense is fairly common in Shakespeare's work.
Compare:

> *The expedition of my violent love*
> *Outrun the pauser reason.*   *Macbeth*, II.3.107–8

66 *yet* nevertheless, still, even so

72 *Christophero.* This is the reading of the Second Folio.
The First has 'Christopher', which is unmetrical.

76 *wit* understanding, mental faculties

77 *knew but* only knew

80 *By my fay* by my faith
goodly considerable

81 *of all that time* in all that time

82 *idle* meaningless, empty, silly

83 *goodly* fine, well-proportioned

84 *beaten out of door* driven out of the house

86 *present her at the leet* bring her up for trial before the
manorial court. The leet was the equivalent of the
modern Police Court.

87 *sealed quarts* quart measures officially stamped to show
that they held the correct quantity. Sly is suggesting,
of course, that the 'stone jugs' are a swindle, because
they hold less than they are supposed to.

88 *Cicely Hacket.* Compare note to Induction.2.20.

89 *the woman's maid of the house* the mistress of the house's maid, the landlady's maid
    house inn, tavern

91 *reckoned up* mentioned, enumerated

92-3 *Stephen Sly ... John Naps ... Peter Turph ... Henry Pimpernell.* These could well be the names of real people. A Stephen Sly was living at Stratford in January 1615. (See E. K. Chambers, *William Shakespeare*, Oxford, 1930, volume II, p. 144.)

92 *Greece.* It has been suggested that this is a misreading of Greet, a hamlet not far from Stratford, but there were Greeks in England in the sixteenth century, and 'John Naps' might be the English version of a Greek name.

95 *nor no man* nor any man. Shakespeare frequently uses the double negative for the sake of emphasis.

96 *amends* recovery, improvement in health

97 (stage direction) *One gives Sly a pot of ale.* This direction, which does not appear in the Folio, is called for because Sly has asked for 'a pot o'th'smallest ale' some twenty lines earlier, and he now thanks one of the servants.

99-100 *How fares ... I fare well.* There is a quibble here. The Page enquires about Sly's state of health, and Sly replies that he is well supplied with 'fare' in the sense of drink.

100 *Marry.* Derived originally from the name of the Virgin Mary, used as an oath or asseveration, this exclamation meant no more in Shakespeare's day than 'why, to be sure'.

104 *goodman* husband

114 *abandoned* banished

115 (stage direction) *Exeunt Lord and Servingmen.* The Folio provides no direction here, but, as Dover Wilson points out, one is required, because Sly has just expressed his desire to be left alone with his 'wife', and because the upper stage must be cleared of all except the three 'Presenters' before the play proper can begin.

121 *In peril to incur* on peril of your incurring
123 *stands for* is valid as, can be accepted as
124 *it stands* (a bawdy quibble alluding to the erection of the male organ)
     tarry wait, stay
126 *the flesh and the blood* sexual desire
     (stage direction) *Enter the Lord as a Messenger*. The Folio reads: '*Enter a Messenger*'. In this edition the role of the Messenger has been assigned to the Lord for the following reasons: first, the Lord has had the play put on in order to enjoy Sly's reactions to it, and must, therefore, be in a position where he can best observe them; secondly, in *The Taming of a Shrew* it is the Lord who announces the play to Sly in the following words, which are very close to the Messenger's first two lines:

> May it please you, your honour's players be come
> To offer your honour a play,

and he remains on the upper stage until the play is almost done; thirdly, if the Lord is with Sly and the Page, the reference to 'The Presenters above', in the stage direction at I.1.245 makes much better sense than it does if he is not; and, finally, who but the Lord could appear on the upper stage, and, in his role as servant to Sly, give the necessary parallel to the Lucentio–Tranio relationship?

128 *pleasant* merry
129 *For so* because
     meet suitable, fitting, right
130–31 *Seeing too much sadness ... frenzy.* For the general attitude to the relationship between physical and psychological states compare *King John*, III.3.42–4:

> Or if that surly spirit, melancholy,
> Had bak'd thy blood and made it heavy-thick,
> Which else runs tickling up and down the veins. ...

131 *nurse* nourisher

134   *bars* prevents

135   *Marry, I will. Let them play it. Is not a comonty . . . ?*
        The Folio reads: 'Marrie I will let them play, it is
        not a Comontie', which does not make satisfactory
        sense, since 'comonty' must be Sly's blunder for
        'comedy'.

136   *gambold* frolic, caper

137   *stuff* matter, material (in its literary sense)

138   *household stuff* furnishings. Sly, in his drunken state,
        has taken the word 'stuff' in its most literal sense.

139   *history* story, narrative

141   (stage direction) *They sit.* This does not appear in the
        Folio, though clearly demanded by the dialogue.
        (stage direction) *A flourish of trumpets to announce the
        play.* The Folio reads simply: '*Flourish*', and places
        this direction at the head of what is, in modern editions,
        I.1.

The Play

I.1   The opening of this scene is a rather primitive piece of
        exposition, of the kind that Sheridan guyed so well in
        The Critic. Lucentio tells Tranio many things that
        Tranio should know already, for the benefit of the
        audience, who need to know where the scene is and
        what the two characters are doing there. The scene
        comes to full dramatic life only with the entrance of
        Baptista, his daughters, and their suitors. At this point
        the purveying of information is replaced by action.
        (stage direction) *Tranio.* This name appears in Plautus's
        Mostellaria, the character who has it being a wily
        townsman. It is quite possible that it was associated
        in Shakespeare's mind with the word 'train', meaning
        'deceit' or 'trickery'.

1   *for* because of, owing to

2   *fair Padua, nursery of arts.* Shakespeare knew what he
        was writing about. The university of Padua, founded in
        1228, was one of the oldest in Europe, and was still in

the sixteenth century the main centre for the diffusion of Aristotelian teaching.

3   *I am arrived* for I have arrived in. In Shakespeare's time 'be' as well as 'have' was commonly used to form the past tense of verbs of motion.

8   *breathe* live, settle down
     haply institute auspiciously begin

9   *ingenious studies* intellectual studies, liberal studies

11   *Gave me . . . first* first gave me

12   *of great traffic through* with much business throughout

13   *come of* descended from

14–16 *Vincentio's son, brought up in Florence,* | *It shall become to serve all hopes conceived* | *To deck his fortune with his virtuous deeds.* The sense of this rather stilted and Latinate sentence is: 'It is right that Vincentio's son, brought up in Florence, should fulfil the hopes men have of him by adorning his prosperity with virtuous deeds.'

17   *for the time* at present

17–18 *study* | *Virtue,* . The Folio reads: 'studie, | Vertue'. The change in the position of the comma makes the statement much more pointed.

19   *apply* pursue, devote myself to
     treats of deals with

19–20 *happiness* | *By virtue specially to be achieved.* The idea of achieving happiness through virtuous action is central to Aristotle's *Ethics*.

23   *plash* pool, puddle

25   *Mi perdonato* excuse me (Italian)

26   *in all affected as* in entire agreement with

29   *admire* regard with reverence

31   *stoics* rigorists, people who despise pleasure; *stocks* senseless unfeeling people. There is a quibble on the two words.

32   *devote* devoted, addicted
     checks restraints, counsels of moderation

33   *As that*

33   *Ovid* (Latin poet who lived from 43 B.C. to about A.D. 17. In his *Ars Amatoria* Ovid calls himself *praeceptor amoris*, the Professor of Love, and it is in this capacity that Tranio cites him here.)

34   *Balk logic* chop logic
      acquaintance acquaintances, friends

35   *common talk* ordinary conversation

36   *to quicken you* to refresh yourself, as recreation

38   *Fall to them as you find your stomach serves you* take them up when you feel so inclined. *Fall to* means literally 'begin eating', and [*when*] *your stomach serves you* 'when you have an appetite'. The metaphors indicate the practical bent of Tranio's mind.

39   *No profit grows where is no pleasure ta'en*. These words are an adaptation of Horace's celebrated comment, which was the foundation of Renaissance aesthetics: *Omne tulit punctum qui miscuit utile dulci* – the most successful artist is the man who has contrived to mix the pleasurable with the instructive (*Ars Poetica*, 343). *ta'en* taken (colloquial)

40   *affect* love, enjoy

41   *Gramercies* many thanks (Old French *grant merci*)

45   (stage direction) *Katherina*. This name appears under the forms *Katerina*, *Katherina*, *Katherine*, and, of course, *Kate* in the Folio.
      (stage direction) *a pantaloon*. The pantaloon (*pantalone* in Italian) was a stock figure, and indeed the central figure, in the Italian *Commedia dell'arte* (Comedy of skill). He was always portrayed as an old man, a Venetian by origin and dialect, and invariably appeared clad in tights, a red jacket, a long black sleeved gown, and black slippers. His main role was to serve as an obstacle to the lovers. (For a full discussion of the character and the part see Allardyce Nicoll, *The World of Harlequin*, Cambridge, 1963, pages 44–55.) Gremio is explicitly referred to as 'the old pantaloon' by Lucentio at III.1.36.

47   *show* play, spectacle, pageant

50   *bestow* give in marriage

55   *To cart her*. 'Carting' – undergoing a whipping while
      being drawn through the streets either in, or at the tail
      of, an open cart – was the punishment inflicted on
      bawds and whores. There is, of course, a quibble on
      'court' in the previous line.

      rough bad-tempered

56   *will you* do you want

58   *a stale of me amongst these mates* a laughing-stock of me
      among these contemptible fellows (with a quibble on
      stale meaning 'harlot')

59   *Mates ... No mates* (1) contemptible fellows; (2)
      husbands

60   *mould* frame, nature

62   *Iwis it is not halfway to her heart* certainly marriage (with
      you) is not a matter that she takes even half seriously

63   *doubt not her care should be* be sure she would take care

64   *comb your noddle* give you a dressing, beat you about the
      head

65   *paint your face* scratch your face till it bleeds. In *The
      Taming of a Shrew* (scene V, line 24) Katherina
      threatens to set her 'ten commandments' (finger-nails)
      in Ferando's face.

      use treat

68   *Husht* be quiet, not a word

      toward on hand, about to begin

69   *wonderful froward* incredibly disobedient, perverse

73   *Mum!* keep quiet!

74   *make good* perform, carry out

78   *peat* pet, spoilt darling

78-9 *It is best | Put finger in the eye, an she knew why* the best
      thing she can do is to make herself weep, if she knew of
      some excuse. 'To put finger in the eye and weep' was a
      proverbial expression. Shakespeare uses it again in *The
      Comedy of Errors*, where Adriana says:

> *Come, come, no longer will I be a fool,*
> *To put the finger in the eye and weep.*   II.2.202–3

80   *content you in my discontent* take pleasure in my sorrow
81   *pleasure* will, command
     subscribe submit
82   *instruments* musical instruments
84   *Minerva* (the goddess of wisdom)
85   *strange* distant, unfriendly
86   *effects* causes
87   *mew her up* shut her up, confine her
88   *for* on account of
90   *content ye* compose yourselves, be satisfied
92   *for* because
97   *Prefer* direct, recommend
     cunning well qualified, skilful
103 *be appointed hours* be given a time-table
105 *the devil's dam* the devil's mother (proverbially thought
     of as worse than the devil himself and as the archetype
     of shrews)
     gifts endowments, natural qualities
106 *hold* retain, keep
     There ! Love. The Folio reads: 'Their loue', which could
     mean 'the love of women', but confusion of 'their' and
     'there' is common in early texts of the plays, and Gremio
     is fond of 'There' as an exclamation (compare line
     56).
106–8 *Love is not so great . . . but we may blow our nails together,*
     and fast it fairly out. The general sense of this passage
     is: 'Our rivalry over Bianca is not so important that we
     can't remain on friendly terms while we wait for things
     to improve.'
107 *but* but that
     blow our nails wait patiently
108 *fast it fairly out* pass our period of abstention from love
     in a friendly manner
     Our cake's dough on both sides our efforts have ended in

182

failure for both of us. 'My cake is dough' was a proverbial way of announcing failure. Gremio uses the
phrase again at V.1.128.

110 *light on* find, come across

111 *wish him* commend him, invite him to offer service

113–14 *yet never brooked parle* never yet allowed of negotiations
between us

114 *upon advice* on careful reflection

it toucheth it concerns, it is a matter of importance to

117 *labour and effect* strive to carry out

123 *so very a fool to* such an absolute fool as to

125 *pass* exceed, go beyond

127 *good fellows* rogues, needy adventurers. Compare Introduction, page 30.

an if, provided that

129 *I cannot tell* I don't know what to say

as lief as soon, as readily

130 *high-cross* (market-cross in the centre of a town)

133 *bar in law* legal impediment (Baptista's refusal to allow
them to court Bianca)

134 *it shall be so far forth friendly maintained till* our agreement shall be kept up in a friendly manner until

136–7 *have to't afresh* let us renew our rivalry, to battle again

137 *Happy man be his dole* may the best man win. This
proverbial expression for wishing someone good luck
means, literally, 'may his lot be that of a happy man'.

137–8 *He that runs fastest gets the ring.* This proverb is given
by John Heywood in 1546 under the following form:
'Where wooers hop in and out, long time may bring |
Him that hoppeth best, at last to have the ring [wed-
ding-ring].' Shakespeare seems to have given the old
saying an original twist here by relating it to the joust-
ing-game in which each of a number of riders attempted
to carry off on the point of his lance a circlet of metal
suspended from a post.

139 *would I* I wish that I. Gremio is continuing with the
metaphor of 'running at the ring'.

141   *woo her, wed her, and bed her*. This is another proverb, very common in the sixteenth century, describing the progress of a love affair from the wooing to the consummation.

    rid free. Gremio has added a bit of his own to the original proverb.

144   *take such hold* take such firm root, gain such a hold of a man

148   *love in idleness*. Lucentio is playing with two ideas: (1) the proverb, 'Idleness begets lust'; (2) 'Love-in-idleness' as another name for the pansy, or Heartsease, as it was called. Compare Oberon's description of it as 'a little western flower' (*A Midsummer Night's Dream*, II.1.166–8).

149   *plainness* frankness

150   *as secret* as intimate, as much in my confidence

151   *As Anna to the Queen of Carthage was*. In Virgil's *Aeneid* (IV.8–30) Dido, Queen of Carthage, confides to her sister Anna that she has fallen in love with her guest Aeneas. The scene between the two sisters had been dramatized by Christopher Marlowe in his play *The Tragedy of Dido, Queen of Carthage* (III.1.55–78), published in 1594.

153   *achieve* win

157   *Affection is not rated from the heart* it's no use trying to expel love from the heart by scolding it

158   *naught remains but so* there's nothing left to be done but this

159   *Redime te captum quam queas minimo* free yourself from captivity at the lowest ransom you can. Shakespeare took this line from Lily's *Latin Grammar* and not from the original source, Terence's *Eunuchus* (I.1.30), where it appears under a slightly different form.

160   *Go forward, this contents* carry on, this is the right sort of advice

162   *longly* persistently

163   *marked* noticed

163   *the pith of all* the central issue, the main point of it all

165   *the daughter of Agenor* Europa. According to Ovid (*Metamorphoses*, ii, 846–75), Jupiter fell in love with her, and, in order to win her, appeared to her as a snow-white bull. He knelt before her, and behaved so gently that eventually she mounted on his back. He promptly rose, rushed into the sea, and carried her off from Tyre, where her father was king, to Crete.

167   *Cretan strand* shore of Crete. It looks as though Shakespeare thought Europa had been carried off *from* Crete, instead of to it.

176   *Bend* apply, strain (as in bending a bow)
      Thus it stands this is the situation

177   *curst and shrewd* waspish and difficult

180   *closely mewed her up* confined her strictly to the house

181   *Because she will not* in order that she shall not
      annoyed with molested by

183   *art thou not advised* didn't you notice

185   *marry* indeed, to be sure

186   *for my hand* by my hand

187   *Both our inventions meet and jump in one* our two plans concur and operate as one

190   *device* scheme, plot

193   *Keep house* entertain in the appropriate style
      ply his book study

194   *countrymen* fellow-countrymen (natives of Pisa)

195   *Basta* enough (Italian)
      I have it full I've hit on the answer

200   *port* state, manner of life suiting my station

202   *meaner* poorer (than I really am)

204   *Uncase thee* take off your outer garments
      coloured hat and cloak (the dress of an Elizabethan gentleman, as distinct from the 'blue coats', IV.1.81, worn by servants)

206   *charm him first to keep his tongue* first give him strict orders not to blab

207   *So had you need* you need to. The broken line here gives

the impression that there has been a cut, especially as Tranio does not explain why it is so necessary to keep Biondello quiet, but continues his speech with the inconsequential words 'In brief'.

208 *sith it your pleasure is* since it is your will

209 *tied* obliged, bound

211 *serviceable* diligent to serve

212 *in another sense.* It did not occur to Lucentio's father that his son would require Tranio to change places with him.

216–17 *And let me be a slave t'achieve that maid | Whose sudden sight hath thralled my wounded eye.* The paradoxes here are the conventional ones of Elizabethan love-poetry.

217 *Whose sudden sight* the sudden sight of whom
thralled enslaved

224 *frame your manners to the time* suit your behaviour to the occasion

226 *countenance* manner

229 *descried* seen, observed

230 *as becomes* as is fitting, in the proper manner

231 *make way* go

232 *Ne'er a whit* not in the least

236–41 *So could I . . . Lucentio.* Printed as prose in the Folio, these lines are, in fact, doggerel verse of a kind that is also to be found in *The Comedy of Errors* (III.1.11–83) and in *Love's Labour's Lost* (IV.2.21–33).

236–7 *after . . . daughter.* These two words, probably pronounced as 'arter' and 'darter', rhymed in Shakespeare's day. Compare the Fool's lines in *King Lear* (I.4.318–22):

> *A fox, when one has caught her,*
> *And such a daughter,*
> *Should sure to the slaughter,*
> *If my cap would buy a halter.*
> *So the fool follows after.*

243   *rests, that thyself execute* remains for you to carry out

244-5 *To make . . . weighty* (another patch of doggerel verse)

244   *make one* become one

245   *Sufficeth* it is enough to say, I need only say

       (stage direction) *The Presenters above speak.* The presenter, who was a fairly common figure in Elizabethan drama (see, for example, Kyd's *The Spanish Tragedy*, Robert Greene's *James IV*, and Ben Jonson's *Every Man Out of His Humour*), was the character, either human or allegorical, who was responsible for the presentation or putting-on of a play. He normally sat 'above', and often commented on the progress of the action. In this play the Lord, whose idea it is that the show should be put on before Sly and his 'wife', has the best title to the role, while they can also be considered as 'Presenters' by virtue of their remarks on the play.

246   LORD. The Folio reads: '*1. Man.*', but no provision has been made for anyone other than a Messenger to be present with Sly and the Page, and neither a Messenger nor a Servant can really be called a 'Presenter'. See note to Induction.2.126.

       mind attend to, take notice of

247   (stage direction) *coming to with a start.* Though not in the Folio, this piece of business is obviously demanded by the context.

248   *matter* subject, story

       surely no doubt

249   *but* only just

251   *Would* I would that, I wish

       (stage direction) *They sit and mark.* These words clearly imply that the three 'Presenters' were to remain in their places. The problem of why they say nothing further, especially after Sly has made his views on it all so plain, is a difficult one. See Introduction, pages 15 and 44.

I.2   (stage direction) *Petruchio.* The spelling of this name,

with the 'ch' pronounced as in 'Charles', represents
Shakespeare's attempt to find an English equivalent for
the Italian name *Petruccio*. There is a servant called
Petrucio in *Supposes*.

(stage direction) *Grumio*. Shakespeare may have got
this name from Plautus's *Mostellaria*, where one of the
characters, a downright countryman, is so called, but it
could also be the result of an effort to give the English
word 'groom' an Italian appearance.

1–4   *Verona . . . house*. Like Lucentio at the opening of the
previous scene, Petruchio begins with a bit of self-
explanation, but on this occasion it is kept down to a
bare minimum and gives way almost at once to dramatic
action. The relationship between Petruchio and Grumio
here forms a nice contrast to that between Lucentio and
Tranio in I.1.

2   *but of all* but especially, but above all

4   *trow* believe, know

      his house. Having come on to the stage by one of the
main doors, Petruchio and Grumio cross to the other
main door, which now becomes the entrance to Hortensio's house.

5   *knock* rap for admittance. Grumio takes the word in its
other sense of 'beat' or 'strike'.

7   *rebused* (Grumio's mistake for 'abused')

8   *Villain* slave, wretch

      knock me here soundly. The *me* here is a relic of the old
dative meaning 'for me' – Grumio, of course, takes it as
the accusative – but by Shakespeare's time it had become a device for lending life and colour to a statement
and amounted to 'mark me' or 'I tell you'.

13–14   *I should knock you first . . . worst* you are asking me to
strike you, so that you can then have an excuse for giving
me a drubbing

16   *an* if

      I'll ring it I'll ring. The *it* is superfluous, as it is also in
sing it, and there is a quibble on 'ring' and 'wring'.

17 *sol-fa* sing

  (stage direction) *He wrings him by the ears* he twists Grumio's ears

21 *How do you* how are you

23 *part the fray* separate the combatants, stop the brawl

24 *Con tutto il cuore ben trovato* with all my heart well met (Italian)

25-6 *Alla nostra casa ben venuto,* | *Molto honorato signor mio Petruchio* welcome to our house, most worshipful Petruchio

27 *compound* amicably settle

28 *'leges* alleges

  in Latin. Grumio, despite his name, is a good solid English character who does not know the difference between Latin and Italian.

31 *use* treat

32-3 *two and thirty, a pip out*. This is a jesting allusion to the card-game of 'one-and-thirty', the 'pips' being the marks on the cards. According to John Ray in his *Collection of English Proverbs* (1678), to be 'one-and-thirty' meant to be drunk. It seems more likely to the present editor, however, that Grumio is saying that his master, like a gamester who has overshot the mark by scoring thirty-two instead of thirty-one, is 'not quite right – in the head'.

36 *A senseless* an unreasonable

38 *for my heart* for my life

41-2 *come you now with* do you now come along with

44 *pledge* surety

45 *this's* this is (colloquial). The Folio reads 'this'.

  heavy chance sad misunderstanding

46 *ancient* of long standing

  pleasant merry, entertaining

51 *in a few* in short, to be brief

54 *maze* chancy business (of looking for a wife)

55 *Haply* with luck, fortunately

  to wive and thrive. Two proverbs, both of which help

to explain why Petruchio thinks of his enterprise as a *maze*, are relevant here: 'It is hard to wive [get married] and thrive both in a year,' and 'In wiving and thriving a man should take counsel of all the world, lest he light upon a curse while he seeks for a blessing.' Petruchio takes counsel, but then wisely disregards it.

58   *come roundly* speak plainly

59   *And wish thee to a shrewd ill-favoured wife* and commend you to a sharp-tongued ill-conditioned wife. *Ill-favoured* must mean 'endowed with bad qualities', rather than 'ugly', because at line 85 Hortensio describes Katherina as 'beauteous'.

60   *Thou'dst* thou wouldst

62   *th' art* thou art (abbreviated colloquial form)

67   *burden* (musical accompaniment)

68   *foul* ugly, plain
    Florentius' love. Florentius is a knight in Gower's *Confessio Amantis*. His life depends on his answering the riddle 'what do women most desire', and he agrees to marry a loathsome old hag on condition that she tells him the answer. The same story is told by Chaucer in *The Wife of Bath's Tale*.

69   *Sibyl.* In the *Metamorphoses* (xiv. 130–181) Ovid has the Sibyl of Cumae tell Aeneas how Apollo granted her as many years of life as the number of grains of sand that she could pick up in a handful.
    curst and shrewd waspish and shrewish

70   *Xanthippe* (wife of Socrates, notorious for her bad temper)

71   *moves me not* can't make any impression on me, can't alter my plans

71–2   *or not removes at least | Affection's edge in me* or at least she can't destroy the keenness of my desire

76   *flatly* plainly, downright

77   *mind* intention

78   *aglet-baby* (small figure, often in the shape of a death's-head, forming the tag of a lace)

78   *old trot* decrepit old woman, hag

80–81   *so money comes withal* provided money comes with it

82   *are stepped thus far in* have gone so far

83   *that I broached* that which I began

88   *intolerable* intolerably

90   *state* fortune

94   *board* woo. Compare Sir Toby Belch's similarly figurative use of the naval word 'board' when he tells Sir Andrew, ' "Accost" is front her, board her, woo her, assail her' (*Twelfth Night*, I.3.52–3).

       chide scold

95   *crack* go off with a bang (like a gun)

97   *An affable* a polite, kind

103–4   *let me be thus bold with you | To give you over at this first encounter* let me take the liberty of leaving you at this our first meeting

107   *O' my word* on my word

108   *do little good upon* have little effect on

110   *an he begin once, he'll rail in his rope-tricks.* This is one of the most obscure passages in the whole play. The present editor thinks it means 'if he once begins, he'll scold in his outrageous rhetoric'. The nonce-word *rope-tricks* is probably Grumio's version of 'rope-rhetorics', a term used by Thomas Nashe in his pamphlet *Have with You to Saffron-Walden*, published in 1596. There Nashe writes of Gabriel Harvey's 'Paracelsian rope-rethorique', apparently meaning 'bombastic rhetoric for which the author deserved to be hanged' (*The Works of Thomas Nashe*, edited by R. B. McKerrow, London, 1904–10, volume III, page 15). In view of the interest the Elizabethans had in 'the tropes of rhetoric', it is quite possible that the word 'trope-tricks', meaning 'subtleties of rhetoric', may well have existed as a slang term, though there is no record of it. If it did, the transition to 'rope-tricks' would have been an easy one.

111   *stand* face, resist, withstand

111–14   *he will throw a figure in her face, and so disfigure her with*

       it that she shall have no more eyes to see withal than a cat.
       The general sense of this passage is that Petruchio will
       use figures of rhetoric to such effect that Katherina will
       be quite overcome.

112   *throw a figure in her face.* Grumio is probably quibbling
       on two senses: (1) hurl a figure of speech at her; (2)
       subject her to the influence of the kind of spell-binding
       figure used by conjurers and magicians.
       disfigure deform, mar. But perhaps the word is used
       metaphorically to mean 'change her attitude'.

113–14 *than a cat.* Shakespeare may be ridiculing the casual and
       unthinking use of terms such as this.

116   *keep* keeping, custody

117   *hold* safe-keeping

119   *other more* others besides. 'Other' was a common form
       of the plural.

122   *For those defects* on account of those faults
       rehearsed recited

124   *this order* these measures

129   *do me grace* do me a favour

132   *Well seen* well served, well qualified

139   *the rival of my love* my rival in love (Gremio)

141   *A proper stripling and an amorous!* Grumio is being
       ironical at Gremio's expense.
       proper fine, handsome

142   *note* list of the books

143   *them* the books
       fairly handsomely

144   *see that at any hand* see to that in any case

145   *read no other lectures* give no other lessons

148   *mend it with a largess* improve it with a donation
       paper (the 'note' or list of line 142)

149   *them* the books

154   *as yourself were still in place* as if you yourself were
       present all the time

158   *woodcock* dupe, simpleton. The Elizabethans thought of
       the woodcock as a stupid bird.

161   *you are well met* I'm glad to meet you

162   *Trow you* do you know, can you guess

167   *turn* needs

170   *help me to* assist me in obtaining

175   *bags* money-bags, wealth

176   *vent* give vent to, utter

178   *news indifferent good for either* news that is equally good for each of us

180   *Upon agreement from us to his liking* on our agreement to conditions that suit him. The conditions, that Gremio and Hortensio bear the cost of Petruchio's wooing, are mentioned later (lines 212–14).

183   *So said, so done, is well* it's fine when actions come up to promises

187   *What countryman?* where do you come from, where's your home?

191   *were strange* would be surprising

192   *if you have a stomach, to't a God's name* if you have an inclination to try, get on with it in God's name

194   *Will I live?* certainly!

195   *Will he woo her? Ay, or I'll hang her.* Compare Feste's remark: 'Many a good hanging prevents a bad marriage' (*Twelfth Night*, I.5.18).

196   *but to that intent* except for that purpose

200   *chafèd* annoyed, enraged (the sweat of the hunted boar being compared with the foam of a stormy sea)

201   *field* battle-field

204   *'larums* alarums, calls to arms made with drum and trumpet

206   *to hear.* So the Folio; but the emendation 'to th'ear', first suggested in the eighteenth century, makes good sense.

208   *fear boys with bugs* frighten boys with bugbears (bogies or hobgoblins)
       fears none is afraid of none

211   *yours.* So the Folio. The reading has been emended to 'ours' by some editors, so obscuring the dramatic point

that Gremio is eager to shift any expense involved on to Hortensio.

213   *charge* expense

215   (stage direction) *bravely dressed*. The Folio reads: '*braue*', that is, 'richly attired'.

216   *be bold* take the liberty

217   *readiest* easiest, quickest

219–20   *He that has the two fair daughters – is't he you mean?* Biondello's remark has been prearranged as part of Tranio's opening gambit.

222   *her too?* The Folio reads: 'her to –', denoting either that a word is missing or that the compositor could not make out the sense of what he had printed. If a word is missing, it must be 'woo', but this does not fit Tranio's answer. 'Too' on the other hand, which is interchangeable in Shakespeare texts with 'to', follows naturally on Biondello's 'you mean' (line 220) and fits in perfectly with Tranio's reply.

223   *What have you to do?* what is that to you?

224   *at any hand* in any case

233   *choice* chosen, appointed

235   *Softly* gently, just a moment

236   *Do me this right* do me this justice

238   *not all* not altogether

239   *And were his daughter fairer* and even if his daughter were more beautiful

241   *Fair Leda's daughter* the lovely daughter of Leda (Helen of Troy). The 'thousand wooers' was probably suggested by Marlowe's famous line 'Was this the face that launched a thousand ships?' (*Dr Faustus*, scene xiii. 91)

242   *one more* one more than she has already

244   *Though Paris came* though Paris (the son of Priam, King of Troy, who stole Helen away from her husband Menelaus) were to come

    in hope to speed alone hoping to be the winner

246   *give him head, I know he'll prove a jade* give him free scope, I know he'll soon tire. The language here is that

of horsemanship – to give a horse its head is to cease checking it, and a jade is a poor worthless horse that soon grows tired.

248 *as ask* as to ask

253 *let her go by* leave her alone

254-5 *Hercules . . . Alcides' twelve.* Hercules, otherwise known as Alcides, was the legendary hero of classical mythology who carried out twelve stupendous tasks, or labours as they were called. Gremio calls Petruchio Hercules, and implies that he has taken on an even greater task.

255 *let it be more than* admit that it surpasses

256 *understand you this of me in sooth* take this from me for certain

257 *hearken for* lie in wait for, seek to win

263 *Must stead* who must help, who must be of use to

266 *whose hap shall be* he whose good fortune it shall be

267 *so graceless be to be ingrate* be so lacking in all decency as to be ungrateful

268 *conceive* understand the situation

270 *gratify* reward, requite

271 *rest generally beholding* remain without exception under an obligation

272 *slack* remiss, backward

273 *contrive* spend, while away

274 *quaff carouses* drink toasts

277 *motion* proposal

279 *ben venuto* literally, 'welcome' (Italian). Hortensio means that he will pay for Petruchio's entertainment.

1 (stage direction) *Enter Katherina, and Bianca with her hands tied.* The Folio, which has neither Act nor scene heading here, reads: '*Enter Katherina and Bianca*', but Bianca's first speech clearly indicates the state in which she appears.

1 *wrong* (1) harm; (2) disgrace

3   *gauds* pieces of finery, gewgaws. The Folio reads 'goods'.

12   *fancy* like, love

13   *Minion* spoilt brat

14   *affect* love

17   *fair* fine, well dressed

18   *envy* (pronounced with the stress on the second syllable) hate, feel jealous of

23   *dame* mistress, madam (implying a rebuke)
     whence grows this insolence? what is the reason for this disgraceful behaviour?

25   *meddle not* have nothing to do with

26   *hilding* base wretch, baggage

28   *cross* contradict, annoy

29   *flouts* mocks, shows contempt of

31   *suffer me* let me have my own way

33   *I must dance bare-foot on her wedding-day.* An elder sister who remained unmarried was supposed to dance bare-foot at her younger sister's wedding. The phrase thus became proverbial for being unmarried.

34   *lead apes in hell.* This is another proverbial occupation of old maids – they led apes in hell because they had no children to lead into heaven. Compare Beatrice's remarks on the same subject in *Much Ado About Nothing*, II.1.34–41.

36   *occasion of* opportunity for

37   *grieved* afflicted

38   (stage direction) *Enter Gremio ... with Hortensio ... books.* The Folio direction, omitting all mention of Hortensio, reads as follows: '*Enter Gremio, Lucentio, in the habit of a meane man, Petruchio with Tranio, with his boy bearing a Lute and Bookes.*'
     habit of a mean man dress of a poor man. Compare Lucentio's description of the disguise he intends to assume, given at I.1.202.
     (stage direction) *Cambio* (a significant name, since it is the Italian for 'exchange')

45 *go to it orderly* go about the business in a proper orderly manner

46 *give me leave* excuse me

49 *affability* kindness, gentle behaviour

54 *for an entrance to my entertainment* as an entrance-fee for my reception, to show that I am in earnest

57 *sciences* branches of knowledge

59 *Accept of* accept

61 *Y'are* you are (colloquial)

62 *for* as for

63 *She is not for your turn* she will not come up to your requirements, she's not the girl for you

65 *like not of my company* don't approve of me

67 *What may I call your name?* what is your name?

71 *Saving* with all respect for, no offence meant to

73 *Baccare!* stand back! give place! A sixteenth-century proverb ran: 'Backare, quoth Mortimer to his sow.' The word, always used in a jocular sense, seems to have been made up from the adverb *back* with the addition of *-are*, the ending of the Latin infinitive.

74 *I would fain be doing* I am eager for action (probably with a quibble on 'doing' in the indelicate sense)

76 *grateful* agreeable, welcome

80 *Rheims.* The seat of a university founded in 1547.

86 *walk like a stranger* seem to be on your own, not one of the party

93 *In the preferment of* in giving precedence to

95 *upon knowledge of* when you know about

98 *toward* as a contribution to

102 (stage direction) (*opening one of the books*). This direction, which is not in the Folio, seems necessary in order that Baptista may see Lucentio's name, which has not yet been mentioned, on the fly-leaf.

104 *mighty* illustrious, important, leading

109 *To my daughters, and tell them both.* The line is unmetrical, and something has probably been omitted from it; but it is impossible to say what the missing

word was. The Second Folio reads: 'To my two
daughters'.

112   *dinner* (the main meal of the day in Shakespeare's
England, served between eleven o'clock and noon)
passing very, most

114   *asketh* requires, demands

122   *in possession* in immediate possession

123–4   *for that dowry I'll assure her of | Her widowhood* in
exchange for that dowry I'll guarantee her her widow's
rights. *Widowhood* here means 'the estate settled upon
a widow' in the marriage contract.

126   *Let specialties be therefore drawn between us* let explicit
detailed contracts between us therefore be drawn up

130   *father* father-in-law. Petruchio's self-assurance is
splendidly brought out here.

131   *peremptory* (always accented on the first syllable in
Shakespeare)

133   *the thing that feeds their fury.* The fuel Petruchio is
referring to is Katherina's shrewishness.

134–5   *Though little fire grows great with little wind, | Yet
extreme gusts will blow out fire and all.* Petruchio makes
it plain, through his use of this analogy, that he thinks
Katherina's headstrong temper has been encouraged
by the feeble opposition (*little wind*) that it has encountered hitherto. His own opposition (*extreme gusts*) will
be of a sterner kind, and so more effective.

138   *happy be thy speed* may the outcome be fortunate for
you

139   *unhappy* harsh, inauspicious

140   *to the proof* so as to be invulnerable

141   *shakes* shake (the old plural)
(stage direction) *broke* bruised and bleeding

143   *I promise you* let me tell you, I assure you

145   *prove a soldier* (a quibble on (1) become a soldier, and
(2) put a soldier to the test)

146   *hold with her* stand up to her handling, not break in her
hands

147   *break her to the lute* train her to play the lute (as a horse is broken to the bit). This is the first of a number of analogies in which the taming of Katherina is compared to the taming of a high-spirited animal or bird.

148   *broke the lute to me.* The comic effect of these lines is much increased if Hortensio appears with the broken lute draped round his neck like a horse-collar.

149   *frets* (rings of gut or bars of wood upon the lute to regulate the fingering)

152   *Frets* vexations (quibbling)
       fume be in a rage (as in 'fret and fume')

156   *pillory* (an instrument of punishment, consisting of a pair of movable boards raised on a post, with holes through which the culprit's head and hands were thrust so that he appeared to be framed in wood)

157   *rascal* base, good-for-nothing

158   *Jack* (term of contempt used of a base or silly fellow)

159   *As had she studied to misuse me so* as though she had given a lot of careful thought to how she might abuse me so

160   *lusty* merry, high-spirited

164   *Proceed in practice* carry on your lessons

168   *attend* await

170–80   *Say that she rail, why then I'll tell her plain . . . married.* Petruchio, to enable the audience to enjoy the ensuing scene to the full, announces his plan of campaign.

172   *clear* serenely beautiful

176   *piercing* moving

177   *pack* be gone

179   *deny* refuse

183   *heard . . . hard.* The two words were both pronounced 'hard', giving a pun.

186   *bonny* fine, strapping

189   *dainties are all Kates* (quibbling on 'cates' meaning 'delicacies')

190   *consolation* comfort

192   *sounded* proclaimed, praised aloud

193   *deeply as to thee belongs* loudly as you deserve

194   *moved* impelled

195   *in good time!* indeed, forsooth! Katherina is taking *moved* in its literal sense.

196-7   *I knew you at the first | You were a movable* I recognized you from the start for (1) the piece of movable furniture that you are; (2) a person given to change

198   *A joint-stool* a wooden stool made by a joiner. The proverbial remark used by the Fool in *King Lear*, III.6.51, 'Cry you mercy, I took you for a joint-stool,' was a taunting apology for overlooking a person, as Katherina affects to do here.

199   *to bear* to carry burdens. Petruchio gives the words a bawdy turn in the next line.

201   *jade* a horse (of either sex) that soon tires. Katherina is impugning Petruchio's virility.

202   *burden* (1) lie heavy on; (2) make accusations against. For the second sense, which is the more important here, compare *The Comedy of Errors*, V.1.209, 'this is false he burdens me withal'.

203   *light* (1) slight, slender; (2) wanton

204   *Too light for such a swain as you to catch* too quick-witted to be caught by a country bumpkin like you

205   *as heavy as my weight should be* the right weight for one of my standing. Katherina has switched the allusion to money. Clipped and counterfeit coins were 'too light'. She is saying that she is good sound currency; her reputation as a woman is untarnished, and therefore no charge of lightness can touch her.

206   *Should be? Should – buzz!* Petruchio is quibbling here, first on 'be' and 'bee', and then on 'buzz' as (1) the noise made by bees, and (2) rumour or scandal. In effect he tells Katherina 'You should just hear what is said about you.'

       ta'en taken, caught

       buzzard (1) useless kind of hawk; (2) according to the O.E.D., 'a worthless, stupid, or ignorant person'. In the opinion of the present editor, however, 'scandal-monger' or 'tale-bearer' fit this context much better. A similar use of the word will be found at *Richard III*, I.i.133, 'kites and buzzards prey at liberty'.

207   *turtle* turtle-dove (the symbol of faithful love)

208   *Ay, for a turtle, as he takes a buzzard.* The best explanation of this difficult passage is given by Dover Wilson, who paraphrases it thus: 'the fool will take me for a faithful wife, as the turtle-dove swallows the cock-chafer [yet another meaning of 'buzzard']'.

215   *tales* rumours, discreditable gossip (with, of course, a pun on 'tails' meaning 'backsides')

216   *What, with my tongue in your tail?* Apart from its obvious lewdness, this means 'What, are you going to turn tail on my repartee?'
  come again (1) come back; (2) let's renew the combat. Compare *Hamlet*, V.2.295, 'Nay, come again.'
  (stage direction) *He takes her in his arms.* Not in the Folio, but clearly indicated by Katherina's remark at line 219.

217   *try* test, make trial of

219   *loose your arms* (1) relax your hold; (2) lose your coat of arms (the mark of a gentleman)

222   *in thy books.* To be in the herald's books was to be registered as a gentleman, but there is also a pun on being in someone's good books.

223   *crest* (1) figure or device borne above the shield and helmet in a coat of arms; (2) a tuft of feathers or the like on an animal's head
  coxcomb (a fool's cap, like a cock's comb in shape and colour)

224   *so* provided that

225   *craven* (a fighting-cock that is not game)

227   *crab* (1) crab-apple; (2) sour-tempered person with a sour-looking face

231   *Well aimed of such a young one* a good guess for one so raw

232   *too young* too strong

234   *scape* escape

235   *chafe* (1) vex, annoy; (2) excite, heat

236   *passing* very, extremely

238   *a very liar* an absolute liar

239   *pleasant* merry
        gamesome sportive, gay

240   *But slow in speech* not a bit sharp-tongued

241   *askance* scornfully, with disdain

243   *cross* given to contradiction, perverse

244   *entertain'st* receivest

245   *conference* conversation

251   *whom thou keep'st command* order your own servants
        about, not me

252   *Dian* (Diana, the goddess of chastity and hunting)
        become adorn, grace

255   *sportful* amorous, wanton

256   *study* learn off by heart

257   *mother-wit* natural intelligence

258   *A witty mother, witless else her son* a wise mother she
        must be, for without her help her son has no wits of his
        own

259   *Am I not wise? Yes, keep you warm.* The retort is an
        allusion to the proverb 'He is wise enough that can keep
        himself warm.' Katherina means that Petruchio has the
        bare minimum of intelligence necessary for existence,
        and no more.

263   *'greed* agreed

264   *will you, nill you* whether you will or whether you won't

265   *for your turn* to fit your needs, exactly right for you

267   *like* love

270   *wild Kate* (with a pun on 'wild-cat')

271   *Conformable* tractable, compliant
        household domestic

274   *how speed you* how are you getting on, what progress are
        you making

276   *speed amiss* not make good progress

277   *In your dumps?* are you feeling down-hearted?

278   *I promise you* I can tell you

282   *to face the matter out* to get his own way by sheer effrontery

285   *for policy* as a deliberate policy, for her own purposes

286   *froward* difficult, refractory

287   *hot* violent, passionate

288   *a second Grissel.* The famous story of Patient Griselda, the model of wifely obedience, is the subject of Chaucer's *The Clerk's Tale.* Borrowed by Chaucer from Boccaccio's *Decameron*, it was subsequently treated in numerous tales and ballads in English. Two plays on the theme had been written by the time Shakespeare was two years old, and another, entitled *Patient Grissell*, by Dekker, Chettle, and Haughton was first acted in 1600.

289   *Roman Lucrece.* The tale of Lucrece, the legendary Roman heroine who committed suicide after having been raped by Tarquin, is told by Shakespeare himself in his elaborate narrative poem *The Rape of Lucrece*, first published in 1594.

294   *speeding* success

        good night our part farewell to our share in the business

302   *vied* redoubled. To 'vie' was a technical term in card-playing meaning 'to raise the stakes'.

303   *twink* twinkling, instant

304   *'Tis a world to see* it's a treat to see

306   *meacock* spiritless

        shrew. The sixteenth-century pronunciation of this word is indicated by the Folio spelling 'shrow' at V.2.187, and confirmed by the rhymes at IV.1.196–7 and V.2.28–9.

308   *'gainst* (colloquial form of 'against') in readiness for

310   *fine* handsomely dressed, in her finery

311–13 *give me your hands ... witnesses.* This brief ceremony before witnesses was the essential part of an Elizabethan marriage. Once this pre-contract, as it was called, had been made, neither party could marry another person. Compare the Duke's words to Mariana in *Measure for Measure*, IV.1.70–1:

> *He* [Angelo] *is your husband on a pre-contract.*
> *To bring you thus together 'tis no sin. . . .*

315   *apace* quickly, soon

318   *clapped up* fixed up in a hurry, arranged in an improvised manner

320   *desperate mart* reckless and chancy business arrangement – one that is probably doomed to failure

321   *'Twas a commodity lay fretting by you* it (referring to Katherina) was a piece of goods that was deteriorating in value while it remained on your hands. There is a quibble on *fretting* (1) decaying through moth and rust; (2) chafing with vexation.

323   *quiet in.* The Folio reads: 'quiet me', the compositor having taken 'inne' for 'me'. The same mistake occurs again at IV.2.71.

330   *Youngling* stripling, novice

332   *Skipper* light-brained skipping fellow. Compare *1 Henry IV*, III.2.60, where the King contemptuously describes Richard II as 'The skipping king'.

      nourisheth provides the good things of life

333   *flourisheth* prospers, thrives

334   *compound* compose, make an amicable settlement of

335   *deeds* (1) actions; (2) legal deeds, title-deeds

      he of both the one of you two

336   *dower* (the land and goods which the husband settled on his wife at marriage in order to provide for her widowhood in case she survived him)

340   *plate* utensils of silver

341   *lave* wash

342   *hangings* (draperies with which beds and walls were hung)

343   *crowns* (coins worth five shillings each)

344   *arras counterpoints* counterpanes of Arras tapestry

345   *tents* bed-testers or canopies

346   *bossed* embossed, studded

347   *Valance of Venice gold in needlework* valances (fringes on the canopy of a bed) adorned with Venetian embroidery in gold thread

348   *belongs* (the old plural)

350   *milch-kine to the pail* cows whose milk goes to the dairy (not to feed calves)

352   *answerable to this portion* corresponding to an estate on this scale

353   *struck in years* advanced in age, old

356   *came well in* was mentioned at the right time, was very apropos – since Tranio now makes great play with the fact that he is an only son
        list listen

360   *rich Pisa walls* the walls of rich Pisa

362–3 *two thousand ducats by the year | Of fruitful land* fertile land bringing in an income of two thousand ducats a year. A ducat was a Venetian gold coin worth about nine shillings.

363   *her jointure* the estate settled on her to provide for her widowhood

364   *pinched you* put you in a tight corner, gained an advantage in the argument

366   *My land amounts not to so much in all* the capital value of my land does not come to that

367   *argosy* (merchant-vessel of the largest size, especially one from Ragusa – whence the name – or Venice)

368   *Marseilles road* the roadstead (sheltered anchorage) at Marseilles. The Folio reads: 'Marcellus roade', and thus indicates the sixteenth-century pronunciation of 'Marseilles'.

371   *galliasses* (heavy, low-built vessels, larger than galleys)

372   *tight* sound, water-tight

378   *out-vied* out-bidden. A card-player was 'out-vied' when he refused to stake any more on his hand.

383   *but a cavil* merely a captious objection

393   *gamester* adventurer, gambler. Gremio has picked up
the allusion implicit in Tranio's use of the word 'out-
vied' at line 378.

395   *Set foot under thy table* live on your charity
a toy! sheer nonsense!

398   *faced it with a card of ten* brazened the matter out by
playing a card with ten pips. To 'outface with a card of
ten' was a proverbial phrase for bluffing.

399   *'Tis in my head* I have a scheme

400   *I see no reason but* I see it is necessary that
supposed the pretended, the substitute

402   *wonder* miracle

403   *get* beget

404   *I fail not of my cunning* I don't lose my ingenuity

III.1   This scene is headed '*Actus Tertia.*' in the Folio, though
there is no indication there of where the second Act
begins. It shows a side of Bianca's character that has not
been apparent up to this point.

1–3   *Fiddler, forbear, you grow too forward, sir ... withal?*
From these lines it looks as though Hortensio, when
the scene opens, is holding Bianca's hand to 'teach her
fingering', as he sought to do with Katherina at
II.1.150.

2   *entertainment* reception

3   *withal* with

4   *But, wrangling pedant, this is.* The line is metrically
defective, but it is impossible to say what has been
omitted from it.

6   *prerogative* precedence

8   *lecture* lesson

9   *Preposterous.* The word is used here in its literal sense,
meaning 'one who inverts the natural order of things,
one who puts the cart before the horse'.

10   *ordained* created, instituted

12   *usual pain* customary toil, normal work

14   *serve in* serve up (Lucentio's way of voicing his contempt for Hortensio and his music)

15   *braves* bravadoes, ostentatious displays of defiance

18   *no breeching scholar in the schools* no schoolboy liable to be flogged

19   *'pointed* appointed

22   *the whiles* the while

25   *That will be never.* Lucentio is deliberately taking 'in tune' in the sense of 'being in a good temper'.

28-9   *Hic ibat Simois, hic est Sigeia tellus … senis.* These lines from Ovid (*Heroides*, i. 33-4) mean 'Here ran the [river] Simois; here is the Sigeian land [Troy]; here stood the lofty palace of old Priam.'

35   *port* state, style

36   *the old pantaloon* Gremio. See note to stage direction at I.1.45.

38   *fie* (an exclamation of disgust)

39   *Spit in the hole, man, and tune again.* This is a perversion of the proverb that was used to encourage someone to make a second attempt, 'Spit in your hands and take better hold.' Lucentio is showing his ignorance of music, because to spit in the sound-hole of a lute would not help to tune it.

46-56   *How fiery and forward our pedant is … you both.* In the Folio the speeches in this section of the dialogue are wrongly assigned as follows:

> *Luc.* How fiery …
>   … I mistrust.
> *Bian.* Mistrust it …
>   … grandfather.
> *Hort.* I must …
>   … you both.

The prime cause of the confusion was probably the use of *Lic.*, the shortened form of Hortensio's assumed name Licio, in the speech headings, since *Lic.* would be very difficult to distinguish from *Luc*. Similar confusion occurs at IV.2.4–8 (see note).

48   *Pedascule* (a nonce-word coined as a contemptuous diminutive of 'pedant' on the analogy of '*didaskalos*' – the Greek for 'master')

50–51   *Aeacides | Was Ajax . . . grandfather.* Ajax Telamonius, one of the Greek heroes in the Trojan War, was also known as Aeacides from the name of his grandfather Aeacus. Lucentio, in an attempt to blind Hortensio with Ovid, has moved on to the next line of *Heroides*, i, which begins '*Illic Aeacides*'.

55–6   *Good master, take it not unkindly, pray, | That I have been thus pleasant with you both.* Bianca is addressing Hortensio, who alone has reason to be displeased; and *pleasant with you both* stretches her apology to cover Lucentio's chaff, and her laughter at it.

57   *give me leave* (a polite way of saying 'Please go')

59   *formal* punctilious, concerned for your professional rights

60   *withal* at the same time
    but unless

63   *order* method

65   *gamut* the musical scale
    briefer sort quicker fashion

66   *pithy* condensed
    effectual effective

71   *ground of all accord* basis of all harmony

74   *ut* (corresponds to the 'doh' of modern usage)

75   *one clef, two notes.* It has been suggested that the 'one clef' is love and the 'two notes' Hortensio's real and his assumed personality.

78–9   *so nice | To change* so capricious as to exchange

79   *odd inventions* fantastical new ideas

80   SERVANT. The Folio heads this speech '*Nicke.*', which some editors have taken as the name of the actor who first played the part. In fact, however, it seems most improbable that Shakespeare would have had a particu-

lar actor in mind for a part that only amounts to three
lines.

87–8   *if thy thoughts, Bianca, be so humble | To cast* if your
inclinations, Bianca, are so low that you cast

88   *stale* decoy, lure. The metaphor, from falconry, is
carried on in the next line. Hortensio is beginning to
see Bianca as a hawk that will stoop to anything.

89   *Seize thee that list* let anyone who wishes have you
ranging (1) straying (of a hawk); (2) being inconstant
(of a lover or wife)

90   *will be quit with thee by changing* will get even with you
by loving another

I.2   (stage direction) *Enter Baptista . . . Lucentio as Cambio
. . . Katherina.* The Folio direction reads: '*Enter
Baptista, Gremio, Tranio, Katherine, Bianca, and others,
attendants.*' The omission of Lucentio from it is probably due to the fact that he says nothing until line 137.

5   *To want* to be without

10   *rudesby, full of spleen* rough unmannerly fellow full of
whims and caprices

14   *to be noted for* in order to be known as, to get a reputation as

16   *Make feast, invite friends, and.* The Folio reads: 'Make
friends, inuite, and', which is neither good sense nor
good metre. The reading adopted in this edition is
based on Petruchio's line at II.1.309 'Provide the feast,
father, and bid the guests'.

22–5   *Upon my life, Petruchio means but well . . . honest.* At
some stage in the evolution of *The Taming of the Shrew*
these lines must have belonged to Hortensio, who is
Petruchio's friend and therefore knows a good deal
about him. They are out of place in the mouth of
Tranio, who, from this point onwards, appears to have
taken over much that must originally have been written
for Hortensio.

23   *Whatever fortune stays him from his word* whatever
      accident prevents him from keeping his promise

25   *merry* facetious, a bit of a joker
      honest one who keeps his word

26   (stage direction) *Exit weeping, followed by Bianca and the
      other women.* The Folio direction '*Exit weeping*' is
      simpler and more dramatic, since it emphasizes that
      Petruchio has already met with some success in his
      effort to make Katherina acknowledge her own feminine
      nature, but it has to be expanded in order to get the
      bridal train off the stage.

27   *now to weep* for weeping now

29   *of thy impatient.* The Folio reads: 'of impatient', but
      the necessary 'thy' appears in the Second Folio.

30   *such old news.* The Folio reads: 'such newes', but
      Baptista's comment in the next speech shows that 'old',
      meaning 'good old' or 'rare old', has been omitted.

42   *what to* what of

44   *jerkin* short outer coat or jacket

45   *boots that have been candle-cases* boots too old for wear
      that have been used to keep candle-ends in

47   *chapeless* lacking a sheath. The 'chape' was literally the
      metal plate on a scabbard that covered the point of a
      sword.

48   *points* (tagged laces used for fastening the hose to the
      doublet)
      hipped lamed in the hip

49   *of no kindred* that don't match, that are not a pair

49–50 *possessed with* affected by, suffering from

50   *the glanders* (a contagious disease in horses, marked by
      swellings beneath the jaw and discharge of mucous
      matter from the nostrils)
      like to likely to
      mose in the chine. The word 'mose' is not known outside
      this passage and is probably corrupt. 'To mourn of the
      chine' was to suffer from the final stage of 'glanders',
      and this is probably what is meant here.

51   *lampass* (a disease of horses in which the fleshy lining behind the front teeth swells and hinders mastication)

    fashions farcy (a horse-disease similar to glanders)

52   *windgalls* (soft tumours on a horse's legs just above the fetlocks)

    sped with ruined by

    spavins swellings of the leg-joints

    rayed soiled, befouled

    yellows jaundice

53   *fives* strangles (a swelling of the parotid glands)

    stark spoiled with absolutely wrecked by

    staggers (a horse-disease marked by giddiness)

54   *begnawn* gnawed at

    bots (a disease caused by intestinal worms)

    swayed strained. The Folio reads 'Waid'.

54–5   *shoulder-shotten* with a dislocated shoulder

55   *near-legged before* knock-kneed in the front legs

55–6   *half-cheeked bit* bit on which the cheeks (the rings or side pieces attaching the bit to the bridle) had got broken

56   *headstall* (the part of the bridle covering the horse's head)

    sheep's leather (not so strong as pigskin or leather of cowhide, which were normally used)

57   *restrained* drawn tight

58   *new-repaired*. The Folio has 'now repaired', but the context makes it clear that this operation has been done not once but time and again.

    girth (the leather band going round a horse's belly and drawn tight to hold the saddle in place)

59   *pieced* mended

    crupper (strap, normally of leather, ending in a loop which passes under the horse's tail and prevents the saddle from slipping)

    of velure made of velvet

60   *two letters for her name fairly set down in studs* her two

initials handsomely marked on it in studs (probably of brass or silver)

61   *pack-thread* string

63   *for all the world caparisoned* in every respect harnessed, dressed in trappings exactly

64   *stock* stocking
       kersey (coarse woollen cloth)

65   *boot-hose* (over-stocking which covers the leg like a jack-boot)

66   *list* strip of cloth
       the humour of forty fancies. This must be an allusion to some kind of fashionable affectation, but precisely what it was no one knows.

66–7   *pricked in't* pinned to it

69   *odd humour pricks* strange whim that incites

78   *all one* one and the same thing

79–83   *Nay, by Saint Jamy ... many.* This jingle is printed as prose in the Folio.

80   *I hold you* I bet you

87   *I come not well?* I don't arrive opportunely? (Petruchio has noticed the look of displeasure on Baptista's face.)

88   *you halt not.* Taking 'come' in the literal sense of 'walk', Baptista points out that Petruchio's entrance has been unceremonious.

90   *Were it not better.* The Folio reads: 'Were it better', which does not make very good sense.

92   *Gentles* gentlefolk, gentlemen

94   *wondrous monument* strange portent

95   *Some comet.* Comets were regarded as omens of disaster. Compare *Julius Caesar*, II.2.30–31:

> *When beggars die, there are no comets seen;*
> *The heavens themselves blaze forth the death of princes.*

       prodigy omen

98   *unprovided* unprepared, improperly dressed

99   *habit* dress, outfit
       estate rank, social status

101   *occasion of import* matter of consequence, important reason

105   *Sufficeth* it is enough that

106   *digress* (1) go out of my way; (2) deviate from my promise

110   *wears* is passing, wears on

111   *unreverent* disrespectful, unseemly

115   *Good sooth* yes indeed, truly
        ha' have (colloquial)

117   *wear* wear away, use up. The allusion is bawdy.

122   *lovely* loving

123–5   *He hath some meaning in his mad attire . . . church.* These words, which give the impression that Tranio is about to follow Petruchio, were almost certainly written for Hortensio in the original version of the play. There can be little doubt that the part of Hortensio has been rather clumsily excised from this scene, and that his words have not very appropriately been given to Tranio.

126   *event* upshot, outcome

127   *But, sir, to love.* The Folio reads: 'But sir, Loue' which does not make sense. Some editors change this to 'But to her love' which certainly makes the meaning much clearer.
        The abrupt beginning of this speech, together with Tranio's remaining on the stage after his previous remarks, and with the presence of Lucentio, who is not included in the Folio entry at the beginning of the scene and who has not said a word hitherto, all point to cobbling. There is every indication that something has been cut between Baptista's exit and the beginning of this speech.

127–8   *to love concerneth us to add | Her father's liking* it is essential for us to win her father's good will and join it to her love for you

131   *It skills not much* it doesn't matter much, it makes no difference

138   *steps* movements, actions

139   *to steal our marriage* to make a secret marriage

140   *let all the world say no* even though it meets with universal opposition

143   *watch our vantage* look out for a favourable opportunity

144   *overreach* dupe, get the better of

145   *narrow-prying* inquisitive

146   *quaint* crafty, scheming

147   (stage direction) *Enter Gremio.* The very short space of time allowed for the marriage – a mere twenty lines – adds to the evidence that the dialogue between Tranio and Lucentio has been heavily cut.

148   *came you* have you come

149   *As willingly as e'er I came from school.* Like much that Gremio says, this expression was a proverbial one.

150   *And is the bride and bridegroom coming home.* Shakespeare often uses the singular form of the verb when the subject is two singular nouns. Compare 'Hanging and wiving goes by destiny' (*The Merchant of Venice*, II.9.83).

151   *a groom indeed* a really rough individual just like a servingman

156   *a fool* a gentle innocent (term of pity as often in Shakespeare)

157   *Sir Lucentio.* In Shakespeare's day foreigners belonging to the gentry were often addressed as 'Sir'. Lucentio, like Vincentio at IV.2.106, is regarded as a foreigner because he comes from Pisa.

158   *Should ask* asked, came to ask. 'Should' is sometimes used by Shakespeare to denote a reported statement – compare *As You Like It*, III.2.167–8, 'But didst thou hear without wondering how thy name should be hanged and carved upon these trees?'

159   *by gogs-wouns* by God's wounds (a common oath)

161   *again to take it up* to take it up again

162   *took him* struck him, gave him

164   *Now take them up.* 'Them' here refers to the bride's dress. Petruchio is explaining his conduct by saying

214

that he suspected the bending priest of trying to interfere with Katherina's underwear – compare Grumio's remarks to the Tailor at IV.3.154–9. Such a suspicion would have some plausibility for an Elizabethan audience, since it was customary after the marriage ceremony for the young men present to rush forward and pluck off the elaborate emblems made of ribbons that the bride wore on her dress, and also to remove her ribbon garters.

164   *if any list* if anyone cares to (an obvious threat to any who sought to follow the custom described in the previous note)

165   *rose up again.* The Folio reads: 'rose againe' which is unmetrical. Another way of curing the defect is by reading 'arose again'.

166–82 *Trembled and shook . . . minstrels play.* These lines are printed as prose in the Folio.

167   *cozen* cheat, deceive (by some irregularity that would make the marriage invalid)

169   *He calls for wine.* At the conclusion of the marriage service in Shakespeare's time a cup of muscadel (see note below) with cakes or sops in it was drunk by the bride, the bridegroom, and the company.

171   *muscadel* (a sweet wine. Petruchio leaves none for anyone else.)

174   *hungerly* sparsely, having a famished undernourished look

180   *rout* company, crowd of guests

184   *think* expect

190   *Make it no wonder* don't be surprised

202   *not stay* not content to stay
       how you can how you may

203   *horse* horses. 'Horse', the old form of the plural, was still common in Shakespeare's time.

204–5 *they be ready – the oats have eaten the horses* the horses are fresh (ready to gallop) because they have had more oats than they could eat

210 *You may be jogging whiles your boots are green* be off while your boots are fresh (proverbial expression for getting rid of an unwelcome guest)

212 *a jolly* an arrogant, overbearing

213 *That take it on you at the first so roundly* since you assume authority so unhesitatingly from the outset

214 *content thee* compose yourself, keep your temper

215 *what hast thou to do?* what business of yours is it, what right have you to interfere?

216 *stay my leisure* wait till I'm ready

223 *domineer* feast riotously

226 *for* as for

227 *Nay, look not big, nor stamp, nor stare, nor fret.* These words are almost a concealed stage direction to Katherina – it is what she should be doing – but Petruchio, affecting not to see her, speaks them angrily to the rest of the company.
big angry, threatening

229–31 *She is my goods, my chattels, she is my house ... any thing.* Much of this echoes the Tenth Commandment. Petruchio wittily accuses the company of coveting Katherina.

233 *I'll bring mine action on the proudest he* I'll take legal proceedings against the proudest man

238 *buckler* shield, defend

240 *Went they not* if they had not gone (subjunctive)

244 *is Kated* has caught the 'Kate' (as though it were the name of a disease). Compare Beatrice's remark: 'God help the noble Claudio! If he have caught the Benedick, it will cost him a thousand pound ere 'a be cured' (*Much Ado About Nothing*, I.1.81–3).

245–6 *wants | For to supply* are not here to fill

247 *there wants no junkets* there is no lack of delicacies

249 *room* place, seat

250 *bride it* play the bride

1   The Folio marks no Act division at this point, though the move to Petruchio's house in the country is the first real change in the location of the action since the play proper began. Shakespeare makes it abundantly plain in Grumio's first speech that the move has taken place, and that this house is a very different place from Padua. Even the weather is on Petruchio's side.

1   *jades* vicious worthless horses

2   *foul ways* dirty roads

3   *rayed* dirtied

5   *a little pot and soon hot.* Grumio is quoting a well-known proverb which means that little men soon grow angry. That Grumio was imagined by Shakespeare as a little man is also evident from his reference to 'a taller man than I' (line 9) and from Curtis's calling him 'you three-inch fool' (line 23).

7   *come by* get, find

11   *so coldly* like one benumbed with cold

16–17   *fire, fire, cast on no water.* This is a reference to the catch

> *Scotland's burning, Scotland's burning,*
> *See yonder! See yonder!*
> *Fire, fire! Fire, fire!*
> *Cast on water! Cast on water*

Grumio, unlike Scotland, wants to burn.

18   *hot* angry, violent

20   *winter tames man, woman, and beast.* This is an allusion to the proverb 'Winter and wedlock tame both man and beast.' Grumio significantly adds woman to the list.

23   *I am no beast.* By naming himself third Grumio has equated himself, and therefore his fellow-servant Curtis, with the beasts. Hence Curtis's rejoinder.

24–5   *thy horn is a foot, and so long am I at the least.* The inevitable retort – Grumio says that he is big enough to have made Curtis a cuckold.

26   *complain on* complain about

217

28   *hot office* duty of fire-making

32   *Do thy duty, and have thy duty* do thy duty and take thy due

36   '*Jack boy, ho boy!*' An allusion to a catch which begins

> *Jack boy, ho boy, News:*
> *The cat is in the well.*

36–7   *as wilt thou* as you could wish

38   *cony-catching* trickery, evasion (perhaps with reference to Grumio's fondness for catches)

41   *rushes strewed.* The strewing of fresh rushes on the floor was an essential part of the preparation for a guest.

42   *fustian* (a coarse cloth made of cotton and flax)

43   *Jacks* (1) men-servants; (2) leather drinking-vessels

44   *Jills* (1) maid-servants; (2) metal drinking-vessels
        the carpets laid (on tables and chests rather than on the floor, which was strewn with rushes)

52   *ha't* have it (colloquial)

56   *feel* experience, suffer

57   *sensible* (1) capable of being felt; (2) easily understood

59   *Imprimis* first, to begin with (Latin)

61   *Both of* both on

64   *crossed* interrupted

67   *bemoiled* covered with mud and dirt

73   *of worthy memory* worthy of remembrance, that ought not to be forgotten

74   *unexperienced* in ignorance of them

76   *more shrew* more of a shrew (*shrew* could be applied to either sex)

78   *But what* but why

80   *slickly* smoothly, sleekly

81   *blue coats* (normal uniform of servants)

82   *of an indifferent knit* of a reasonable pattern, not too showy

82–3   *curtsy with their left legs* (as a token of submission – to put the best foot first was a sign of defiance)

84   *horse-tail* horse's tail

84   *kiss their hands.* To kiss one's own hands was a mark of respect to a superior.

87-8   *to countenance* to grace, to honour

91   *calls.* This is the second person singular. Shakespeare, who wrote his words to be spoken, not read, often avoids the '-est' form.

93   *credit* honour, do credit to. Grumio, of course, takes the word in the other sense of 'provide credit for'.

101   *spruce* lively, brisk

103   *All things is ready.* 'All things' is thought of as a collective equivalent to 'everything'.

105   *Cock's passion* (a corruption of 'by God's Passion')

111   *logger-headed* thick-headed, stupid

115   *peasant swain* country bumpkin

       whoreson (literally 'son of a whore', but commonly used as a term of contempt and reprobation)

       malt-horse drudge (slow heavy horse, used to grind malt by working a treadmill)

119   *all unpinked* entirely without their proper ornamentation. To 'pink' leather was to decorate it by punching out a pattern on it.

       i'th' in the (colloquial)

120   *link* (blacking made of the material of burnt torches, or 'links', as they were called)

121   *sheathing* being fitted with a scabbard

126   *Where is the life that late I led?* This is the first line of a song that is now lost, and *Where are those* appears to be the continuation of it. The existence of the song is known, because an answer to it, entitled 'Dame Beauty's Reply to the Lover late at Liberty', was published in Clement Robinson's *A Handful of Pleasant Delights*, 1584. The song would be appropriate to Petruchio's newly-married state.

127   *Where are those –.* The Folio reads: 'Where are those?'

128   *Food, food, food, food!* The Folio reads: 'Soud, soud, soud, soud.', which makes no sense whatever. 'Food', however, is exactly what Petruchio wants, and if it

were spelled 'foud' in the manuscript, as it well may have been, the mistake is easily intelligible, since the letter 'f' and the 'long s' [ſ] closely resembled each other.

129   *when, I say* (common expression denoting impatience)

131   *It was the friar of orders grey . . . way.* These lines are the beginning of another lost ballad. The friar in question is a Grey friar or Franciscan.

133   *Out* (expression of anger)

134   *mend* make a better job of

135   *Some water here.* Washing of the hands before meals, especially important at a time when people ate with their fingers, was carried out at table in Shakespeare's England.

(stage direction) *Enter one with water.* The direction is rightly placed at this point in the Folio, and there is no need to move it, as many editors have done, four lines down to make it follow Petruchio's second demand. The house is admirably organized and runs like clock-work, so making all his complaints doubly ridiculous; which is, of course, exactly how he wants them to appear, since the essence of his plan is to bring Katherina over to the side of order by showing her the folly of ill-tempered outbursts of choler.

137   *my cousin Ferdinand.* This looks like a loose end, for the cousin never turns up.

143   *beetle-headed* thick-headed. A 'beetle' is a heavy wooden mallet.

flap-eared with heavy pendulous ears

144   *stomach* appetite

145   *give thanks* say grace

149   *dresser* (kitchen-table on which food was prepared)

151   *trenchers* (wooden platters used for serving up meat)

152   *heedless joltheads* careless blockheads

153   *I'll be with you straight* I'll be after you, I'll chastise you
(stage direction) *Exeunt Servants hurriedly.* The Folio provides no direction here, but one is plainly needed

both as a consequence of Petruchio's threat and so that the Servants can '*Enter severally*' at line 164.

154   *disquiet* upset, in a temper

155   *well* good, satisfactory

158   *For it engenders choler.* For the belief that over-cooked meat produced an excess of choler, and so stimulated anger, see *The Comedy of Errors*, II.2.59–62, where Dromio of Syracuse begs his master not to eat dry unbasted meat, 'Lest it make you choleric, and purchase me another dry basting'.

160   *of ourselves* by nature

162   *mended* put right

163   *for company* together

164   (stage direction) *severally* one by one

166   *He kills her in her own humour* he outdoes her (and so masters her) in her own special line of tantrums

169   *Making a sermon of continency to her* giving her a lecture on the virtues of moderation and restraint

170   *rates* scolds, lays down the law
       that so that

174–97   *Thus have I politicly begun my reign ... to show.* This speech, addressed direct to the audience, is central to the play, because in it Petruchio explains his plan for taming Katherina and, at the same time, through the image of the falcon, gives his estimate of her character.

174   *politicly* prudently, like a clever statesman
       begun my reign. This is an allusion to the idea that the wife was the husband's subject. Compare V.2.145–6, 'Thy husband is thy lord ... thy sovereign.'

176–82   *My falcon now is sharp and passing empty ... obedient.* The methods used in the training of a wild hawk or haggard, as she was called, in order to make her 'meek, and loving to the man', are thus described by a contemporary of Shakespeare:

'All hawks generally are manned after one manner, that is to say, by watching and keeping them from sleep, by

a continual carrying of them upon your fist, and by a
most familiar stroking and playing with them, with the
wing of a dead fowl or such like, and by often gazing
and looking of them in the face, with a loving and gentle
countenance, and so making them acquainted with the
man.' Gervase Markham, *Country Contentments* (1615),
fourth edition, London, 1631, pages 36–7.

176   *sharp* sharp-set, famished
        passing extremely

177   *stoop* fly to the lure
        full-gorged allowed to feed her fill

178   *looks upon* regards, takes notice of
        lure (apparatus used by falconers to recall their hawks,
        being a bunch of feathers attached to a cord, within
        which, during its training, the hawk finds its food)

179   *man my haggard* tame my wild hawk

181   *watch her* keep her awake
        these kites those falcons

182   *bate and beat* flutter and flap their wings

189   *hurly* commotion
        intend pretend, try to make out

190   *reverend* reverent, respectful

191   *watch* stay awake

193   *still* constantly

194   *to kill a wife with kindness.* To 'kill with kindness' was a
        proverbial phrase for harming someone by excessive
        and mistaken indulgence. Petruchio is using it ironically
        for to 'give her a taste of her own medicine'.

197   *charity to show* to show public spirit. The rhyme 'shrew
        – show' indicates how 'shrew' was pronounced.

IV.2.3   *she bears me fair in hand* she deceives me in a very con-
        vincing fashion

4–8   *Sir, to satisfy you in what I have said ... Love.* The
        Folio distributes these lines wrongly, giving lines 4–5
        to Lucentio, line 6 to Hortensio, line 7 correctly to

Bianca, and line 8 to Hortensio. For a possible explanation of how the confusion may have arisen see the note to III.1.46–56.

4   *to satisfy you in* to convince you of

5   (stage direction) *Enter Bianca, and Lucentio as Cambio.* The Folio reads: '*Enter Bianca.*' – a consequence of the mistaken attribution of the previous speech to Lucentio.

8   *that I profess* that which I practise

     The Art to Love (Ovid's witty poem the *Ars Amatoria*, in which love is presented as a science)

11   *Quick proceeders* apt students. The allusion is to 'proceeding' from B.A. to M.A. – compare 'master of your art' in line 9.

15   *wonderful* surprising, incredible

18   *scorn* scorns. The verb agrees with the antecedent 'I' instead of with the relative 'that'.

20   *cullion* base fellow, rascal

23   *entire affection to* pure unalloyed love for

24   *lightness* wantonness, loose behaviour

31   *fondly* foolishly

     withal with

34   *how beastly* in what animal fashion

35   *Would all the world but he had quite forsworn!* Hortensio spitefully wishes that Cambio were Bianca's only suitor. It does not occur to him that she could ever think of marrying the apparent menial.

37   *a wealthy widow.* The sudden mention of this new character, of whom there has not been a word so far, is another sign that the part of Hortensio has undergone some cobbling.

38   *which* who. The two words are often interchanged in Shakespeare.

39   *haggard* wild intractable hawk – used metaphorically here for a light woman. Compare *Othello*, III.3.257, 'If I do prove her haggard', meaning 'unfaithful'.

43   *In resolution* with fixed purpose, fully determined

45   *'longeth to* belongs to, suits with

46   *ta'en you napping* caught you in the act (of billing and cooing)

53–8   *Ay, and he'll tame her ... chattering tongue.* Tranio knows far more about Hortensio's plans than Hortensio has just told him. This passage is yet more evidence that the part of Hortensio has been much altered.

57   *tricks eleven and twenty long* tricks of exactly the right kind. The allusion is to the game of cards called 'one-and-thirty' that Grumio refers to at I.2.32.

58   *charm* use a magic spell in order to silence (compare I.1.206)

60   *dog-weary* dog-tired, worn out

61   *An ancient angel* a fellow of the good old stamp. An *angel* was a gold coin, worth ten shillings, carrying as its device the archangel Michael and the dragon. Biondello may also be thinking of the Pedant as the angel who has come in answer to his prayer.

62   *Will serve the turn* who will serve our purpose

63   *marcantant* (Biondello's version of '*mercatante*', the Italian for 'merchant')

67   *trust my tale* believe my story

71   *let me alone* rely on me

73   *farrer* farther. The Folio reads 'farre', which editors render as 'far', but 'farrer' makes better sense and is supported by Shakespeare's use of this old form of the comparative in *The Winter's Tale*, where Polixenes tells Florizel, in the Folio text:

> *wee'l barre thee from succession,*
> *Not hold thee of our blood, no not our Kin,*
> *Farre then Deucalion off.* ...   IV.4.421–4

77   *What countryman. . .?* where do you live?

79   *careless of* regardless of

80   *that goes hard* that's a serious matter

81–7   *'Tis death for any one in Mantua ... proclaimed about.* Tranio's story looks to be borrowed from Shakespeare's own *The Comedy of Errors*, I.1.16–20.

83   *stayed* held up
84   *For private quarrel* on account of personal dissension
86   *'Tis marvel* it's strange. Two constructions are involved
      here. Tranio begins to say 'It's strange you haven't
      heard', but then changes abruptly to another way of
      putting it, as people often do in speech.
      but that you are newly come but for the fact that you have
      only just arrived
87   *about* up and down the city
88   *than so* than you think
89   *bills for money by exchange* bills of exchange, promissory
      notes
95   *Pisa renownèd for grave citizens* (a repetition of I.1.10)
101   *As much as an apple doth an oyster* (a well known
      proverb)
102   *and all one* just the very same
107   *credit* reputation
      undertake assume, take on you
109   *Look that you take upon you as you should* see that you
      play your part properly
112   *accept of* accept
113   *repute* consider, think of
115   *make the matter good* put the plan into effect
117   *looked for* expected
118   *pass assurance of* settle, make a binding promise of

.3   The Folio marks the beginning of this scene as the
      opening of Act Four, heading it 'Actus Quartus. Scena
      Prima.' See the head-note to IV.1.
2   *The more my wrong* the greater the injustice done to me
5   *Upon entreaty have a present alms* have only to ask and
      they receive alms immediately
9   *meat* food in general
11   *spites* mortifies, vexes
13   *As who should say* as if to say, as though he were saying
44   *present* immediate

15 *some repast* something to eat

16 *so* so long as, provided that

17 *a neat's foot* the foot of an ox

19 *choleric* productive of anger, prone to make one irascible

20 *broiled* grilled, cooked over the coals

22 *I cannot tell* I don't know what to say

26 *let the mustard rest* don't worry about the mustard

32 *the very name* the mere name, the name and nothing else

36 *sweeting* darling, sweetheart

all amort down in the dumps, sick to death (French *à la mort*)

37 *what cheer?* how is it with you?

as cold as can be as cold a reception, as poor entertainment, as can be imagined (quibbling on the other sense of 'cheer')

43 *all my pains is sorted to no proof* all my labour has been in vain, has been taken to no purpose. 'Pains' is always singular in Shakespeare.

45 *poorest* slightest, most insignificant

46 *mine before.* The ellipse of the verb 'be' is common in Shakespeare, otherwise 'mine be 'fore' would be an attractive reading.

48 *to blame* too blameworthy, too much at fault. This use of 'to blame' as though it were 'too blame' was common in Shakespeare's day. Compare the Nurse's reproof to Old Capulet, 'You are to blame, my lord, to rate her so' (*Romeo and Juliet*, III.5.169).

51 *do it* may it do

52 *apace* quickly

54 *as bravely* in as splendidly dressed a manner

56 *ruffs* (articles of neckwear elaborately fluted and stiffly starched)

farthingales hooped petticoats

57 *bravery* finery

58 *this knavery* tricks of dress like those, that sort of trumpery

59 *stays* awaits

60 *ruffling* swaggering, gay

62–140 *Lay forth the gown . . . Ay, there's the villainy.* Some interesting parallels to this attack on fashions in dress are to be found in *Life in Shakespeare's England*, ed. J. Dover Wilson, Penguin Books edition, 1968, pp. 161–73.

63 HABERDASHER. The Folio heads this speech '*Fel.*'
  bespeak order

64 *moulded on* modelled on, shaped like
  porringer (small basin from which soup, porridge, and the like were eaten)

65 *A velvet dish* a dish made of velvet
  lewd and filthy (Elizabethan equivalent of 'cheap and nasty')

66 *cockle* cockle-shell

67 *knack* knick-knack, silly contrivance
  toy piece of nonsense
  trick bauble, practical joke

69 *fit the time* suit the fashion

75 *endured me say* suffered me to say

76 *best you stop* it were best for you to stop

82 *custard-coffin* (crust of pastry in which a custard was baked)

83 *in that* because, inasmuch as

86 (stage direction) *Exit Haberdasher.* The Folio gives the Haberdasher no exit, but now that the business of the cap is over there is no reason for his remaining.

87 *masquing stuff* clothes that look suitable for use in a masque. Strange and elaborate costumes were a feature of the masque.

88 *demi-cannon* large gun with a bore of about six and a half inches. The sleeve in question is of the leg-of-mutton variety that became popular around 1580. It was often slashed, as well as being padded and stiffened with embroidery – hence Petruchio's subsequent attacks. Men's dress, it should be added, was equally elaborate.

91   *censer*. The usual explanation of this rare word – that it was a fumigator, consisting of a brazier with a perforated lid to emit the smoke of burning perfumes – is not very satisfactory in this context, but until a better is found it must serve.

92   *a devil's name* in the name of the devil

94   *bid* (past tense)

96   *Marry, and did* indeed I did
    be remembered recollect

97   *mar it to the time* ruin it for ever

98   *hop me* hop, I say
    kennel gutter, surface-drain of a street

99   *hop without* lose. Compare *2 Henry VI*, I.3.133–5:

> *Thy sale of offices and towns in France,*
> *If they were known, as the suspect is great,*
> *Would make thee quickly hop without thy head.*

100   *make your best of it* do what you like with it

102   *quaint* artfully made, elegant

107   *nail* (a measure of length for cloth, being one sixteenth of a yard)

108   *nit* egg of a louse. There is no need to assume from these abusive terms, as some editors have done, that the part of the tailor was played by a small man or by a boy. Petruchio is practising the rhetorical art of diminution, encouraged, no doubt, by the common proverb 'Nine tailors make a man'.

109   *Braved* defied, challenged
    with by

110   *rag* (1) tattered bit of cloth; (2) shabby person
    quantity scrap

111   *bemete* measure (with a quibble on 'mete out punishment')

112   *As thou shalt think on* that you will think twice about

121   *faced* (1) trimmed with braid, velvet, or some other material; (2) impudently confronted, bullied

123   *braved* (1) provided fine clothes for; (2) defied, set yourself up against

126   *Ergo* therefore, consequently (term much used in logic)

129   *The note lies in's throat* (1) the note tells a black lie; (2) the musical note is in his throat, meaning 'the words come from his mouth'

130–31 *loose-bodied* (1) loosely fitting; (2) of the kind worn by 'loose bodies', meaning 'harlots'

132–3 *bottom of brown thread* ball of brown thread. The *bottom* was really the core or bobbin on which thread was wound.

135   *compassed* cut so as to fall in a circle

137   *trunk sleeve* large wide sleeve

139   *curiously* (1) carefully, accurately; (2) elaborately. Petruchio takes the word in the second sense, of course.

141   *bill* (1) the 'note' of line 127; (2) bill of indictment, accusation

143   *prove upon thee* establish by fighting you. The allusion is to trial by combat. Compare *Richard II*, IV.1.44–8:

> *Aumerle, thou liest; his honour is as true*
> *In this appeal as thou art all unjust;*
> *And that thou art so, there I throw my gage,*
> *To prove it on thee to the extremest point*
> *Of mortal breathing.*

145   *an* if

145–6 *in place where* in a fit place, in the right spot

147   *for thee straight* ready to do battle with you at once

       bill (1) note; (2) kind of pike or halbert used by watchmen

148   *mete-yard* measuring yard

149   *God-a-mercy* God have mercy!

150   *odds* advantage, superiority (probably with a quibble on the odds and ends left over from a garment which were the tailor's perquisites)

153   *take it up unto thy master's use* take it away and let your master make what use he can of it

154-5 *Take up my mistress' gown for thy master's use!* See note on III.2.164.

155 *use* sexual purposes

156 *conceit* idea, notion, innuendo

157 *think for* imagine

163 *Take no unkindness of* don't imagine there is any ill-will in

166 *mean habiliments* poor clothes

167 *proud* puffed up

170 *peereth in* can be seen peeping through

174 *painted* richly coloured
     contents pleases, delights

176 *furniture* outfit, dress
     array attire

178 *frolic* be merry

180 (stage direction) (*to Grumio*). This is not in the Folio, but Petruchio would never give an order of the kind that follows to Katherina.

184 *dinner-time* (between eleven o'clock and noon)

186 *supper-time* (between half-past five and half-past six. Petruchio and Katherina are substantially agreed, if on nothing else, that it takes about four hours to get to her father's.)

188 *Look what* whatever, no matter what
     think to do intend to do, think of doing

189 *still crossing* always contradicting, constantly thwarting
     let't alone forbear, take no further action about the matter

192 *so* apparently, according to what he has said. This line leads on very neatly to the opening of IV.5, the next scene in which Petruchio and Katherina appear.

IV.4   (stage direction) *Enter Tranio as Lucentio, and the Pedant, booted, and dressed like Vincentio.* The Folio reads: '*Enter Tranio, and the Pedant drest like Vincentio.*' For the addition of the word *booted*, meaning 'wearing riding boots', see the note to line 17.

1   *please it you* may it please you

2   *what else?* of course

      but unless

4   *Near* nearly

5   *Where we were lodgers at the Pegasus.* The Folio prints this as the first line of Tranio's speech – the result of a careless alignment of the speech heading in the manuscript, or, perhaps, to indicate that the line is to be spoken by the Pedant and Tranio simultaneously as a sign of their complicity.

      at the Pegasus. Pegasus, the winged horse of classical mythology, was a popular inn-sign in Shakespeare's London.

6   *hold your own* play your part well

9   *schooled* instructed in his part

10   *Fear you not him* don't be worried about him

11   *throughly* thoroughly, properly

      advise instruct, caution

12   *right* real, true

16   *looked for* expected

17   *Th' art a tall fellow, hold thee that to drink* you're an able chap, take that to get yourself a drink

      (stage direction) *Enter Baptista, and Lucentio as Cambio.* The Folio reads: '*Enter Baptista and Lucentio: Pedant booted and bare headed.*' As the Pedant is already on stage at this point, it looks as though this direction may well be something left over from an earlier version in which the scene began here.

18   *Set your countenance* look like a grave father

21   *stand* be, show yourself

23   *Soft* gently, just a moment

24   *having come* I having come. The omission of the noun or pronoun on which a participle depends is fairly common in Shakespeare. Compare 'Coming from Sardis, on our former ensign | Two mighty eagles fell . . .' (*Julius Caesar*, V.1.79–80).

26   *weighty cause* serious matter

28   *for* because of

30   *to stay him not* in order not to keep him waiting

32-3   *to like | No worse than I* to be no less satisfied than I

35   *With one consent* in entire agreement
       bestowed matched, married

36   *curious* over-particular in a matter of business, niggling

45   *pass* settle upon

46   *done* settled

48-50   *Where then do you know best | We be affied and such assurance ta'en | As shall with either part's agreement stand?* where, in your opinion, may we best be betrothed and such legal arrangements be made as will be agreeable to both parties?

52   *Pitchers have ears.* This proverb, which Shakespeare uses again in *Richard III*, II.4.37, puns on the 'ears' or handles by which water-vessels were lifted, and means 'there may be listeners'.

53   *hearkening still* still watching his opportunity

54   *happily* haply, perchance

55   *an it like* if it please

56   *lie* lodge

57   *pass* settle

58   (stage direction) *He winks at Lucentio.* This is not in the Folio, but clearly demanded by Biondello's remark at line 74.

59   *scrivener* (notary, one publicly authorized to draw up contracts)

60   *slender* slight, insufficient

61   *pittance* fare, diet

62   *hie you* get you, hurry off

63   *straight* immediately, straightway

68   (stage direction) *Enter Peter, a Servingman.* This direction is based on the Folio, which reads: '*Enter Peter.*' Although Peter says nothing, his purpose is almost certainly to indicate to Tranio, by a gesture, that the meal is ready.

70　*One mess is like to be your cheer* one dish is likely to be your fare

76　*'has* he has

78　*moralize* explain the meaning of

79　*safe* safely out of the way

80　*deceiving* sham
deceitful sham

86　*command* service

89　*assurance* legal settlement
Take you assurance make sure

89-90　*cum privilegio ad imprimendum solum.* This inscription, frequently found on the title-pages of books printed in Shakespeare's time, meant originally 'with the privilege for printing only', but it was later taken to mean 'with the sole right to print', which is the significance Biondello has in mind here. There is a pun on printing in the sense of 'stamping one's own image on a person by getting her with child'.

91　*some sufficient* enough, the right number required by law

92　*that you look for* that which you long for

99　*against you come* in preparation for your coming

100　*appendix* appendage (meaning Bianca)

103　*I'll roundly go about her* I'll approach her without ceremony

104　*It shall go hard if Cambio go without her* Cambio is not going to lose her if he can possibly help it

IV.5　The location of this scene, established in the first two lines, is somewhere on the road between Petruchio's house and Padua. No Elizabethan audience would trouble its head over whether the travellers are in that 'Long-lane', mentioned by Petruchio at IV.3.181, or whether they are somewhere further along the main road, walking up a hill to rest their horses. The audience would know that the characters must be on foot, because horses did not appear on the Elizabethan stage.

7   *list* please, choose

8   *Or e'er* before ever

14   *rush-candle* (candle of feeble power made by dipping a rush in grease)

20   *And the moon changes even as your mind* (a nice touch showing that Katherina has lost neither her spirit nor her sense of humour)

23   *go thy ways* go on, carry on (used as a term of approbation)

25   *against the bias* against its natural inclination. The bias is the weight lodged on one side of the wooden ball, or bowl, used in the game of bowls, in order to make it swerve when rolled.

27   *where away?* where are you going?

29   *fresher* more youthful

31   *spangle* brightly adorn

35   *'A* he (colloquial)

36   *the woman.* So the First Folio, though most editors prefer to follow the Second and read 'a woman'. The allusion is, however, to the theatre, where the part of the woman was played by a boy. Petruchio, says Hortensio, is assigning the old man the woman's role in the little play he is staging. Compare *Coriolanus*, II.2.93–5:

> *In that day's feats,*
> *When he might act the woman in the scene,*
> *He proved best man i'th' field. . . .*

38   *Whither away, or where.* This is the reading of the Second Folio; the First has 'Whether away, or whether'. Since 'where' was a contracted form of 'whether', the mistake is easily understood.

41   *Allots* (the old plural)

47   *green* (1) green in colour; (2) fresh, new, youthful

54   *encounter* manner of address, greeting

61   *father* father-in-law. Petruchio is rather stretching the meaning.

62–3 *The sister to my wife, this gentlewoman, | Thy son by this hath married.* Neither Petruchio nor Hortensio, who adds his assurance at line 74, can possibly know this, since it has not yet happened. Moreover, Hortensio has every reason to think it never will, because Tranio, who for him, as for Petruchio, is Lucentio, joined with him in forswearing Bianca for ever. Though these discrepancies are likely to go unnoticed in the theatre, they do point, nevertheless, to the same kind of cobbling that is evident in the conduct of so much of the subplot.

64 *of good esteem* of good reputation, highly respected

66 *qualified* endowed with good qualities

    beseem befit

71 *or is it else* or else is it

72 *pleasant* merry, facetious

    break a jest play a practical joke

76 *jealous* suspicious

77 *put me in heart* encouraged me

78 *froward* difficult, refractory

79 *untoward* unmannerly, unforthcoming

1 The Folio marks no Act division at this point, but since the action has now moved back to Padua, where it will remain for the rest of the play, this is obviously the right place for the last Act to begin

    (stage direction) *Enter Biondello, Lucentio as himself, and Bianca. Gremio is out before.* So the Folio, except that it fails to indicate that Lucentio is no longer in disguise. The very unusual direction '*Gremio is out before*', which has all the appearance of an afterthought, means that Gremio comes on first, and the rest follow after a brief interval. Why he is waiting for Cambio (see line 6) is never made clear, but his failure to notice him when he does come on is accounted for by the fact that Lucentio is not now 'in the habit of a mean man'.

4   *I'll see the church a your back* I'll see the church at your back (meaning 'I'll see you safely married')

7–8   *Sir, here's the door, this is Lucentio's house ... market-place.* These two lines are a strong indication that for the part of the action that takes place in Padua one of the main doors leading on to the stage is thought of as the entrance to Lucentio's house and the other as the entrance to Baptista's house.

10   *You shall not choose but* you must

11   *your welcome* a welcome for you

12   *some cheer is toward* some good cheer is to be expected

13   (stage direction) *Pedant looks out of the window.* This stage direction has been adapted from a similar one in Gascoigne's *Supposes*, where in the corresponding scene (IV.3) Dalio, the cook in the house of Dulipo (Tranio), 'cometh to the window, and there maketh them answer' when the true father of the hero turns up. The window in question was probably above the stage door that served as the entrance to Lucentio's house.

17   *withal* with

23–4   *To leave frivolous circumstances* to have done with point-less talk, to cut the cackle

27   *from Mantua.* The Folio reads: 'from *Padua*' which does not make very good sense, since they are in Padua. A much better comic effect is produced by letting the Pedant forget his role for a moment and give the name of the place he has really come from.

32   *flat* downright, bare-faced

34–5   *'a means to cozen* he plans to cheat

35   *under my countenance* by pretending to be me

37   *God send 'em good shipping* may God grant them a good voyage (a proverbial phrase for wishing someone good luck)

38   *undone* ruined

40   *crack-hemp* rogue deserving to be hanged, gallows-bird

41   *I hope I may choose* I trust I may suit myself (meaning 'be allowed to go on my way')

56   *offer* dare, have the effrontery

58   *fine* richly dressed

59   *copatain hat* sugar-loaf hat

60   *good husband* careful economical manager

65   *habit* appearance

66   *what 'cerns it you . . . ?* how does it concern you, what business of yours is it?

67   *maintain* afford

69   *Bergamo.* This town, some twenty-five miles to the north-east of Milan, is an improbable place for a sail-maker to live, but it is exactly the right place for Tranio to come from, since it was the traditional home of Harlequin, the facetious servant of the Italian *Commedia dell'arte.*

82   *an officer* a constable

        (stage direction) *Enter an Officer.* Not in the Folio though required by the dialogue and the action.

84   *forthcoming* ready to stand his trial when required

89-90   *cony-catched* cheated, swindled, made the victim of a confidence-trick

96   *dotard* drivelling old fool

97   *haled and abused* dragged about and wrongfully treated

99   *spoiled* ruined

101   (stage direction) *Exeunt . . . as fast as may be.* There is a parallel to this picturesque bit of description in *The Comedy of Errors*, IV.4.144, where the Folio direction reads: '*Exeunt omnes, as fast as may be, frighted.*'

106   *counterfeit supposes* false suppositions caused by the exchange of identities. There is an obvious reference here to Gascoigne's *Supposes.*

        bleared thine eyne deceived your eyes

107   *Here's packing, with a witness* here's plotting, and no mistake

119   *I'll slit the villain's nose.* The slitting or cutting-off of the nose was a recognized form of revenge. Compare Othello's words about Cassio, 'I see that nose of yours, but not that dog I shall throw it to' (*Othello*, IV.1.142-3).

123   *go to* come, don't worry

128   *My cake is dough* I have failed. See note to I.1.108.

129   *Out of hope of all* with no hope of anything

141   *Better once than never, for never too late.* Petruchio has rolled two proverbs into one: 'Better late than never', and 'It is never too late to mend'. 'Once' here means 'sometime'.

The last few lines of this scene, when Petruchio and Katherina have the stage to themselves, are some of the most important in the play, for it is here that Katherina addresses Petruchio for the first time in an affectionate manner and gives him the kiss that sets the seal on their union.

V.2   The Folio heads this scene '*Actus Quintus.*', disregarding the change of location that has occurred a scene before, and leaving the last Act rather thin.

(stage direction) *Enter Baptista . . . banquet.* The Folio reads: '*Enter Baptista, Vincentio, Gremio, the Pedant, Lucentio, and Bianca. Tranio, Biondello Grumio, and Widdow: The Seruingmen with Tranio bringing in a Banquet.*' Tranio, it will be noticed, is mentioned twice, while Petruchio, Katherina, and Hortensio are not mentioned at all. A direction such as this can hardly be the work of the author, and it would certainly not have passed muster in the theatre.

(stage direction) *banquet* (dessert of fruits, sweetmeats and wine, served after supper)

1   *long* late, after a long time

agree harmonize

3   *scapes* escapes

overblown gone by, that have blown over

4–5   *My fair Bianca, bid my father welcome . . . thine.* Lucentio is giving the banquet at his house, to which they have all adjourned after enjoying the wedding feast at Baptista's.

5   *kindness* the feelings proper to kinship, goodwill

8   *Feast with* feast on

9   *close our stomachs up* put the finishing touches to our meal. Cheese is normally used for this purpose today, but our ancestors had different ideas.

13   *affords this kindness* offers this as the natural thing

14   *kind* affectionate, kindly. Petruchio is thinking of Katherina.

16   *fears* (1) is afraid of (the sense in which Petruchio uses it); (2) frightens (the sense in which the Widow takes it)

17   *Then never trust me if I be* I can tell you I am not

18   *sensible* judicious, discriminating
       sense meaning

20   *He that is giddy thinks the world turns round* people are prone to attribute their misfortunes to others. The saying was proverbial.

21   *Roundly* (1) outspokenly; (2) glibly

22   *Thus I conceive by him* that's the state I think he's in

23   *Conceives by me!* (the obvious quibble)

24   *conceives her tale* interprets her remark

25   *mended* rectified

31   *mean* petty, trivial

32   *I am mean, indeed, respecting you* I am moderate in behaviour by comparison with you

33   *To her* have at her, assail her

35   *marks.* A mark was worth thirteen shillings and four-pence.
       put her down (1) get the better of her; (2) have sexual relations with her – the sense Hortensio gives the phrase. There is a similar quibbling exchange between Don Pedro and Beatrice in *Much Ado About Nothing*, II.1.259–62.

36   *office* employment

37   *like an officer* like one who does his duty

39   *butt together* butt each other. The Folio reads: 'But together', which many editors change to 'butt heads together' in order to prepare the way for Bianca's retort.

This, however, makes the line unmetrical, and is not strictly necessary, since the use of the head is implicit in the act of butting. Shakespeare employs the same analogy between young people exchanging witticisms and cattle butting each other in *Love's Labour's Lost*, where Longaville tells Katharine:

> Look how you butt yourself in these sharp mocks!
> Will you give horns, chaste lady?   V.2.251–2

40   *Head and butt!* head and tail! 'Butt' here means 'bottom'.
       hasty-witted body quick-witted person

41   *your head and butt were head and horn* your butting head was a horned head (a reference to the cuckold's horns)

45   *bitter* shrewd. The Folio reads: 'better'.

46–7   *Am I your bird? I mean to shift my bush,* | *And then pursue me as you draw your bow.* The reference is to the Elizabethan method of fowling with bow and arrows. The target had to be a sitting one; therefore, if the bird moved to another tree or bush, the fowler had to follow.

49   *prevented* forestalled, escaped from

52   *slipped* unleashed

54   *swift* prompt, quick

56   *your deer does hold you at a bay* your deer (with a quibble on 'dear') shows fight and holds you off. A stag is said to be 'at bay' when it turns on the dogs and defends itself with its horns.

57   *hits you* gives you a shrewd blow, catches you on the raw

58   *gird* taunt, gibe

60   *'A* he (colloquial)
       galled me scratched me, given me a surface wound

61   *did glance away from* ricocheted off

63   *in good sadness* in sober earnest

65   *for assurance* to make sure

72   *of* on

75–6   *That will I. Biondello,* | *Go. . . .* The Folio reads: 'That will I. | Goe *Biondello*. . . .', which is metrically unsatisfactory. The transposition of the two words, 'Biondello' and 'Go', puts the metre right, while leaving the sense unaltered.

77   *I'll be your half* I'll go half-shares with you in the risk and the profit of betting that

81   *How?* really? (expression of surprise)

84   *I hope better* I have better expectations

97   *The fouler fortune mine, and there an end* the worse my luck, and that's that

98   *by my holidame* by all I hold sacred, by my halidom

101   *conferring* chatting

102   *deny* refuse

103   *Swinge me them soundly forth* beat them soundly, I tell you, and make them come hither

105   *wonder* miracle

106   *bodes* portends, presages

108   *awful* commanding due respect
       right supremacy supremacy that deserves the name

110   *fair befall thee* good luck to you, congratulations to you

114   *as she had never been* as if she had never existed, out of all recognition

117   *obedience.* So the Folio, but the repetition of the word is suspicious. It has probably been caught by the compositor from the end of the previous line.

127   *a hundred crowns.* The Folio reads: 'fiue hundred crownes', though Lucentio's bet, made at line 74, was only for one hundred. The best explanation of the mistake is C. J. Sisson's; he thinks that the manuscript read 'a hundred', which the compositor took as 'v hundred'.

128   *laying* laying a bet, wagering

135   *unkind* harsh, in a manner contrary to nature

138   *blots* disfigures, destroys
       meads meadows

139   *Confounds thy fame* ruins your reputation
       shake shake to pieces

141   *moved* annoyed, in a bad temper

142   *ill-seeming* unpleasant to look at
       thick turbid

143   *none so dry* no one no matter how dry, no one however
       dry

147   *maintenance; commits.* The Folio reads: 'maintenance.
       Commits', which many editors change to 'maintenance
       commits', assuming that it is in order to maintain his
       wife that the husband 'commits his body | To painful
       labour'. In this edition the punctuation of the Folio is
       substantially adhered to, because it brings out a general
       contrast between the life of the husband and the life
       of the wife, the one exposed to the dangers of the world,
       the other safe at home.

148   *painful* hard, toilsome

149   *watch* be on guard through, be on the alert through

158   *foul* wicked

159   *graceless* depraved, sinful

160   *simple* foolish, unintelligent

161   *offer* begin, declare

165   *Unapt to* unfit for

166   *conditions* qualities, temperaments

168   *unable* weak, impotent

169   *My mind hath been as big as one of yours* my inclination
       has been as strong as that of either of you

170   *heart* courage
       haply perhaps, maybe

171   *bandy* exchange (as a ball is hit to and fro in tennis)

173   *as weak* (as weak as straws)

174   *That seeming to be most which* seeming to be that in the
       highest degree which

175   *vail your stomachs* lower your pride
       it is no boot it is of no avail, there is no help for it

176   *And place your hands below your husband's foot.* There
       may well be a reference here to some traditional act of
       allegiance, but the basic idea is clearly set out in the
       Homily entitled 'Of the State of Matrimony', where
       wives are advised to submit to their husbands 'in respect

of the commandment of God, as St Paul expresseth it
in this form of words: *Let women be subject to their
husbands, as to the Lord; for the husband is the head of the
woman, as Christ is the head of the church.* Ephes. v'
(*Sermons or Homilies*, London, no date, pp. 553–4).

178   *do him ease* give him satisfaction

180   *go thy ways* well done

     ha't have it, meaning 'have the prize', 'be acknowledged
     as the winner'

181   *a good hearing* a nice thing to hear, a pleasant spectacle

     toward docile, tractable (the exact opposite of 'froward')

184   *sped* done for, defeated

185   *the white* the white ring at the centre of the target (with
     a quibble on the name Bianca, the Italian for white)

186   *being* since I am. Petruchio, like a successful gamester,
     goes off while his luck still holds.

AN ACCOUNT OF THE TEXT

IN 1594 a quarto was published, entitled *A Pleasant Conceited Historie, called The taming of a Shrew. As it was sundry times acted by the Right honorable the Earle of Pembrook his seruants.* This volume, however, though it was regarded by the publishing trade throughout the rest of Shakespeare's life and, indeed, even as late as 1631, as being commercially identical with *The Taming of the Shrew*, has, it is generally agreed, no authority whatever. The exact nature of its relationship to Shakespeare's play is still a matter of dispute – in the view of the present editor, it is essentially a 'bad quarto', a very garbled version of the original, put together, probably by an actor or actors, from memory, eked out by extensive patches of verse culled from *Dr Faustus* and *Tamburlaine* – but the crucial point is that, no matter what its origin, it does not go back for its text to a Shakespeare manuscript, or to any copy of such a manuscript. In these circumstances, the sole primary text of the play is that given in the Folio of 1623 (F), where it was printed for the first time.

It is very difficult to determine the kind of copy that the printers of the Folio had at their disposal when they came to set up this particular play. It cannot have been the prompt-book used in the playhouse, because neither entrances nor exits are properly or adequately marked. To take a glaring example, the stage direction at the opening of V.2 reads as follows: '*Enter Baptista, Vincentio, Gremio, the Pedant, Lucentio, and Bianca. Tranio, Biondello Grumio, and Widdow: The Seruingmen with Tranio bringing in a Banquet.*' Tranio, who has only four lines to speak, is mentioned twice, while Petruchio and Katherina, much the most important characters in the scene, are not mentioned at all, nor is Hortensio. As a direction to the actors, this is quite useless. Other instances of entrances and exits that have been omitted will be found in the Commentary. Furthermore, the causes that have led to the muddles about who says what, which occur at III.1.46–56 and at IV.2.4–8, would, of necessity, have been cleared up in a prompt-book.

It seems equally impossible that the text can have been set entirely from the author's manuscript. The stage direction at IV.2.5, '*Enter Bianca.*', instead of '*Enter Bianca and Lucentio*', which is what is required, must be the work of someone who has been misled by the wrong assigning of lines 4 and 5 to *Luc.* into thinking that Lucentio is already on stage. The curious stage direction at the beginning of V.1, '*Enter Biondello, Lucentio and Bianca, Gremio is out before.*', is also suspect. The last four words in it, meaning that Gremio comes on before the other three characters, look distinctly like an afterthought by someone, evidently not the author, who has discovered, on reaching line 6, that Gremio has been on stage all the time, though hitherto he has said nothing. Yet there are other features that do point to the author's manuscript. Some of the stage directions are, from a purely theatrical point of view, unnecessarily elaborate and descriptive, rather as though Shakespeare is reminding himself of who is who; which is what he seems to be doing at I.1.45, where we find '*Enter Baptista with his two daughters, Katerina & Bianca, Gremio a Pantelowne, Hortentio sister* [for *suitor*] *to Bianca. Lucen. Tranio, stand by.*' Other directions are of the vague and indefinite sort normal in a manuscript draft, such as '*Enter foure or fiue seruingmen.*' at IV.1.94. It is the Servingmen's first entrance, and Shakespeare has not yet made up his mind how many of them he will need.

The most attractive theory to account for, and even to reconcile, these contradictory kinds of evidence (the one pointing to some sort of outside interference with Shakespeare's manuscript and the other to that manuscript itself) is the view that what the printers of the Folio were using was not the manuscript itself, but a transcript of it, made by someone other than Shakespeare. Further support for this theory is to be found in state the of the text itself. The most obvious and troublesome feature of it is the large number of lines of verse that have been made unmetrical by the omission of a small word, or even part of a word. At Induction 2.2, for example, the Folio reads: 'Wilt please your Lord drink a cup of sacke?' which is neither good metre nor idiomatic English. As early as 1632 it was recognized that something was wrong here, and those who were responsible for the preparation of the Second Folio (F2), which came out in that year, put the matter right – much as they did in a number of similar cases – by substituting 'Lordship' for 'Lord'. In prose, errors of this kind are much more difficult to detect, but when Baptista asks Biondello, at III.2.32, 'Is it new and olde too? how may that be?' it is clear that the word 'olde' must have appeared somewhere – it is impossible to be sure exactly where – in Biondello's previous speech, though there is no sign of it in the Folio text. As the compositors who set the Folio were not, to judge from the evidence of other verse plays in it, very prone to this kind of mistake, it follows that the copy they were using was probably at fault. One only has to imagine that they were working from a transcript of Shakespeare's manuscript, made rather hurriedly and carelessly, to see how it could all have come about.

The Taming of the Shrew is closely connected with a period of great turmoil and change in the history of the Elizabethan acting companies. The worst plague of the reign broke out in 1592, and continued, with a short break, right on into 1594. For the greater part of this time the theatres in London were closed, and the companies tried to make ends meet by touring the provinces. Some of them split up, others lost their identity altogether. Among these latter were the Earl of Pembroke's men, for whom this play seems to have been written. A company that was breaking up into two different groups might well need hurried transcripts of the most popular plays in its repertory, so that each group could act them; and, in the final stages of the company's disintegration, its more indigent members, cut off from all access to its 'books', could easily have been driven to the expedient of vamping up a text from memory for some such occasion as that which Shakespeare depicts in his Induction.

The copy used for the Folio text of *The Taming of the Shrew* is probably a result of the first process, and that used for *The Taming of a Shrew*, published in 1594, perhaps a result of the second.

COLLATIONS

1

The following list contains the substantial additions and alterations that have been made in the present edition to the stage directions, and Act divisions and speech headings, of the Folio. The reading of the present text is to the left of the bracket, and that of the Folio to the right of it.

(a) *Stage directions*

Ind. 1.	0	*Enter Christopher Sly and the Hostess*] *Enter Begger and Hostes, Christophero Sly.*
	8	*He lies on the ground*] not in F
	10	*Exit*] not in F
	71	*Sly is carried away*] not in F
		A trumpet sounds] *Sound trumpets.*
	72	*Exit Servingman*] not in F
	136	*Exeunt*] not in F
Ind. 2.	0	*Enter aloft Sly*] *Enter aloft the drunkard*
	23	*A Servingman brings him a pot of ale*] not in F
	24	*He drinks*] not in F
	97	*Enter Page as a lady, with attendants. One gives Sly a pot of ale*] *Enter Lady with Attendants.*
	100	*He drinks*] not in F
	115	*Exeunt Lord and Servingmen*] not in F
	126	*Enter the Lord as a Messenger*] this editor; *Enter a Messenger.*
	141	*They sit*] not in F
I.1.	45	*suitor*] sister
	91	*Exit Bianca*] not in F

248

IV.1. 141   *He strikes the Servant*] not in F

151   *He throws the food and dishes at them*] not in F

153   *Exeunt Servants hurriedly*] not in F

173   *Exeunt*] not in F

IV.2.   5   *and Lucentio as Cambio*] not in F

10   *They court each other*] not in F

43   *Exit*] not in F

71   *Exeunt Lucentio and Bianca*] not in F

IV.3.   40   *He sets the dish down*] not in F

86   *Exit Haberdasher*] not in F

180   *(to Grumio)*] not in F

192   *Exeunt*] not in F

IV.4.   0   *Pedant, booted, and dressed*] *Pedant drest*

17   *Lucentio as Cambio*] *Lucentio: Pedant booted and bare headed.*

58   *He winks at Lucentio*] not in F

66   *Exit Lucentio*] not in F

93   *He turns to go*] not in F

V.1.   3   *Exeunt Lucentio and Bianca*] *Exit.*

5   *Exit*] not in F

52   *Exit*] not in F

53   *Exit from the window*] not in F

82   *Enter an Officer*] not in F

129   *Exit*] not in F

V.2.   0   *Petruchio with Katherina, Hortensio*] not in F

48   *Exeunt Bianca, Katherina, and Widow*] *Exit Bianca.*

104   *Exit Katherina*] not in F

121   *She obeys*] not in F

186   *Exeunt Petruchio and Katherina*] *Exit Petruchio*

188   *Exeunt*] not in F

(b) *Act divisions and speech headings*

Induction] *Actus primus. Scœna Prima.*

Ind. 1.   1   SLY] *Begger.*

3   (and before all subsequent speeches) SLY] *Beg.*

80   FIRST PLAYER] 2. *Player.*

Ind. 1. 86   FIRST PLAYER] *Sincklo.*

    2. 99   (and in all subsequent speeches) PAGE] *Lady.*

      127   LORD] this editor; *Mes.*

I.I.   0   I.I] not marked in F

    246   LORD] this editor; I. *Man.*

II.I.   0   II.I] not marked in F

III.I. 46–9   How fiery and forward our pedant is . . . mistrust]
            assigned to *Luc.* in F

    50–51   LUCENTIO] *Bian.*

      52   BIANCA] *Hort.*

      80   SERVANT] *Nicke.*

IV.I.   0   IV.I] No Act division here in F

     23   CURTIS] *Gru.*

IV.2.   4   HORTENSIO] *Luc.*

      6   LUCENTIO] *Hor.*

      8   LUCENTIO] *Hor.*

     71   Take in your love, and then let me alone] F heads
           this line *Par.*

IV.3.   0   IV.3] *Actus Quartus. Scena Prima.*

     63   HABERDASHER] *Fel.*

IV.4.   5   Where we were lodgers at the Pegasus] assigned to
           Tra. in F

V.I.   0   V.I] no division here in F

V.2.   0   V.2] *Actus Quintus.*

2

The following list is of words that have been added to, or, more
rarely, omitted from, the text of the Folio, in order to regularize
the metre or improve the sense. Most of these changes were first
made in the seventeenth and eighteenth centuries – many of
them in one or the other of the three seventeenth-century
reprints of the Folio (F2, F3, and F4); these are noted. The
reading to the left of the bracket is that of this edition; that to
the right, of the Folio.

Ind. 1. 62   he is Sly, say] he is, say
    2. 2   lordship] F2; Lord
 I.2. 45   this's a] this a
      72   she as] F2; she is as
   119   me and other] me. Other
 II.1. 8   charge thee tell] F2; charge tel
    79   unto you this] vnto this
III.2. 16   Make feast, invite friends] Make friends, inuite
    28   a saint] F2; a very saint
    29   of thy impatient] F2; of impatient
    30   such old news] such newes
    90   Were it not better] Were it better
  127   But, sir, to love] But sir, Loue
  129   As I before] As before
  165   rose up again] F2; rose againe
IV.2. 60   I'm] I am
    86   are newly] are but newly
  121   Go with me, sir, to] F2; Go with me to
IV.3. 81   it is a paltry] F2; it is paltrie
    88   like a demi-cannon] F2; like demi cannon
IV.5. 78   she be froward] F2; she froward
 V.1. 115   arrived at last] F2; arriued at the last

3

Below are listed other departures in the present text from that of the Folio. Obvious minor misprints are not noted, nor are changes in lineation and punctuation unless they are of special significance, nor cases in which the Folio prints verse as prose, or prose as verse. Most of these emendations were made by editors in the eighteenth century. Those suggested by modern editors are gratefully acknowledged. The Folio reading is to the right of the bracket.

The Characters in the Play] not in F
Ind. 1. 9–10 thirdborough] Headborough
      15   Breathe] (C. J. Sisson, 1954); Brach F

Ind. 2. 52 wi'th'] with
72 Christophero] F2; Christopher
135 I will. Let them play it. Is not] I will let them play,
it is not

I.1. 13 Vincentio come] *Vincentio's* come
17–18 study | Virtue] studie, | Vertue
25 *Mi perdonato*] *Me Pardonato*
106 There! Love] Their loue
204 coloured] F3; Conlord
241 your] F2; you
I.2. 18 masters] mistris
24 *Con tutto il cuore ben trovato*] *Contutti le core bene trobatto*
25–6 *ben venuto, | Molto honorato*] *bene venuto multo honorata*
51 grows. But] growes but
170 help me] helpe one
188 Antonio's] *Butonios*
222 her too?] her to –
264 feat] seeke
279 ben] F2; *Been*
II.1. 3 gauds] goods
75–6 wooing. | Neighbour] wooing neighbors
90 a suitor] as utor
104–5 Pisa. By report | I] *Pisa* by report, | I
186 bonny] F4; bony
241 askance] a sconce
323 quiet in] quiet me
368 Marseilles] Marcellus; Marsellis F2
III.1. 28 and 41 *Sigeia*] F2; *sigeria*
32 *Sigeia*] F2; *Sigeria*
79 change true rules for odd] charge true rules for old
III.2. 33 hear] F2; heard
54 swayed] *Waid*
58 new-repaired] now repaired
152 grumbling] F2; grumlling

IV.1. 42   their white] F3; the white

       128   Food, food, food, food!] J. Dover Wilson, 1928;
              Soud, soud, soud, soud.

IV.2. 13   none] me

        31   her] F3; them

        71   Take in] Take me

        73   farrer] this editor; farre

        78   Of Mantua? Sir,] Of *Mantua* Sir

IV.3. 177   account'st] accountedst

IV.4.   1   Sir] Sirs

        88   except] expect

        90   *imprimendum solum*] F2; *Impremendum solem*

IV.5. 18   it is] F2; it in

        38   Whither away, or where] F2; Whether away, or
              whether

        41   Allots] F2; A lots

V.1.   5   master's] mistris

        27   Mantua] *Padua*

        47   master's] F2; Mistris

      135   No, sir] Mo sir

V.2.   2   done] come

        37   ha' to thee] F2; ha to the

        39   butt] But

        45   bitter jest or two] better iest or too

        62   two] too

        65   therefore for] F2; therefore sir

     75–6   That will I. Biondello | Go] this editor; That will
              I. | Goe *Biondello*

      127   a hundred] fiue hundred

      131   you're] your

      147   maintenance; commits] maintenance. Commits

4

The following list contains emendations of the Folio text which
have some measure of plausibility, but which have not been
adopted in this edition. The reading to the left of the bracket

is that of this edition; the reading to the right of it is the un-adopted emendation.

Ind. 1. 15   Breathe] (Brach F); Broach (J. Dover Wilson, 1928)

    2. 135   comonty] commodity (J. Dover Wilson, 1928)

  I.1. 181   she] he

       202   meaner man] mean man

  I.2. 151   go to] go

       191   O sir] Sir

       206   to hear] to th'ear

       211   yours] ours

  II.1. 109   To my daughters, and tell them both] In to my daughters; tell them both from me

       141   shakes] shake F2

       168   I'll] I will

       201   such jade] such a jade

       337   have my Bianca's] have Bianca's F2

  III.2.   16   Make feast, invite friends] (Make friends, inuite F); Make friends invited

       127   But, sir, to love] (But sir, Loue F); But to her love

       165   rose up again] (rose againe F); arose again

       208   tomorrow – not till] (to morrow, not till F); tomorrow, till

  IV.1.   37   wilt thou] thou wilt F2

        56   This 'tis] This is

      106   at door] at the door

  IV.5.   26   soft, company] soft, what company

        36   the woman] a woman F2

  V.1.27–8   and here] and is here

  V.2. 105   of a wonder] of wonder

      147   maintenance; commits] maintenance commits

NEW PENGUIN SHAKESPEARE

General Editor: T. J. B. Spencer